STITCHED SMILE PUBLICATIONS PRESENTS

UNLEASHING THE VOICES WITHIN

ANTHOLOGY

EDITED BY

DONELLE PARDEE WHITING

AMANDA SHORE

VERONICA SMITH

COVER ART BY

LISA VASQUEZ

ISBN-10: 1-945263-02-4
ISBN-13: 978-1-945263-02-6

You'll find links and more to all of our authors on our website. If you've enjoyed reading their works, we invite you to leave a review and seek out more by visiting us at:

www.stitchedsmilepublications.com
www.facebook.com/stitchedsmilepublications
www.stitchedsmilepublications.wordpress.com

Dedicated:

To all of the fans and readers that have made STITCHED SMILE PUBLICATIONS such a great home.

To all the beta readers that support authors and do whatever they can to get the word out.

To Donelle Pardee Whiting for the long hours and "girl talk" when I wanted to scream or cry.

To Amanda Shore for sticking it out and giving it her all against all roadblocks.

To Veronica Smith who has been there since the beginning, before she even knew it.

To the authors that donated their stories to a no name publisher just coming to life.

To my family for putting up with my face in a computer for hours on end.

THIS IS THE HOUSE THAT STITCH BUILT

Contents

Janie's Got a Gun by Lisa Vasquez

Janie sat in her last class of the day and watched the sunlight filter in from the north-facing window. The clock ticked out the seconds on the standard, round clock above the professor, who prattled on about formulas and reactions. His voice began to muffle and the incessant ticking grew even louder, drowning out everything else.

Tick. Tick. Tick. Tick.

Her eyes began to grow heavier, and Janie covered her mouth to stifle a yawn just as the familiar itch came back. She hissed and began to scratch at her temple. Gentle at first but then with more fervor. Ever since she was a child, "the itch" was present. Doctors ran a battery of tests and could never find out what was causing it.

Some days, it was non-existent, and other days, it would go on and on until she was huddled in the corner of her bed, praying for relief.

On this day, the itching caused her the usual anxiety, so she reached in her bag on the floor for her bottled water and medication. Her attempt at discretion was put off when her fingers pushed past the stacks of books and papers only to come up empty.

Shit. Where is it?

Janie leaned over a little further now and captured the full attention of her professor. "Miss Adler? I assume you are looking for your notebook to take notes since your previous test score indicates that you hadn't done so."

The class had a laugh at her expense, and Janie's cheeks flushed with both embarrassment and fury. Fuck you, Mr. Science Guy.

The itching began to move in deeper, making her hand tremble. She wanted to scratch at it so bad, but the entire classroom's eyes were lingering on her.

Tick. Tick. Tick. TICK. TICK.

She was about to unleash a scream and ask them what the fuck they were all looking at when the bell sounded. Janie needed no extra motivation to snatch her bag up and rush out, shouldering anyone that got in her way.

Racing down the hall, she found shelter in the furthest bathroom. No one came in there; it was too isolated from the other classrooms and the parking lot. Slamming the stall door shut, she forced the sole of her shoe against it and began to scratch at her head. The more she scratched, the more it itched. It was crawling so deep she could barely stand it!

It's going to get into my brain…

"What?" came a voice from the neighboring stall.

Janie was panting. She didn't see anyone else when she came in, and she had checked under every door.

"Hello?" Janie called out.

"You said it was going to get into your brain. Are you okay in there?"

"I…" How the fuck was she supposed to answer that?

She didn't. Instead, she burst out of the bathroom and down the hall like a bull. One of the other teachers saw her and called out.

"Janie? Janie, wait," Mrs. Prescott called out. "Janie! Stop!"

Janie's hand was trembling so hard her entire arm ached as she stopped mid-step. With a slow pivot, she turned and faced her English professor.

"Oh my God. Are you okay?"

Mrs. Prescott was standing in front of her now, reaching out to turn Janie's head to the side for a better look.

"You're bleeding, Janie. What happened?" she asked.

Janie reached up and felt the warm, wet trail of blood on her fingers before lowering them to eye level to confirm what her professor saw. The very sight of the dark crimson made Janie's stomach churn and her head swim. The last thing she remembered was the arc of fluorescent lights overhead as she fell to the floor.

When her eyes fluttered open, Janie could hear the nurse and doctor talking over her chart. The steady beep of the heart monitor beside her made her cringe. She hated hospitals. The smell of the sterile sheets made her skin crawl. She didn't dare move yet. If she was awake, there'd be questions. There was movement to the side of her, and she shut her eyes, hoping they hadn't noticed.

"Ms. Adler?" The male voice was soft.

Janie didn't respond.

"Ms. Adler, I'm Dr. Shani. You were brought in by ambulance this morning."

Playing 'possum wasn't going to work. With a sigh, Janie opened her eyes before squinting. The doctor looked exactly like one of her other doctors. In fact, it was the same one! So why was he using the name Dr. Shani?

"Dr. Patel?" she asked in confusion.

The doctor smiled. Perfect, straight white teeth contrasting to his dark skin did nothing to set her at ease.

"It's Dr. Shani," he repeated. "How are you feeling now?" he asked, jotting something in the chart.

He put it in your head, Janie. "Shut up," she growled.

Dr. Shani's brows rose, and he looked up at her. "I'm sorry?"

Janie cleared her throat and avoided his question. "You're Dr. Patel. My psychologist. Why are you here?"

Dr. Shani lowered the clipboard and glanced at the nurse, who held it for a few seconds. The two broke their gaze and turned back to Janie.

"Janie, do you know where you are?" the nurse asked.

"Duh, I'm in a hospital," Janie answered. *Look at how she stares at you. Don't trust her. She's in on it.*

The itch was flaring up, and Janie let out a hiss before bringing her hand up to scratch, but it was stopped just shy of reaching her head. Panic swooped in, and she glanced down at her wrist, which was secured by a strap.

"Uhh…wanna tell me what the fuck is going on?" Janie's voice grew louder. "Seriously, why am I being restrained?"

She wasn't waiting for an answer as she tugged at the cuff and rattled the chain against the bed's rail. The doctor jotted something else down then set the clipboard on the counter beside him. He stood at her bedside and leaned on the opposite rail.

"Have you blacked out like this before, Ms. Adler?"

The nurse was still staring at her. *They know you tried to take it out.* The two of them staring at her made the itch insatiable, and her irritation mounted until Janie finally exploded.

"Let me out!"

Dr. Shani looked at the nurse and nodded. The nurse took a step back then left the room. Janie did not want to be alone with this doctor, so she pulled at the restraints harder, causing the bed to rock. *They're going to put it back! Get out of here! Get out!!*

The itch at her scalp throbbed and jabbed like a needle digging and weeding into her brain. She could feel the heat of it searing at the gray matter, invading the soft tissue and worming further in. *It's in! Oh God, it's going to kill us!*

"Let. Me. Out!!!" Janie screamed, throwing herself back against the bed repeatedly.

The chains rattled in cadence to her shouts, and the doctor tried to subdue her. He was saying something that she couldn't make out because his voice was drowned by both her own screams and the screams from inside her. She could see the nurse run back in with a syringe accompanied by two more nurses. Both of them were male.

She tried to pull away, but they were on her in an instant.

"No! Please? No, stop!"

The world spun into darkness again.

< >

She had no idea how long she was out, but before consciousness fully invaded the sweet depth of her dreams, Janie could smell the lavender fabric softener she loved so much. Was she home? Her fingers crept along the sheets. One thousand thread count, Egyptian cotton.

What the Hell was going on?

"Morning, beautiful."

His voice was the soft rays of sun on her cheeks. He warmed her body from her toes all the way to the ends of her long, brown hair. Despite how groggy she was, she pushed through the dark world of dreamland to find the surface of daylight. The smell of his skin drew her toward him, and she nuzzled against his chest, placing a kiss there.

His fingers brushed through her hair and cupped her cheek, pulling her face upward and into a soft, sweet kiss. She moaned quietly against his mouth, and he smiled.

"How about breakfast?" he purred back against her lips. "Some eggs. Some fresh-squeezed juice."

He pecked at her mouth between each sentence. She was drunk on his voice alone.

"Mmm-yes," she cooed then extended her arms over her head and arched her back to stretch.

She kept her eyes shut the whole time. Opening them meant she had to wake up and come out of her dream. She felt the mattress sink then lift, followed by the sound of Adam's footsteps to the kitchen. *He's so perfect.*

The smell of eggs began to fill the room, and she sighed in surrender. Janie opened her eyes and gazed out of the window to the view of the city stretched beyond. The loft's windows were floor-to-ceiling, two-way glass. They could see out, but no one could see them. It offered all the protection and privacy they needed.

Janie threw the sheets off of her and slid her legs over the side of the bed. The chill of the air caused her skin to dimple, and she crossed her arms over her naked chest. Using her palms, she brushed her hands up and down each bicep to warm herself up again. When she stood, she had the sluggish feeling that occurred after a long night of drinking. Was she buzzed?

Looking to her left, she spotted the bottle of champagne, and her brows came together. Why didn't she remember what happened?

The itch started again. *There's something in the glass. Look!*

Dropping her eyes, Janie saw the flutes. Bubbles were still rising to the top. A small, open black box sat next to them. Wait… She was engaged?

She tore her eyes from the flutes and looked down at her hand. On her ring finger was a huge center diamond surrounded by a halo of pink ones. It was the most beautiful ring she'd ever seen in her life. *Check the goddamned flutes!!*

The itch grew and poked at her scalp incessantly. She didn't want to look. It was too perfect. She tried to fight it, but the voice grew louder. *He drugged you! He wants to put it back!*

Janie's fingers began to claw at the itch now. Desperate to make it stop, she forced her nails in deeper and cried out in pain.

From behind, the patter of Adam's footsteps grew closer until he stopped at the door. "Janie? What is it? Are you okay?"

She couldn't stand it anymore. Janie curled forward as if she'd been struck in the stomach and let out a sob.

"I can't make it stop!"

Janie stopped to turn around, cradling her hand covered in blood. When she caught sight of Adam, she let out a scream and backed up against the window. The sudden action knocked over the champagne flutes and sent shattered glass everywhere.

"Where's Adam? What did you do with my Adam?!"

"What? It's me, Janie! What's going on?" he said, moving closer with caution.

"You are not Adam! You're Dr. Patel!"

Adam stood there incredulously. He was afraid to move closer, watching her back up into the glass as if she might push through it. All around her were the shards of broken crystal embedding into the soles of her feet. She continued to press her heels into the floor to try and back further away, causing more blood to smear against the boards.

"Please, Janie. Let me help you. You're bleeding."

The itch was so bad that her left eye began to twitch and try to close itself. *He poisoned you! Get out! Get OUT!*

Janie glanced around for a way out, but Adam was still standing by the doorway. He was moving in very slow steps toward her, hands outstretched and palms open.

"Janie… Janie, it's me, baby. It's Adam. Please… Please let me help you."

She was hysterical now. Her sobs were so intense each gulp of air hitched between pulls. *He's going to take you back. Can you feel the poison? It's crawling into your veins!*

She tried to fight the urge to scratch, but it had control of her. It festered in her head like a white-hot wire, stretching out to the other side. It was no use trying to resist it. She brought her nails to her head and clawed at it again. Bits of her flesh clumped under her fingernails.

"Oh my God. Janie, stop!" Adam yelled.

When she wouldn't, he leapt at her and tackled her against the glass. There was a shatter and a gust of air before they both began to fall. The look of fear on Adam's face was the last thing she saw before the pain of her bones hitting pavement brought the comfort of darkness.

< >

"Janie?"

The girl stirred, but she remained unawake.

"Janie, you're going to be alright. Hang on," the voice said.

"What did you take, Janie?" Another voice from the other side of her.

The darkness was the only place she didn't feel any pain. Why did she ever have to leave it? The voices were trying to call her back again.

"Stay with us, Janie. We're going to get you to the hospital," it said.

"Blood pressure dropping—we need to get a line in," said the other.

"Janie, we need to know what you took," said the first.

They're going to do it again. Taking you away to put the bug inside. It's going to eat your brain.

She began to stir again. Something was wrong.

"Lie still, Janie. Can you talk?" the voice asked.

Why couldn't she move? Janie tried to open her mouth, and something welled up from inside, causing her to choke and cough. It was like water but thicker. Her mouth filled with the taste of metal.

"I need an aspirator!" the second voice said.

Her body was being rolled onto her side, but she was frozen, unable to move freely. She was strapped to something hard beneath her. A board? She was growing so cold. Janie tried to move her head to look around, but she couldn't open her eyes. Who were those voices? Where did they come from?

She could still hear the voices surrounding her, but all of them sounded like they were underwater, and there was that beep again...

Beep. Beep.

Beep.

Beeeeeeep.

"She's flatlining!" the first voice boomed.

"Begin compressions."

"Janie, hang on! Fight, Janie..."

< >

Janie was just a girl when the itching started.

The scrape of her nails leaving red ribbon trails across her forehead. Bumpy scabs made it impossible for her mother to pull her hair back. It didn't matter anyway; Janie would always pull the rubber band out and let her the strands hang in her face.

The doctors said it was just anxiety. Had she suffered any traumatic event lately?

Janie. There's something inside of us. She's putting it in your food. She wants you to go away.

Often, the girl would stare off into nothing and refuse to eat for days. She was frail and underweight. When she was 14, her mother took her to the psychologist. Dr. Shani was a soft-spoken, quiet man. His skin was darker than hers, and he had a perfect smile.

"You don't have to say anything you don't want to, Janie," he said.

"It's eating my brain," she finally said, breaking the silence.

"What's eating your brain?" Dr. Shani asked.

He had the same look on his face as everyone else. He thinks you're a freak. They all do. They want you to go away.

"Nothing," Janie said sharply.

"Do you think there's something inside of you, Janie?"

The girl sat there in silence. Her fingers twitched as the sensation coiled under the skin again. She slapped her other hand over them to hide it.

"Janie?"

From experience, she learned to find "that other place" and play in the darkness when she didn't want to talk or deal with anyone. They were always looking at her like a science project. Always making her feel like she was a freak or crazy.

The darkness was the only place she felt safe.

< >

"Blood pressure is 75/40. Patient is unresponsive."

Janie was still strapped to something hard and struggling to move, but she was immobilized.

"I'm here!" she screamed from inside.

Why couldn't she get out of the dark this time?

We're finally free. You did it, Janie. They can't put it inside of you anymore.

Janie's body began to convulse, and she could feel several other bodies struggling to hold her down. There were drops that began to fall from above her — was it raining? — and she tried to look up. She remembered the rain from the summer she met Adam.

The sun had just begun to fall into the horizon, splashing the sky with streaks of violets and oranges. She was on a trip to Hawaii with her friend Nicole, who'd run off with some guy she met the day before. Janie could see her friend and the guy making out in the sand. She tried to pretend she wasn't looking.

She was always getting left behind while Nicole found her next conquest. She was just there to keep her company until then. Glancing down at the oversized drink on her thigh, Janie picked up the umbrella and pulled the chunk of pineapple off the end then twirled the colorful paper by the stick between her fingers.

"Your friend shouldn't leave you alone like that," said a male voice from behind her.

"Why not? She's having fun," Janie said over her shoulder.

"Because you're not."

Janie was about to turn around and give this guy a piece of her mind when her eyes locked onto his. It was over. Her body went limp, and she almost dropped her drink to the sand.

"Woah!" Adam laughed.

His reflexes were quick, and he caught it before it toppled.

"I'm so embarrassed... I'm such a klutz," Janie chided herself.

That summer was the best time of her life. Adam was everything to her. She gave her body to him as well as her heart. When he bought her the ring, she was over the moon. Everything she had ever wanted was finally real.

She and Nicole shopped for wedding dresses and honeymoon clothing until they couldn't carry anything more. Even the itching was silent for a little while.

Everything changed one week from the wedding on the night of Janie's bachelorette party.

"Nicole, where the fuck are you?"

Those were the last words she'd ever speak. She was fifteen minutes late picking Nicole up for the bachelorette party. Everyone else was already there and on their way to being buzzed. They were calling her from the club, asking where she and Nicole were while shouting over the dance music blaring in the background.

Getting out of her car, Janie walked to the door of Nicole's parent's home. The daughter of a lt. colonel in the United States Marines, Nicole was often left alone while "daddy" was on business. Even though they'd been friends since the fourth grade, Janie always knocked before entering.

She knocked three times to no answer before she turned the knob and entered. Music was playing from Nicole's bedroom, but other than that, it was too still. Janie headed down the hallway and heard Nicole's laughter, which pissed her off even more. Why was she the one waiting on Nicole for her own party?

Janie shoved the door open, and before she could speak, she got a front-row seat to her fiancé plowing into her best friend from behind. She stood there for what seemed like forever until Adam looked up and threw himself back in horror. Nicole looked up at Janie in the doorway and smirked.

"Oh my God," she said in her fake voice.

She pretended to cover herself as Adam stood there, mortified.

Janie turned and walked back the way she came down the hallway. She could hear Adam shouting at Nicole and then running after her.

Janie hurried her steps and ducked into the first room she could, slamming her back against the door and locking it. Adam was on the other side, banging and shouting apologies. Behind him, Nicole was trying to pull him away.

"Jesus, Adam, let her go!"

"Fuck you, Nicole! Janie, please open up! I'm sorry."

Janie slid down to the floor and began scratching at her head subconsciously. She couldn't stop the rush of tears that followed. *All that bitch does is take! She's taken everything from you! Make her pay! Make all of them pay!*

Janie let out a scream and jumped to her feet. The meticulously kept room was too perfect. Just like Adam. Just like Dr. Patel's smile. She felt the undeniable urge to destroy all of it. Throwing her hands across the dresser, the lt. colonel's belongings were flung in the air. A picture frame smashed into the corner, and a clock met with the wall. She jerked every single drawer out of the dresser and began pulling out clothing, using her fingernails to rip through the measured, square rows of white t-shirts.

She was making her way through the second drawer when she heard a thud at her feet.

Adam and Nicole were still arguing while he banged on the door. She was still trying to convince him to leave Janie and be with her.

Crouching, Janie felt the cold metal in her fingertips. It was hard and dangerous in her hands, and the rush made her body feel feathery and light. She was possessed by something… Revenge. Fury. Jealousy. Hurt.

All of the above.

She walked slow and calm to the door and turned the knob. She didn't open it at first. The two on the other end were suddenly quiet.

"Janie?" Adam said in a cracked voice.

Janie opened the door, leading the way with the barrel of the .45 ACP Recon that barely fit in her hand. Seeing the gun, Adam threw his hands up and began backing away. Nicole became incensed at the condition of her father's room and his gun in Janie's hand.

"What the fuck, Janie!!" she screamed. "My fuckin' dad is going to kill you! You stupid cu —"

BANG!

Nicole gasped and flew back the short distance to the wall before falling onto her ass. She was in total shock. With her arms still held up, she looked down at the hole in her stomach, which was oozing blood into her lap.

"Holy FUCK!" Adam shouted, pressing his back against the wall behind him.

The asshole was still naked and standing there in nothing but his socks. He looked over at Nicole as if to make sure what he thought happened really did before he began to cry.

"Janie, I'm sorry! Oh God, you shot her!" he said, the panic beginning to rise. "You fucking shot her! She's fucking dying, Janie... What the f —"

BANG!

Adam's head slammed against the wall in a spray of bone and bits of brain matter on the white paint behind him. His eyes were still wide open and staring at her. She could hear the sirens in the distance closing in, and the needling of the itch began to creep in once more. Janie took one hand off the gun and scratched at her head, but it was too painful. She scratched harder and faster until she was scraping her scalp with deep lacerations. Blood poured down, following her cheek until it clung to the bottom of her chin. It grew into a fat droplet then fell onto her shirt. She looked down to see it spreading through the fibers.

Make the itch stop, Janie. The dark is the only place that's safe.

With the sirens blaring just outside, Janie could hear the commotion of the police that gathered. Nicole's father was demanding entry, but he was being held off by the officers now surrounding the home. She looked down to her hand covered in blood and the pieces of skin beneath her nail.

"This is the police. We need you to come out with your hands in the air!"

BANG!

I never knew that floating in the darkness was like swimming in the water at night. The white light up above the only sense of direction. The sense of danger all around you and the eeriness of silence depriving all your senses. You float there, knowing that at any moment, something could swim out of the darkness and swallow you. You either swim to the surface...or you take a deep breath and drift away.

END

Night Train Fights By Justin Gowland

I woke up naked in a baggage compartment of a train. Now awaking up naked somewhere wasn't a first for me but waking on a moving train was. Looking round the compartment I saw the usual bags and other traveling items but my clothes were nowhere to be seen. I shivered because of a cold breeze that blew in through the side door of the carriage. It caused the hairs on my arms and legs to stand on end.

A disembodied voice came from somewhere in the carriage "Hello Mr Jacobs and welcome to the night train. You're here for something special and have been chosen to take part."

"Ok I'll bite. What's so fucking special?" I asked looking for cameras.

The voice laughed and said "Mr Jacobs that something special survive of course!"

"What the fuck are you going on about?" I shouted beginning to feel a cold lump in my stomach.

"You have to fight of course. The better you fight, the more chance of getting out alive!" It said.

I sat down on the bags "What if I decide to stay here with the bags?" Now I am no slouch. I've been in plenty fights and I try to look after myself, but I always thought I could do better.

"Then you die, but you need not worry because your first fighter has joined you here." The voice said.

"What the hell are you going on about?"

The door at the end of the carriage opened and out of the darkness a man appeared and not just any man it was a fucking clown with a large bloody meat cleaver. He stood a good three inches taller than me and I'm 5 foot 12. He swung the meat cleaver back and forth with a whistling sound. His bright red curly hair stood out against the pale white makeup on his face, the only other splash of colour was the round bright blue nose he was wearing.

"Please enjoy yourself because we will." Laughed the voice as it faded from the carriage.

I had nothing to defend or fight with. Backing up a little more my eyes darting from side to side as I looked for something to fight back with. The huge clown grinned and then lashed out with the meat cleaver. It hit a travel bag on the rack beside him and the contents spilled out and on to the floor. A rumble came from his chest and I realised that he was laughing. That made my poor parts shrink back inside and I doubted that I would ever be able to coax them back out.

Grabbing a small hard shell bag, I threw it as hard as I could. It just bounced off his large chest and that rumbling laugh came forth. I was nearly at the back of the carriage when I saw what looked like a meat hook. It was buried into the rafter overhead. The clown had stopped in the middle of the carriage and was pointing at my junk and laughing. My cheeks must have gone red because I felt them heat up, and I mean the cheeks on my face. Grabbing at the hook I started to pull, but all it was doing was causing me to swing back and forth. Which of course set the clown off laughing again. The hook was slowly coming free as I heard him stop laughing. I looked between my arms and watched as he slowly lumbered forward.

The hook came free and I fell down on my bare arse and I cried out. Now my arse was red and sore from landing on the wooden floor. Rolling to my side I tried to get up, but I slipped back on to my arse. It was a good thing that I did because the clown's meat cleaver just missed my head and buried itself deep into a large travel case. The clown lifted the cleaver and its accessory up. He stood there looking at the case and cleaver combo, before looking down at me with a puzzled expression on his face.

If this is who I need to kill or maim to get out of here, then who ever put me here must have low expectations. I lashed out with the hook at the clown's right knee and was glad to hear a howl. The hook had buried deep behind the clown's knee. I tugged at it and was greeted with another howl. Yanking at the hook for all I was worth, I finally felt something come away and the hook slipped free. I heard a tearing from above me and I rolled to the right, just as the travel case fell to the floor, right where I had just been. Running around the clown I slashed out with the hook and torn three long bloody gouges out of his large rear end. This time the clown lashed out behind him with the cleaver. I danced back but wasn't quick enough and got a slash mark across my chest which instantly started to weep large tears of blood. The clown turned and tried to walk toward me, but I must have really damaged his knee, because it didn't want to hold his weight anymore.

With a wet tearing sound, he fell down on to his good knee. I swear the whole carriage shook with his bulk hitting the floor. I thought the clown suit was just pretend but there must have been some weight hidden behind it. Whilst I had been wool gathering I started to hear a loud growling. Fearing that they had let a dog in, I span round and looked the other way. That was when he slammed into me from behind. I flew across the carriage and into another rack of cases. They fell on top of me and it went dark. I don't mean knockout dark. I mean just dark from having the cases on top of me.

Pushing and shoving I pulled myself out of the cases. I looked back at the clown and he was also pulling himself to his feet. Blood poured out of the tear on his right knee. He grabbed a shirt out of one of the broken cases and started to strap up his knee. I really didn't want him too. Dashing forward as he looked down at his knee, I lifted the hook high with both hands. I howled out as I brought the hook down with all of my strength.

The clown looked up with such a stupid look of astonishment on his face just as the hook went in through his right eye. The popping of the eye was louder than I would have thought. I sprayed all over my arms and naked chest. The point was grating against the back of his socket and I couldn't get enough leverage to drive it in deeper. He started to howl and his hands came away from his damaged knee and headed toward his head.

Quickly, I swung round to his back and pulled on the wooden handle. I even had to pull my knees up on to his broad back and still pull with all of my strength. Before finally the hook buried further into his skull. Howling he thrashed around and I hung on to dear life, whilst being beaten to a pulp on the racks and baggage.

His thrashing started to ebb and I managed to drop to the floor away from him. I was sure that I had damaged my ribs in some way and my arms felt like they were jelly. I lay there panting as I listened to his dying howls. Like I said earlier, I have been in many fights but never one where I have taken another life. It hit me like a ton of bricks. Rolling over I started to vomit on top of the baggage that was on the floor. I retched until clear bile poured from my mouth and nose. It was after I had been sick, that I noticed how quiet it had become in the carriage. Looking up I could see the clown staring back at me with his one eye, one hook. He didn't blink and wasn't moving.

Now like everyone else in this world I have watched a horror movie or two, and this was usually the point when the monster or killer comes back to life for that one last kill.

"I can assure you that he is dead!" The voice had returned and didn't sound very pleased.

Looking around I said "I've done what you asked. Now let me fucking go!"

There was a pause and another voice spoke "Mr. Jacobs, I'm sorry to say but we liked your fight. So we've decided to keep you on for another."

Shaking my head, I screamed "Another what!? Another fucking murder!? Another mind fuck!?"

"Ah, I don't think you get it. This isn't murder this is sport, sport of the highest calibre. We pitch killers like the clown here against the average public and bet on the outcome. I have to admit you've made me some money tonight!" the new voice said with a sort of smug tone.

"Well fuck you! You can just kill me here and now!" I shouted before crossing my arms and sitting down on a large trunk.

Nothing was said for a while and I my hopes started to rise with each second. "We have discussed your little tantrum and are willing to overlook it. As a bonus for killing Mr. Clown we will let you look through the baggage for clothing before you move on. Oh, and something else Mr. Jacobs, you only have ten minutes otherwise we...how shall I put this!?" There was a slight pause before "Blow you the fuck up!" the voice shouted from where ever it was hidden.

I sat there for a couple of minutes doubting that they would be wanting to blow up part of a train. Of course that's when the light changed to a blood red glow. I scrambled from the trunk and started ripping into the bags and cases around me. I found a pair of tracksuit pants and a horrible snot green coloured t-shirt. Pulling them on I started looking for some shoes or trainers, but there was none. The light started to pulse and ran to where Mr. Clown had taken his last breath and lifted the heavy meat cleaver.

"You have 2 minutes Mr. Jacobs!" Laughed the disembodied voice.

Running the length of the carriage I hit the door and started to yank on the handle. Blood ran from the meat cleaver on to my hand making my grip slid on the handle. I dropped the meat cleaver to the floor and wiped my hands on the tracksuit pants, before going for the handle again. I managed to get a good grip and pulled the handle down. Rushing air greeted me as the door slid to the side. There was a two or three, foot gap between the baggage car and what looked like a night carriage. Stepping across the gap, my I had just pulled myself on to the lip of the next carriage when I heard a loud pop from behind me. Turning round I saw the baggage car slowly falling back.

I watched as it pulled away thinking, I was right they're not blowing anything up! I had just finished the thought when an almighty bang and flash of light lit up the night. My back was slammed hard against the carriage and I slipped. My hands grabbed the first thing that I could hold, the small railing near to the door, but my legs were hanging over the back end of the train. Swinging and kicking my legs, I managed get myself standing again. My heart was nearly beating itself to death against my rib cage. I didn't really have to face another killer, my body itself was trying to kill me. I stood sucking in huge amounts of air, trying to calm myself. I could always jump! I thought.

The track seemed to speed past at such a rate, I could hardly see the railway ties flying past. If I did jump, then I would be either dead or so badly injured it wouldn't be long after the jump that I died. I had to go on, I was too much of a coward to take my own life. Turning I grabbed the door handle. Shit! The cleaver!

Looking back up the track I could see the blazing wreck of the baggage car. It lit the side of the track and I could see that the train was travelling through the countryside. Large hills bracketed the track and I saw no other light but the fire. Well I killed the clown, all be it by luck. Maybe I could do it again. Opening the door, I stepped inside.

It was pitch black inside, I could barely make out two feet in front of me and that was a wooden wall. I placed my hand on the smooth wall and walked to the right straight into another wall and something hit my shins. Bending down on to my heels I reached for what had hit my shins. It was a fire extinguisher. Pulling it free from the hook that held it on the wall, I hefted the weight in my hands. Images from films passed through my mind. I they were correct. I might be able to smash the new killer's skull in with it.

"Hello again Mr. Jacobs! So nice of you to join us, we thought you might have had a little accident in the baggage car!" The voice said with humour in his voice.

I muttered to myself 'If I get my hands on you lot!'

"Pardon Mr. Jacobs?"

"I said that you didn't leave me much choice!"

The voice laughed "No, I suppose we didn't!" he continued to laugh and I could hear other voices laughing in the background. There were male and female voices.

"So what now!?" I shouted into the darkness.

"Do you like the dark Mr. Jacobs?"

"No I get fucking scared!"

"Please Mr. Jacobs!"

I sighed and sat down on the floor next to the door I had come in through.

"This is a test on your senses Mr. Jacobs. Your next opponent is blind you see and we can't let you have the advantage, can we?"

"There is no way I am killing a disabled person for your sick pleasure!" I said.

The voice chuckled "Don't worry about her Mr. Jacobs. She can hold her own against you!"

"You want me to fight to the death with a blind woman?" I shouted.

Again there was a lot of laughter. I heard a door open and then close. Shit they must have let her in! Grabbing the fire extinguisher, I jumped to my feet. Guiding myself along the wall with one hand and swinging the extinguisher in the other I edged along in the darkness. I heard the patter of feet in the darkness and then something tugged at my pants. The footsteps retreated and I heard a girlish giggle. My leg stung and I reached down with my free hand to touch where I had felt the tug, it came away wet and I knew that I had been cut.

The footsteps rushed in again, but this time I lashed out with the extinguisher, which swung through the air to clang off the wall beside me. Another tug at my pants, this time on the other leg and I knew that I had been cut again.

What the fuck! I thought.

The giggle came out of the dark again.

"Where the fuck you at!?" I screamed.

"Oooo naughty words!" a girl's voice answered.

I heard the shuffle of footsteps in the dark just in front of me. I swung out with the extinguisher and felt something crunch into the end. It screamed out and the sound of footsteps retreated back down the carriage. The funny thing was the extinguisher had only reached as high as my hip. A strange sort of huffing came out of the dark.

The blood running down my legs had started to pool under feet and could feel it sticking to the carpet. I'd need to do something about it or I might just end up dying of blood loss. Reaching out to my right I searched the wall. If I was in a night carriage, then there would be small rooms along the corridor. My hand brushed up against a small handle in the door. Turning it I pushed the door open and quickly stepped inside.

I had been right this was a night carriage, I could just make out two couches facing each other. Locking the door, I hobbled over to the others side of the room. Pulling the t-shirt free, I then pulled down my tracksuit pants. Searching in the dark, I found the slashes in my thighs. I ripped the t-shirt in two and then wrapped them around my injured legs.

"Mr. Jacobs, you do realise that this is a fight!" The voice said.

"Fuck you!" I said back. The door was locked and I felt safe inside the small room.

"Mr. Jacobs, you have to understand. That by hiding you are making yourself look bad and in turn making you a bad bet. Now we are going to overlook this and open the door so that the fight can continue." And there was click from over beside the door.

Standing I hobbled toward the door, the feeling in my legs was slowly ebbing away with each pulse. I needed to end this and end it quickly. The voice might send someone to help me if I won this fight.

Pulling the door open, I walked into the hallway. The train rocked and slammed into the wall on the other side. Something breezed past me and I felt a large sharp pain erupt on my side. Grabbing it I felt my blood start to run from a six-inch gash. I heard laughter from behind me and whipped the extinguisher in that direction, but my hands were covered with my own blood and the extinguisher slipped out of my fingers and into the dark. I heard it slam against the rear wall, as I was slashed across my chest.

I howled in pain and slid to the floor. My legs felt like they weren't there anymore and my side and chest burned. Tightness slowly began to grip my chest, as I lay there trying to keep my blood from escaping. The giggling voice returned and I could feel her breath on the side of my face.

"Would you like to see me?" she whispered into my ear.

For some reason the question frightened me more than the fighting had. I tried to say no but I was so groggy with blood loss I couldn't say it. I heard small palms clapping in the dark when I didn't say anything.

Giggling she said "Could nice Mr. Voice turn the lights on please!"

"Certainly my dear, but before we do. Mr. Jacobs, please don't feel bad no one has ever gotten past Cassey, she is very good!" a voice said but I hardly head it.

The lights blazed on and I hand to hold my hand up to my face. A shadow cut out the blinding light and I started at what was leaning over me. It looked like a little girl, but it was no little girl I had ever seen or would wish to ever see again. Dressed in a small yellow stained summer dress she stood looking at me. Large blonde bunches hung from wrinkled green/grey skin. There was one half of an ear on the left side of her head and on the other was a hole that black sticky fluid seemed to leak out of it.

Looking fully at her face I saw the reason that she was blind. One eye had been gouged out and in its place was small leather ball, her other eye was just a blank socket and I could see the white bone of her skull through it. A large metal clipped scar stretched from her left temple across her skull and then straight down to her open nose cavity. The same black goo slowly leaked from her nose and dripped on to my pants. She smiled and her broken green cover teeth broke out between her split and torn lips.

She clapped her hands again and I pushed back away as quickly as my dying body could. She had no fingers at all on those hands. Instead there was a long razor sharp blade. The giggles started again and she leaded forward and I tried to turn away from her.

"You were naughty to me, and you hurt me!" as she spoke she placed one blade on my chest and the other on my groin. "Now it's time for you to hurt!" the daggered hand on my groin slowly pushed down. I tried to lift my hands to slap her away but my strength had left me. All I could do was watch that grinning face as she carved into my groin. The pain seemed to eclipse everything I had ever felt in my life. It seemed to go on and on.

In the end I was begging for her to end my life. Her little dress was covered in my blood and she licked it from the blade that had cut away my privates. Leaning in she kissed me and I felt the blades slide into my chest. I gasped once. The light seemed to dim like we were heading into a tunnel.

I was aware of light on the other side of my eye lids. I was dead wasn't I? I struggled to open my eyes. The baggage carriage streamed into my eyes.

"Hello Mr. Jacobs, are you ready to start your second life?" the voice said.

Final Delivery By Jeff Dawson

PROLOGUE

Gunther Brown spent his hours recalling his grandfather's stories of how Germany should have won the war. He spent his free time poring over the failed tactics Hitler forced his generals to follow. He knew where the mistakes occurred and how, if given the chance, he could change the course of history. Instead of the brave soldiers of the Wehrmacht shivering and dying in the snow-covered landscape around Moscow, with his intuition and tactics, they would have spent the winter of 1941 in warm beds in the confines of the Kremlin.

His obsessions would thrust him back to October 2nd, 1941, where he would join his comrades in their final attack on Moscow. For Gunther, it would be his final delivery for glory or death.

Tula, Russia

September 16th, 2015

Karl always scoffed when I recalled the stories of my grandfather, Frederick. He was proud of his service during the war. Like many of his fellow countrymen, he answered the call to arms with no doubts. The war would purge Europe of a common foe: Communism. It was infecting and sucking the life from every living creature it touched. It flooded the streets like a plague. It was time to end its transgression and vile leaders.

Lenin roared how wonderful his visions were from the cathedrals in Leningrad and Moscow. The teachings of Marx were the only way a country could grow and prosper. Everyone worked for a larger cause: The State, The Motherland, The Rowdina. He always failed to mention how only he and his elite group would benefit from the toils of the masses. Yes, he was no better than the monarchy he brought to its knees.

Unlike Lenin, Hitler knew the true path to victory. He knew who the enemy was, and for Germany to survive, the virus must be eradicated.

"Gunther, stop daydreaming. We're approaching the junction. Contact the trainmaster."

"What?"

"Stop daydreaming, and wake up, man. We don't want to meet another train head-on unless you're ready to meet your maker. I, for one, am not. Now get on the phone, you dolt!"

I hated Karl for his insolence and belittling. If not for me, the railroad would have never hired him. It was my connections which allowed him to…

"Dammit man! Now!"

"Trainmaster, this is Unit 59 approaching outer yard. We are reducing speed to 35 kilometers. Awaiting instructions."

"Unit 59, this is Tula control. Reduce speed to 15 kilometers. Follow green lights to siding."

"Affirmative. Reduce speed to 15 kilometers, and follow green lights to siding."

I shuddered each time we pulled in to this station. What should have been our crowning moment was crushed by the Mongols of Siberia. They came screaming across the frozen plains, routing my fallen brethren. I glanced out the frosty window, ensuring the proper switches were thrown as our train proceeded with caution. The tracks were clear, but something was moving ahead. I could make out men in greatcoats running beside us. They were screaming out *Uns Männer! Uns Männer!* I wiped the snow from my eyes. Surely not? I detected the sound of tank treads pushing against the white landscape. The silhouettes were dark but unmistakable—Kampfwagon IIIs and Sturmgeschützes.

"Slow down, Unit 59. Slow down!" screamed the trainmaster's voice over the intercom. Karl applied the brakes, bringing us to a stop.

"Gunther, one more mistake and I'm reporting you. We almost ran into another train."

"Karl, did you see the men and tanks outside? They were…"

"What? What were they, Gunther? The proud dead bodies of soldiers long forgotten breaching the Kremlin's gates?"

"Why do you mock me, Karl?"

"Because it is a fantasy world you live in. Our world is now; not seventy-five years ago. It's the past, and it should remain there. Your grandfather filled your mind with glories past and conquests which never were. Yet he always forgot to mention the death and destruction that madman brought upon our country and the world."

"Karl, he wasn't a madman. He was a genius, and one day, we shall rise again and resolve the mistakes of the past. I will see to it."

"The only thing you will see to is guiding us to the correct spur. Understood?"

"Yes, Karl, I understand. But one day…" My eyes focused on the green light standard and the tank commander leading his men forward. He looked back at his proud force and yelled, "Kameraden, kommen Sie zu uns (Comrade, come join us)." If only I could.

September 23rd

I was sitting in my small flat reviewing the notes Frederick left for me. No one knew of them but me. My father never understood my fascination with the dead empire that killed over sixty million souls. He didn't understand how I could pore over the tactics of Guederian, Paulus, Manstein, and Peiper. He would tell me, "Son, you are studying men who lost. You should concentrate on those who won: Patton, Montgomery, MacArthur, and Zhukov. These men were winners." I never informed him that the only way they won wasn't based on great strategies or tactics; it was their factories and bottomless manpower pool that made them great. If they had been forced to fight with the same numbers as Germany, their men's remains would litter the battlefields instead of having hundreds of acres of trimmed cemeteries holding their dead. No, they would be forgotten soldiers who died in a lost cause.

Frederick was there. He saw the spires of the Kremlin glistening in the sunlight. His men were hardened and ready for the final push. It wasn't they who failed; it was the meddling of the communists who'd infiltrated OKH. Himmler was responsible for security and background checks on those who surrounded the greatest military mind in history. It should have been him who was shot in Prague, not Reinhard. Yes, if Reinhard had been in control, the traitors would have been rounded up long before July 20, 1944. But then, history didn't always follow a true path. It was recorded so men like myself would learn the lessons of the past and devise the correct plans to ensure victory. Yes — victory would be mine.

I returned to the album, admiring my father's squad of grenadiers. They exhibited the look of grizzled veterans. I could feel the weariness in their faces, but I also saw the glint of victory in each of his men's eyes. They weren't the hollow eyes the allied pictures always depicted. No, these were the faces of seasoned warriors preparing for the final push. They were ready for the task.

Behind his squad sat a squat, powerful Sturmgeschutz. History would show that the short barrel 75mm was no match for head-on assaults with the Russian T-34/76 or the monster KVIIs, but in the hands of the elite panzer formations, their tactics were superior. Outnumbered and outgunned, they littered the battlefields with burning Russian hulks. The commander was looking straight into the camera. I felt he was talking to me. "Kameraden, kommen Sie zu uns." And then his lips moved.

I closed the album and took off for bed, smiling.

September 25th

"Gunther, contact the trainmaster. Gunther!"

"What is it, Karl?"
"The trainmaster. Call the trainmaster. We're approaching the junction."

"Yes, of course."
"If you daydream one more time on your post, I will have no choice but to report your behavior. You are putting us in jeopardy."

"Karl, one day, you will understand what is and isn't important. Until then, tend to the brakes, and let me run this train. Trainmaster, this is Unit 59. We are three kilometers out and slowing to 20kph."

"Unit 59, you are cleared to enter. Reduce speed to 5kph. Watch for caution lights. Tracks are not clear. Repeat, tracks are not clear."

"Understood, trainmaster. Reducing to 5kph. Proceeding with caution to side track." I slid the side window back and breathed in the cold, sharp Russian air. Most of my comrades, like Karl, hated the cold. It burst through your clothes, penetrating every bone and joint. For me, it invigorated my aching soul when I remembered how many fell in the name of victory. They were so close. It was at this junction where the Siberians unleashed their fresh divisions on my ancestors. If Guderian and Halder had known of the reinforcements, they would have planned the offensive differently. They could have absorbed the main blows, eliminated the armored formations, dealt with the waves of infantry, then regrouped and taken the gates of Moscow. Yes, that is how it should have happened.

I peered into the snowy blindness, congratulating myself on planning the perfect strategy. My thoughts were disturbed by the sound of explosions and blinding lights. To my right, I could see endless shells crashing into the hard-packed soil. The counterattack had begun. Didn't the Russians understand the futility of firing shells? Obviously not. Swine. They were only preparing perfect foxholes for the glorious troops of the Wehrmacht. The men would be able to hide in the holes and prepare to repel the onrush. I heard the sounds of engines firing up. Yes, they were ready to meet the red hordes. I saw the tanks moving into some of the larger shell holes. Excellent. They would lower their silhouettes to the enemy gunners and increase their chances of knocking out the charging monsters. Yes, they'd been reading my plans.

The same commander I saw a week before was rallying the men and preparing them for the coming battle. He was calm and cool as he directed the men and machines. His plan was mine. We developed it together. Victory would be…

"Unit 59! Unit 59! You must stop now! Stop now!"

Karl threw the brakes before the intercom disturbed my military prowess. He'd seen the red brake light from the parked tanker car.

"Gunther, consider yourself reported. If we had collided with the fuel train in front of us, the fuel cars we're pulling could have erupted, sending us to our maker. I am not prepared to meet him. I have a family to care for."

"Do what you must, Karl."

I redirected my attention to the raging battle outside. The tank was only five meters from the engine. I could see the Knight's Cross and Cross of Iron decorating this brave leader's neck and tunic. He was peering through his binoculars. A small smile played on his lips. The smile of a commander prepared for battle. He lowered the glasses, scanning the horizon from right to left. When his eyes and mine met, I heard the words. "Kameraden, kommen Sie zu uns."

"Soon, Commander, soon."

September 27th

Once again, I found myself drawn to the old album. Carefully, I turned the pages until the one I sought appeared. Yes, the one with my grandfather was waiting for me. They were no longer looking into the lens. They were spread out amongst the shell holes, waiting—waiting for the enemy to come rushing forward to their doom. The commander scanned the horizon with his binoculars, waiting for the moonlight to glisten off a metallic object to warn him of the impending battle. The muscles on his face were tense yet relaxed. I could feel the tension of battle brewing in his rigid stance. He lowered the glasses, barked out a few commands, then looked at me. "Kameraden, es ist an der Zeit, sich uns anzuschließen (Comrade, it is time to join us)."

"Yes, yes. I wish to be part of this great battle. I can smell the cordite from the shellfire. I can feel the ground rumble as the enemy tanks approach. We are prepared. This time, we shall be victorious." I blinked my eyes. The picture was empty. I blinked again. My eyes couldn't focus on the images. The landscape was black and scorched. The once proud commander was roasting in his metal tomb. T-34s were grinding the remains of the fallen into the hard-packed surface. No! This cannot be. The plans were perfect. We left nothing to chance. Victory was inevitable. I blinked again. The original picture returned; a voice calls out, "Kameraden, kommen Sie zu uns."

September 29th

     I was called to the trainmaster's office. Karl had indeed reported my lapse in concentration. The trainmaster showed leniency. I was two weeks from retirement. If the government released me early, my benefits would be cut in half. Not nearly enough to support myself. He was impressed with my service record. For thirty years, I'd served the railroad with distinction and honor. He agreed to let me finish out my employment and leave the railroad with full pay and benefits. One would think I was pleased with the decision. Outside, I was, but inside, I knew the next trip would be my last. I was going to join my comrades and regale in the victory we deserved. We would sweep away the mongoloid hordes intent on destroying our "God-Given Destiny." We would storm the gates of Moscow and plant our flag on the Kremlin. With the main transportation hub severed, we would be able to deal with Leningrad in the North and Stalingrad in the South at our leisure. In months, all of Eastern Europe would be under the sphere of the swastika and the Third Reich. Then, we could divert our attentions and resources to other bothersome theatres. The plan was so simple it was brilliant. I would not need my pittance of remembrance from my former employer; I would receive a payment they could never understand or provide: Victory!

October 2nd

I could barely contain the excitement welling up inside. This would be my last trip in Russia as a defeated man. This would be a triumphant travel into the pages of history. This time, it would be different. This time, it would be our flags covering the landscape instead of the hated hammer and sickle. This time would be different. But for the plan to be utilized, I had to make the trip alone.

Karl was ever vigilant and the best brakeman I'd worked with, but like many, he was not a believer. I tried many times to educate him to no avail. It pained me, but it had to be done. Our train sped across the desolate, moonlit landscape at a steady 60kph. I found solace knowing it would be painless and quick.

"Karl, I'm showing a loss of pressure between the main engine and dummy #1. Please go check the connection, and make sure it hasn't iced up. I don't want to plow into a sitting train. It wouldn't look good on our records."

Karl studied my face, looking for something he hadn't seen in over a month—concentration.

"Are you sure, Gunther? The lines looked good at Smolensk."

"I'd rather be safe than sorry, Karl. It'll only take a minute."

"You know it's twenty degrees outside?"

"All the more reason to verify the lines are clear."

"Very well." He donned his parka, grabbed his lamp, and moved out of the cab.

I saw his beam dancing between the engines.

"Gunther. What are you doing here?"

"Verifying your findings."

"See for yourself. The lines are clear. Now, let's get out of this accursed cold."

I raised my right hand, revealing the crowbar.

"Gunther, are you mad?" he screamed over the howling wind.

"No, Karl." I struck him over the head and watched his body fall into the enveloping darkness.

"Ich komme, meine Freunde (I am coming, my friends)."

20 Kilometers from Tula Junction

The sounds of the battle resonated in the cab. Flashes of artillery fire lit up the skies. I could see the panzers and grenadiers moving forward, mowing down the enemy as a farmer's sickle does wheat. The reds were on the run now. It was a glorious sight, and there to my right was my commander riding high in his cupola, urging the men and tanks on. Our machines matched speed. He urged me to join them. I waited no longer and sprang from the walkway onto his weapon of victory. He handed me a greatcoat, a helmet, and a rifle. "We've longed for your company. Tonight, we shall live large and enjoy the music and performance of the Bolshoi Opera. Gunther, it will be a glorious day for our Fatherland and Führer. Today, we shall claim our place in the annals of history. Today, the world will shudder as our men and tanks roll into Red Square and vanquish the Communist Stalin and his scum from the face of the Earth. Today, we achieve victory!"

His words inspired us all. We fought and died for the glory of the Reich. Yes, many of our brothers perished in the snow, but less than the enemy. We'd felt the weight of their forces and repelled them with superior tactics and equipment. They withered before our guns, crying for their mothers and fathers. The treads of our tanks silenced their pitiful pleas for mercy and understanding. They understood nothing. They were *untermenschen*. The only tasks they were fit for were polishing our boots, digging cesspools, or dying. I couldn't help but wonder, as we forged ahead, why our numbers never seemed to diminish. I knew we were taking losses, but our ranks never thinned. Reinforcement battalions. Yes, that's what it was. We had broken through, and the generals were releasing the reserves to exploit the breakthrough. Nothing could stop us now. No force on Earth could stop us from achieving our destiny.

We moved across the landscape at a frightening pace. I couldn't help but think back to how the history books mocked our meager, underequipped forces. They only talked of the tired, beaten, worn men who saw no hope with "Operation Typhoon." They were all fools. This time, we did it right. The army was young, fresh, and battle-hardened. We were well-supplied. Our vehicles were fresh from the factories or returned from the work depots. This was how it should have been, but the

Communists who infected our high command issued incorrect orders guaranteeing the offensive would fail. Not this time. No, this time, we would achieve our goals.

We marched on, killing the enemy at every turn and giving them no quarter. We took no prisoners; there was no time for secondary tasks. If some survived, let the rear echelons deal with them. We must reach the summit and hold it.

I wondered at the sight before me. Searchlights danced across the cold, wintry, cloudy sky, illuminating the spires of the Kremlin. I looked around in a daze. "We made it! We have captured the Kremlin!" I shouted.

"Yes, comrade, we have achieved our victory." I turned to see the tank commander standing a few meters behind me holding a victory flag.

"It is yours and his to raise."

"Who do you speak of?"

He stood aside.

"Grandfather. It's you. You made it."

"Yes Gunther, we survived. Let us take our rightful place in history, but first, a warrior should be honored." He reached into his pocket and removed a Knight's Cross. The captain stepped forward, removed the medal from its case, and draped it across my neck. I was filled with a warrior's pride. Victory had been achieved. Grandpapa finished the impromptu ceremony. "Gunther, it is time we…" His words trailed off. The smile from his face disappeared as he dropped the flag to the ground. His energetic eyes were no longer glistening. They were dark and hollow.

The yelling of the trainmaster awoke me from my victory.

"UNIT 59! UNIT 59! YOU ARE GOING TO CRASH!"

My eyes focused too late as the single red light of the parked tanker car raced towards my engine.

A blinding white light filled my eyes. The sounds of Russians dying by the scores filled my mind. Then silence.

* * *

I awoke feeling the icy ground piercing my clothes. My body shivered as snowflakes covered my shaking body. *Where am I?* I rolled on my side. Tears fell and crystallized in the subzero temperatures. I blinked my eyes again. The proud battalion lay dead and scattered over the battlefield. The young, energetic tank commander's body was roasting in his burning hulk. No, we won. We won! This can't be. A moan in the darkness gained my attention. I crawled towards the sound. The voice was familiar yet distant. Yes, I knew the voice. "Grandfather, where are you?"

His voice was shallow and hoarse. "Turn back, Gunther. I was wrong. It's not your war."

"Grandfather, we can win. We can win."

"No, Gunther, I was a fool. Only a fool would believe. I learned too late. Turn back before you too become another casualty. Please, go back before it's too late."

For the first time in my life, I was ashamed to be a German. I was ashamed my grandfather was a traitor. I would rally the forces and urge the men forward. I rose to my feet, picked up a rifle and a helmet, and turned to face the enemy. I turned too late. My eyes were met with the treads of a T-34.

October 3rd

The press and officials were scouring the wreck of Unit 59. The chief inspector was questioning the trainmaster.

"Did Unit 59 ever acknowledge your orders?"

"No, sir."

"Was there any conversation with the brakeman?"

"No, sir."

"Why do you think he disregarded all of your warnings?"

"Inspector, I have no idea."

"This is most unusual."

"Yes, sir; it is."

They directed their eyes onto the charred remains of the engineer. Despite the body being badly burned, there was one unblemished, distinguishing mark: the outline of a Knight's Cross burned into his throat.

END

Cabinet of Truth Written by D. C. Golightly

As much as he tried, Eustace could never silence them.

"Come on, Eustace! They'll be closing soon!"

His mind pulled away from his troubles thanks to his friend shouting. Eustace rounded the corner and tried to forget the other voices. The ones only he could hear.

The young boy sprinted ahead of Eustace, determined to not miss the one attraction of the Paragon Carnival he had traveled to see. The sun was long past set with the silhouette of surrounding hillsides creating a wall around where the wandering circus had sunk its foundations for the time being. The veil was thin, but it covered the crowd and employees alike.

"Right then," Eustace managed to mutter. Instead of thinking about where they were going, though, he was thinking about how long of a distraction this would serve as. How long until he was back home and he could begin hearing them again?

As usual, Eustace was bringing up the rear of their duo. A pudgy boy since birth, he had long ago accepted his physique and wouldn't even bother trying to catch the coattails of his friend. Not that he wore coattails, of course. As 12-year-olds, they hadn't more than a few pennies between them to afford the astounding sights of the carnival.

And astounding they were! From the Flexible Man to the incredible trapeze artists and their daring aerial maneuvers. When the carnival came nearby on a semi-annual basis, Eustace could always account for his best friend to knock on his door with the new flyer in hand.

"Come on!"

"Yes, yes, Michael," Eustace stammered as he rounded the corner of a red and white-striped tent.

Michael, the antithesis of Eustace, if there could be such a thing, stood long-legged and wide-eyed before the side attraction he promised to savor the most this year. Whereas most of the entertainment in the carnival was hidden from public viewing by ancient tent flaps, this particular one was housed within a rather large trailer.

The room on wheels was steadied by legs that were punched into the dirt. No windows would reveal the secrets inside. The roof looked to have been elongated upward, as if unfolded from within, easily doubling the normal height of the trailer. Several extensions of the walls were haphazardly latched on like boils protruding from the main body.

Above it all was a curved sign that read, "Mister Percival's Cabinet of Curiosities" in gold letters that were two feet high.

Eustace chanced a glance at Michael, who was beaming. Pulling his attention away from the new attraction, Michael asked, "What do you think is inside?"

"Don't know," Eustace replied. "I expect we'll find out, yeah?"

Michael laughed and then clapped Eustace on the back. He approached the trailer, or perhaps it was a caravan now that he saw it better, with Eustace once more in tow.

New to the carnival this year, Mister Percival's Cabinet of Curiosities was being promoted as the latest addition to the whimsical expedition and, according to the flyers, was promised to be an instant treasure to all who dared enter. The sketch on the poster had hardly done the thing justice; it was macabre without looking frightening, a trick no doubt accomplished by seeing it in color. The splash of gold lettering at the top looked like a halo when pasted against the reds and blues etching the outlines.

Together, the boys had seen every aspect of the Paragon Carnival since it first began visiting their small mining town. It had become tradition for the pair of youths to explore the newest offerings, critique their authenticity, and generally expand their worldly knowledge. When something new was added, it was typically then the only thing that Michael cared to see.

For Michael, it was a great distraction from the mines themselves; he had joined his father there last summer and already his fingernails were black and chipped away.

For Eustace, it was another kind of distraction, one of the few that would serve to satiate an inner turmoil.

They had gotten a late start on this adventure since Michael had been at the mine since dawn. After a long day of opening vents deep within the mines so that the miners could safely move about the shafts, Michael was released and finally free to explore. By the time Michael had collected Eustace and run to the outskirts where the carnival had set up, they only had an hour before closing to locate Mister Percival's promised entertainment.

Three short steps that had been flipped down from inside the only door led them into a small room, only large enough to fit two people at a time, and it was a tight fit with Eustace being in attendance.

At shoulder-height was a small shelf. The ticket window right above the shelf was closed, and after trading another look with Eustace, Michael politely tapped on the wooden shutter.

It instantly slid open with a thud that startled both boys. Behind the foregone shutter was a man with impossibly white hair and a pointed face. His features seemed to only be present to draw attention to his chin, which was profound. Defying the color of his hair, the man looked young, perhaps only in his twenties. The white hair itself was full and thick, covering his scalp completely without even a widow's peak to reveal his proper age.

"Boys," he said with a smile. "Welcome! How might I be of service to you tonight?"

"We came to see the Cabinet," Michael blurted out. "Are we too late?"

"Late?" the white-haired man replied. "Time is but a symptom of expectation, don't you think? If you fancied to be here just when you arrived, then how could you possibly be too late? No, I think that you have come at precisely the time you were meant to come. Wouldn't you agree?"

"He was working the mines, he means," Eustace said. "Had to hurry over. You aren't closing, are you?"

"The mines, you say. A bit young for that kind of work." The strange man seemed to ponder something as one eye half-closed, but it only lasted a brief moment. "Well, I do always enjoy these blue-collar towns of yours. The twists and turns of the big cities are comforting to me, always welcoming, they are, but I find that your kind of town can quickly become my kind of town if one knows where to look."

Not knowing how to respond, the boys merely looked at one another again, each one hoping that the other could decipher the man's meaning.

"Ha!" he exclaimed. "Never you mind, boys. Come now. You wish to see my Cabinet? I should warn you that inside, you'll find more than just curiosities. Inside here are relics of ancient civilizations that haven't walked our precious grounds for generations, artifacts that prove the unproven, and insight into the very nature of man."

Michael responded with a smile and an extended arm, holding out two tickets to the man. Eustace merely waited beside his friend, a loyal companion who would admit only to himself that he was intrigued.

"Ah, yes. Payment!" The man took the pair of tickets with a flash of movement, depositing them unseen behind the window. "I thank you, young man. And with this transaction, I declare your acceptance into the Cabinet, but do remember my words, and heed these ones: veracity begets epiphany!"

They heard the man stomp his foot, and beside the boys, a door slid back, revealing entry into the deeper portion of the trailer. The darkness inside contained the mysteries of what they were about to witness and added to the overall ambience that Michael was relishing. Eustace pressed his lips together, something he did when he became nervous, but he didn't want Michael to realize that his best friend and most loyal companion was apprehensive about this attraction.

Why should he be nervous, though? So far, this wasn't anything different than what the carnival had offered them in the past. Perhaps it was something that this man, this possible Mister Percival, had said. He couldn't detect any malice, yet here he was, on the precipice of discovery, and he was hesitant.

Michael boldly stepped through the threshold without a second thought, as he always did. Eustace watched the darkness swallow his friend.

"You only need worry if you've something to worry about," the man said beside him.

Eustace opened his mouth to reply, but a snap of wood slapping against wood signaled that the owner of the trailer had shut himself away again. With a deep breath to encourage himself, there was nothing left for Eustace to do but enter the Cabinet.

Once he crossed over the threshold, the door slid shut behind him. Pitch blackness enveloped him and his pulse began to race. Perhaps this wasn't the smartest thing he had done, but this wasn't so different from the carnival's Haunted Maze attraction.

A sizzling sound cut through the silence, quickly followed by a row of gas lamps igniting along the top edge of the room they now stood within. Light thankfully flooded their surroundings and Eustace saw that he was a mere inch away from Michael, who was now taking in the same fantastic scene as him.

The trailer was filled with pedestals and suspended glass tanks, each displaying something odd and irregular. Michael's eyes were open as wide as they could go, and Eustace followed his gaze to the closest item for their consideration.

"Incredible," Michael muttered.

Just a foot or so in front of them was a pillar rising to their navels, holding for them a single item: a decrepit and twisted black animal hand. The fingernails were pointed on the ends and looked deadly. Charred fur lined the top of the hand while the palm was smooth and padded. A plaque fastened to the pillar explained the curious item.

'AUTOCHTHON HAND – *Placed upon a sacrificial table, the inhabitants of an island off the coast of New Zealand would give the hand of a chief to their god in exchange for favor and a good harvest. If the god did not grant his favor, the hand was cleansed in fire.*'

"A chieftain's hand!" Michael exclaimed. "Amazing! Do you think it's real?"

"As real as this Cabinet, I'd say," Eustace replied, which he thought was a clever answer.

Another two paces into the oddly constructed room revealed yet another curiosity. A glass tank suspended from the ceiling by straps of leather held the display at eye level for them to leer into. Inside was an open book, tilted so that they could see the obtuse writing scribbled within. Eustace didn't recognize the language other than it appeared to be Germanic, and he only knew that because of his neighbor, Miss Kauff, and her grocery lists. Another plaque attempted to satisfy their intrigue.

'SECRET MALTESE DIARY – Written by a Carpathian general during the Spanish occupation of Malta by a Spanish Aragonese dynasty in 1291, this diary details the general's plans for returning power to the local constabulary.'

From display to display, the pair of boys made their way through the relatively small Cabinet of Curiosities. While it was true that the space was ultimately limited to the square footage of the trailer, the chambers bolted onto the sides created extra display space alongside the roof extension. The displays created a maze through which the duo slowly traversed, seeking the exit amongst the items of amazement.

The final item was a standing mirror placed against the very back wall of the trailer. Edged in silver, the mirror seemed to hold no obvious context of obscurity. Eustace stood to one side and bent over to read the accompanying plaque.

'LOOKING GLASS OF RECTITUDE.'

There was no description, which set this object aside from all others amidst the bizarre museum. Michael stood in front of the mirror just a few feet back from its clean and shiny surface, sizing himself up.

"Just a regular mirror," he said, his voice proclaiming his disappointment.

Eustace stepped beside him to take in the mirror himself and at first thought nothing but mimicked feelings. When he looked slightly down, however, he was stunned at what he saw.

In the mirror, he gripped Michael's hand tightly. The boys stood just as they were, but otherwise, their digits were firmly intertwined with one another. Eustace took a half step back and looked down at his hands, which were assuredly not grasping Michael's hand.

Again, he looked in the mirror, and again, he saw their hands holding one another. It was a strange sight to see, but a comforting one somehow.

And then *they* started speaking to him again.

From within his very core, perhaps his soul, whispers began to grow. What started as an unintelligible muttering quickly pushed all thought from his mind and overtook him. He could rarely understand what these voices, these inner elocutions, were saying to him. There were too many to separate from one another, and once they began, he typically could not bear them.

Eustace stepped back unwillingly, once again confused and frightened. He glanced at Michael, who was studying the mirror and didn't seem to notice his discomfort.

He realized he was terrified of Michael discovering this plague, this terrible nuisance that he suffered daily. What would Michael think of him if he discovered what a sad wretch he truly was?

Eustace looked into the mirror again, focusing on his entwined fingers, unable to tell which were his and which were Michael's.

But why would he ever feel that way toward Michael? In what realm could he ever hope that he and Michael...that they could...

The voices flared up, and for the first time since he had been visited by them, they shattered his consciousness. Eustace gripped his ears as sweat began to bead on his forehead. The voices now brought with them pain, a head-splitting screech rocked his brains and his eyes rolled into the back of his head.

He stumbled backward as the voices began to form words for the first time:

Disgrace!

Humiliation!

Scorn!

"I suppose he hasn't had time to write up the description for this one then," Michael said, and just as he did, the mirror swung open to reveal the exit.

Blessed silence swept through Eustace. The pain departed, leaving a scar, but still it subsided. He had to blink several times before he could see straight again. The mirror, now angled away from him, looked dark and empty.

Michael stepped out, leaving Eustace alone inside the Cabinet. After a few moments to collect himself, Eustace finally exited as well, and the mirror door shut behind them. They were once more standing in the beaten down grass of the field where the carnival had set up shop.

"Fancy some popcorn before we go home?" Michael asked.

Eustace seemed a little dazed but finally nodded his approval. He breathed deeply to collect himself, hoping that Michael didn't see the troubles he underwent. Michael smirked and raced off into the shanty town of red and white tents to find their evening snack, which they would likely share on the long way back into town.

"You have the look of someone with a revelation unknown," a voice said behind Eustace.

Eustace jumped and whirled around to see the white-haired man, who he presumed was the touted Mister Percival, leaning against the side of his Cabinet. His purple coat was down past his knees and looked immaculate. His white gloves matched his hair.

"Sorry?" Eustace finally said.

"I take it you saw what your friend did not in the mirror? Yes, your face betrays you, my young friend. Know this: the mirror does not lie like you do to yourself."

"I don't understand."

The white-haired man took in a breath before replying, seemingly enjoying the cool night air. "It means," he finally responded, "that you cannot admit how you feel about your friend there."

"Feel? I feel nothing. He's my mate, that's all."

A passing tinge of something in the back of his mind.

A whisper, which thankfully quickly quieted itself.

With a sigh, the man said, "I digress. Have a good evening, young master."

And with that, the white-haired man stepped off into the crowd and disappeared. Eustace looked at the Cabinet, which was now darkened and apparently empty. Within moments of watching the crowd, Michael returned to him, carrying a bag of fresh popcorn for them to share.

As his experience replayed before his eyes, he was now asking himself, was Michael a friend? Or more than a friend? He would always dismiss the thought quickly, given that it was a silly idea. What would his father think, after all?

A fleeting whisper.

This question…now that he thought of the mirror and the occasions when the voices began to impede him, didn't they always speak to him when he knew he would be seeing Michael? Wasn't it true that these expressions of something inside him, something that was apparently growing with efficiency, arose when he *thought* of Michael?

He pushed these questions down as he accepted the popcorn, but found that something pushed them back up again.

Liar!

Escapist!

Abolisher!

"Michael," Eustace found himself blurting out. "Can we talk about something?"

Michael smiled at his friend and tossed a handful of the salty treat into his mouth. "Of course! We best be getting on though. Your mum especially is going to get mad if we're back too late."

They walked side by side, quietly chewing for a few heartbeats before Eustace finally said, "I fancy you."

Michael laughed. "Right! We're best mates, you and me. I know that."

"Sure."

Faith!

Reveal!

Accept!

"I mean no," Eustace quickly said. "I mean I like you more than that. I mean we—"

Within another stride, Eustace realized that Michael had stopped walking. He turned back to see Michael was staring at him, an unreadable look on his face. Eustace felt his stomach turn over and his chest tighten, as if this moment of truth was going to be his unraveling.

But Michael instead stepped forward and placed a hand on Eustace's cheek. The blackened fingernails rested just beneath Eustace's field of vision, and his friend's hand felt warm to the touch.

The voices remained silent.

"I know that, too," Michael said.

END

Blasphemous Tumours By David Court

There's a very old cliché about people feeling like they're having an out-of-body experience whenever they're given very bad news — as though it's all happening to somebody else, as though they're watching themselves from the outside, powerless to act. I can categorically state that in my case no such thing happened. Not *then*, anyway. I'd known that something was wrong when my usually friendly (and often quite flirtatious) GP had calmly walked into the room and refused to make eye contact. She'd quietly and carefully navigated around her desk before sitting down and then — in a very matter of fact way — had tried to deliver her next few sentences with as much sincerity as she could muster. I sat there, and I nodded, going through the motions as I told her that I understood what she was telling me. That was only a partial truth as a great deal of my attention was trying to avoid being distracted by her desk calendar.

Her tone was sombre but felt somewhat forced and practiced — disingenuous, even. She placed particular emphasis on the words "malignant," "brain tumour," "aggressive," and "inoperable" whilst all the time, I was noting the delicious irony of the date even though I'm far from a superstitious man and I'll have no truck with astrology. We Pisces rarely do. *Joke.*

It was June the 21st. The first day of Cancer.

#

I'd carried on working for as long as I could after the initial diagnosis—or at least as long as I could until the concoction of painkillers they'd given me on had dulled my brain so much I could barely string coherent sentences together let alone concentrate long enough to produce bug-free code. My work had begun to suffer, and in a meeting with management—with them being uncharacteristically polite, understanding, and sympathetic—it was agreed that it'd be best all round if I went on garden leave. "We'll continue to pay you," they'd stuttered, "until you…until the end of…"

To be honest with you, odds were I'd be dead way before my three-month notice period had expired at any rate. It just pissed me off that I'd never experience another Christmas again. I bloody love Christmas.

There was an awkward and uncomfortable silence from my usually boisterous and noisy colleagues as I gathered my meagre belongings from work into an old printer box. It was the first time in the decade or so I'd been working there that I could recall there not being at least a background noise of trivial chit-chat, humming, and whistling.

Tom, my cubicle neighbour, had clearly drawn the short straw from the department. As I went to leave, he got to his feet and stood in front of me, refusing to look me in the eye. In his hands, he held out an exotic-looking plant, offering it to me with the timid nervousness of a villager making a sacrifice to a vengeful God.

"We had a whip round," he stammered. "We—we got you this."

To be the source of discomfort in others is a horrible thing. I constantly felt on the verge of apologising for my condition—if only one of them would make eye contact with me long enough. You'd honestly think that cancer could be transmitted from looking at someone affected by it, such was the reticence of anybody to do so.

I took the plant—an ugly looking thing, by all accounts—and mumbled a half-hearted thank you. The pot had one of those stickers on it proudly proclaiming how long it would remain fresh for. Turns out, this bright green morass of odd-shaped leaves would outlive *me*.

I placed my office keys on the front desk and left to an overwhelming chorus of complete silence. A tiny voice in the back of my mind urged me to stay strong.

#

At the advice of my doctor, I started seeing a counsellor, who in turn recommended I start writing down my experiences and my feelings. Our weekly meetings were awkward and stilted—I'd always struggled expressing myself in words, and even with this deadline that fate had suddenly imposed on me, I found myself unable to open up. Despite her attempts to help, I found myself growing increasingly angry and frustrated with my lot in life, with this unfairly rotten hand I'd been dealt.

It was late one evening when I'd downed the best part of three bottles of wine in a half-hearted attempt to see whether I could get my liver to pack up before my brain in some manner of death-match bodily organ tug-of-war. I'd been trying to write a new blog post for hours but couldn't find the correct words and was having difficulty even focussing on the ones I *had* written. I'd decided that it was probably about time to call it a night (which would involve either struggling up the stairs or just collapsing here in my chair, the latter sounding way more achievable) when I heard the *voice*.

An unfamiliar voice from inside the room, as clear as day. It had barked my name as though trying to get my attention.

I spun around on the spot, my ancient desk chair protesting with a series of noisy squeaks. It couldn't have come from the PC; the attached headphones were in the same tangled spaghetti mess of cables they'd lain in for weeks—and there definitely wasn't anybody in here with me. I knew this because there wasn't room to swing a cat—confirmed in a drunken experiment back in 2008 that resulted in the laceration of most of my right arm.

There it was—my name again. Spoken in a northern accent—North English, more precisely, in a broad Bradford accent. I'd always had an unerring knack for recognising dialects.

"I'm not in the room, lad. I'm in your head."

I slumped against the wall, despondent. They'd warned me that as the tumour got worse that I could expect hallucinatory symptoms as it caused an increase of pressure inside my skull, but I'd hoped that the cancer would have done me in before it got that far. This was the beginning of the end and my greatest fear—that I'd spend my last days or weeks on this Earth unable to care for myself and that I'd exist as nothing except as a burden for others.

"I'm not a hallucination, you daft sod," the voice chuckled.

A barrage of thoughts flooded my cancerous brain. How much worse could these hallucinations get? Would they be a constant fixture in what remained of my life now with me unable to tell fiction from reality? And as a proud Midlander born and bred, why was the voice of my hallucination *northern*?

"I've said it before, and I'll say it again. I'm not a hallucination."

Of course you're not, I thought. *I'm clearly undergoing a visitation from a ghost or the invisible man.* I squinted and clutched the sides of my head and screamed at the voice to go away. After a few of moments of blessed silence, I reopened my eyes and looked about myself.

"If you've quite finished," continued the voice, "I'm far from a hallucination. I'm… Well, I guess I could say that I'm your tumour."

A talking cancer. I laughed. Now I'd heard it all.

"I've been here for some time, pal, and I've learned a fair few old tricks. Been trying to have this little chat for days, but I just haven't been strong enough."

This suddenly explained a lot. I'd been suffering from particularly bad headaches for a couple of weeks now and for a little while had been noticing somebody calling my name as though in the distance, but when I'd turned around, nobody was there. I'd forgotten about it at the time, but it all became clear.

Wait—what was I thinking? Was I beginning to entertain this ridiculous premise?

"Why are you... *northern?*"

"Your guess is as good as mine, pal. Not being in possession of any actual vocal chords of course, there's no reason I should have any dialect at all. I'm simply firing my thoughts directly into your own brain, which you're then interpreting as speech. The fact you're hearing me as northern is... Well, it's nothing to do with me; let's just leave it at that."

"So, you're my cancer?"

"That's right"

"And we're having a chat."

"It would certainly *appear* so, my good friend. And not a moment too soon."

"Do you think you could just go away? Just bugger off, and leave me alone, so I'm sort of not actually dying of cancer?"

"Well, that's the trick, isn't it? I'm quite happy with this sentience malarkey now. I like living."

"Well, I'm sorry about that. That really makes this quite awkward."

Awkward. *Awkward?!* He—*it* was killing me. Could I be any more British? I was telepathically apologising to a *fucking cluster of cancerous cells.*

"It does. Because I know for a fact that you're off for an operation early next week. One in which you're off to get a chunk of me taken out in the hope it might delay my spreading and prolong your life."

"How do you —? Oh, of course."

"Tapped into your brain, remember? Haven't you wondered how we've been carrying out this conversation without you so much as moving your lips? I know and see *all*."

"I hadn't thought about it, to be honest. Or rather I had. Stop confusing me."

"Look, let's be honest with each other. I'm here, and I'm here to stay. If you have the operation, it'll give you an extra couple of weeks, but I'll be back with a vengeance. You're riddled with me, to be fair. And have you ever noticed how you can never be riddled with anything good? Nobody ever says, 'Ooh, he's riddled with good luck.' It's only ever for disease or lice or cancer and — anyway, I digress. Cards on the table."

There was a pause whilst my cancer cleared its thoughts.

"If you pop your clogs, it's not a bed of roses for me either. I'll live out the rest of my short existence in a coffin with no company. The diagnosis isn't good for a cancer in a dead host; believe me."

"I've decided I'm being cremated."

"Bloody hell. That's even worse. How had I forgotten that? But you see my point; *it's not in my interest to kill you off*. What I can do, though, is that I can carefully contain how I spread throughout your system. In all fairness, there's no reason that the two of us can't peacefully co-exist. Admittedly, the arrangement can't keep going for as long as it'll take for you to get a chuffin' telegraph for your 100th birthday from the Queen, but we can certainly stretch your life expectancy out for far longer than you thought you'd have had when you woke up this morning."

It sounded reasonable. They'd warned me that the prognosis from the forthcoming operation was poor anyway, so it wasn't even as though he was telling me anything I didn't already know. Assuming, of course, that the conversation *had* actually just taken place and this wasn't entirely a hallucinatory construct. Still, my cards were well and truly marked. What did I have to lose?

#

My doctor was very understanding when I cancelled the operation. To be fair, she'd clearly been trying to talk me out of it since the idea was first introduced to me. I rolled off some rehearsed waffle about "quality of life" and "not wanting to take any unnecessary risks this close to the end," and she nodded and smiled and wished me the best. I couldn't tell her what had actually happened—she'd have had me locked up.

And life for the next few months went on as normal. For the most part, Mr. Cancer (as I'd nicknamed him—for logical reasons, he wanted to be called by my name, but I told him that'd just be confusing) would leave me alone; the headaches went, and he even went that little bit further and did me an enormous favour by blocking out some of the other chronic pain I was experiencing. This bizarre symbiotic relationship appeared to be working well for us both. I found myself sleeping better, and my appetite had increased—all down to his work, I'd imagine.

Whereas we spoke at great lengths in the early days, as time went on, he withdrew a little. Often, he'd sound distracted or simply tired. He'd explained that he didn't want to be too obtrusive—he didn't want to run the risk of us getting irritated by each other's company.

For the first time since the original diagnosis, I was enthusiastic and filled with a new love for life. I fitted more into a few months than I'd managed previously over an entire lifetime. I conquered my fear of heights with insanely tall rollercoasters and skydiving and tried foods that I couldn't pronounce or spell the names of, and Mr. Cancer was there for all of it with me. I was experiencing unique adventures for the first time. Well, we both were, I guess. Me and my malignant travelling companion.

It was a year—a whole *year!*—after the original diagnosis that my doctor got in touch to ask how I was doing and if I'd be willing to pop along to the hospital for a few X-rays. I thought Mr. Cancer would be reluctant to go ahead with that, but he didn't object.

"It's going to be more suspicious if you don't go," he said. "And all they'll see is that I've spread slower than they'd predicted. Nothing dodgy there at all."

#

It was the morning of the hospital appointment. I was showered and ready to leave the house, but Mr. Cancer hadn't made his presence known that morning. He'd usually pop up when I went to have breakfast—he definitely had his cereal preference—and I'd try to arrange it so we had an even share.

Despite the northern accent—which neither of us could ever adequately explain—we'd identified a few differences between ourselves. He loved bananas, whereas I'd never been able to stand them. Texture, taste—everything about them repulsed me on every conceivable level. Every now and then, he'd not unreasonably want to eat some, so I'd have to force some down, wincing with every chew. It was a small price to pay, though, considering the benefits of our *arrangement*. His musical tastes were also slightly more refined than mine; he'd insist on listening to classical whilst bemoaning the amount of guitar-based rock that made up the majority of my own collection.

I was leaving the house and had just started the car when he appeared with a chirpy, "Good morning." We exchanged pleasantries as I drove towards the hospital.

"You seem nervous," he said.

"I am. Maybe just a little. These last twelve months have been…incredible. Incredible and unexpected. I know you keep telling me you've got total control over your growth, but I can't help but worry. What if I'm running out of time quicker than either of us thought?"

"Don't worry," he replied calmly and reassuringly. "Everything is going to be just fine."

#

"It's better than we could ever have predicted," she said as she pointed at a monochrome scan being projected onto the wall. "There's very little growth from the tumour at all."

She pointed at a small dense ball of matter at the edge of the scan. "There, that's it. And the best thing is it that appears to have shrunk back of its own accord. We can remove it with ease. Should be a relatively simple operation, and we can whip the whole thing out."

"See," said Mr. Cancer directly into my head. "You needn't have worried at all. I told you—complete control over my growth."

"I know you were reluctant to do so before," she continued, "but the situation is very different now. I'll need to double-check with my colleagues, but I can confidently say I think we can safely remove it without anything more than minor risk. What do you say?"

"Yeah, cut it out—the sooner the better," I heard myself say, the faint, familiar hint of a northern accent in my voice. Only I hadn't said that; Mr. Cancer had but through my mouth. I tried to speak but couldn't. My body simply wasn't responding. I tried to move my arms, my legs—to do *anything*—but I was no longer in control.

I screamed out in frustration for him to tell me what was happening, that he explain what was going on, but my panicked cries were ignored.

#

And then the oxygen mask was descending, moving closer and closer, and I found myself screaming aloud at Mr. Cancer to do something. As my—or rather my body's—vision faded, I heard his voice in the encroaching darkness.

"Ironic, isn't it. They're going to be cutting out the only part of your brain that *isn't* cancerous. The only bit that's still *you*. I did tell you—complete control."

"Bye."

\#

Only now, at the very end, does that out-of-body experience *finally* happen. The sensible and pragmatic part of me knew that what I was seeing couldn't possibly be real, that it was highly unlikely that I'd been reduced to an ethereal presence staring down at a bright, bloodied pink walnut—a lump of dead matter, all that was me—being splashed unceremoniously into a glass beaker. As the water reddened with swirling eddies of crimson, the darkness returned again—this time to consume me completely. The last thing I ever saw was the eyes of my body flick open, an alien yet somehow familiar presence behind them.

\#

"So we're quietly confident that we've managed to cut out all traces of it," she said as she leaned over, smiling. That hint of flirtatiousness could be heard again in her voice.

"That's brilliant news," I said.

Her hand brushed against my arm as she stood up to check my notes. She nodded as she read over them, smiling all the time.

"You'll need to be in for a day or two whilst we monitor you, but I'm confident you can be home to your normal life in a matter of days. Now, is there anything I can get for you? Anything to eat, drink perhaps?"

"I don't think so," I said as she wandered towards the door.

"Actually, yes there is," I shouted just as she was about to walk out. She turned to face me, an expectant eyebrow raised.

"Might sound like an odd request, but I'd kill for a banana."

END

A Voice in a Box By Katriona E MacMillan

I was in the box for a very, very long time. I was in the box for so long I almost forgot why they put me there in the first place. There was this family, you see, with this little girl and this little boy. The little girl got lost in the dark, and then the family got sucked in alongside her…and then there was only the little girl left. So they put her in the box so she wouldn't hurt anyone else. It was not the little girl's fault… She was just special. She was different in a way that they could not control but only contain. The little girl stayed in the box until she grew up. This is the way of my world.

The box was three feet by three feet. It was made of one-foot-thick, reinforced glass on all sides except for the top. The top was open so that the scientists could come and go and prod and poke with their needles and their metal things that they never let me look at. I didn't mind the scientists…they told me about their families and their friends and their lives, and I hung on their words and remember my own family, and then when they were gone, I cried because mine were gone, and it was because of the little girl. The scientists all wore lights on their heads that were ridiculous and make them look all alien and weird. Underneath, above, and on all sides of the box, there were day lamps to keep everything nice and bright. There were only chains on the floor, chains and me. They had to secure me because if I moved, the shadows would get in, and well…I suppose then they would have to kill me. I only saw faces if I turned my head, and then, it's only the tops of heads. I could recognize people by their hairstyles. It took a long time, and I got confused when they wore hats or dyed their hair.

The only person I ever saw was Winston. Winston fed me with a tube from a meter away. I had a drip in my arm, but it was for water. They thought I benefited from the social interaction, or they would never have let Winston in. I think he was supposed to wear one of those lights on his head, but Winston was different from the rest and wouldn't wear the light. He would drop the tube in and then sit on the floor beside me. He would tell me all about his great-granddaughter and all the lovely things they would do together. They would go to the park and feed the ducks. I had never seen a duck, so Winston brought me a picture so I could see. In the picture was a little blond girl with a half loaf of bread and a pink bubble jacket surrounded by what I now recognized to be ducks. Her hair was in pigtails. One day, Winston didn't come back.

Gary came instead. He lowered the tube from the rim under careful supervision from the scientists, and I couldn't see his eyes because he had a light on his head. I was disappointed. Winston had retired, and Gary was another faceless entity. I had no human connection after that. They installed a computer that I could use with one hand. The computer projected films onto the glass of the box. The image was weak and watery in case the dark came with it. I had an episode where the black ink started to swirl out towards me, but the scientists caught it in time. They switched the machine off and fixed it so that there is no black. After that, it was safe.

One day not long after that (there were no nights in the box), I discovered the world of the internet. There were

all sorts of games out there that would occupy my mind.
There were stories and whole books—most of the
masterpieces were available in PDF. There were websites
of things I might buy if I had money and homes that others
lived in so magnificent it made me wonder what one
person would do with all that space. All of the information
I could ever need—everything I was ever curious about
was right there at the tips of my fingers. There were
photographs and maps of every place in the world. There
were even cameras out there that I might look at links
directly with other places. I began to yearn…I began to
crave. I wanted to feel the sea air on my face and dip my
toes in the water. I wanted to run through the fields, but I
didn't even know if my legs still worked, never mind if I
could run or not. I wanted to go to a restaurant and order
too much food, drink too much wine, and have "friends"
who would hold my hair back when I was sick and would
put me into a car to take me home. I wanted to feed the
ducks in a pink bubble jacket. I wanted to live.

In the box, I flexed the ailing muscles in my arms
and legs and longed for the chance to use them. I couldn't
do more than flex because of the chains, but I started to do
it whilst I watched my movies or read my stories. Flex,
flex, flex along to the beat of the music on screen or the
words of the paragraphs. I ate, I slept, I read, I flexed. I
don't know what I was doing it for. It was just something
to do. As my intelligence increased, so did my desire to get
out of there. The scientists who had once been my saviors
became my tormentors. The people I had given myself to
were no closer after ten years to finding a cure for me than
they had been to begin with. I started to get paranoid
there, suspended in my see-through box with wires
coming in and out to keep me alive. I doubted that they

were even trying to find a cure for me; I started thinking maybe they were there to torture me. They took an awful lot of blood from me, so I suspected they were doing something with it. Something sordid. Maybe they were making something out of it? Something that helped others whilst they were meant to be helping me. It was obvious even to me that my blood has certain qualities to it that needed investigated. My blood is black and bleeds from me like ink from a burst pen…perhaps it cured blindness (or caused it). Maybe they were making it into insomnia pills…I didn't know. I started to get a little crazy in there.

The scientists stopped talking to me when I started asking the wrong questions. I went from asking how their families were to asking who they were thinking of voting for in the next election. They started to worry that I had too much contact with the outside world — that I was getting restless. They were right. They brought Ivan in after that. I liked Ivan immediately. He reminded me of Winston. Ivan let me see his face. There was much more to Ivan than I first thought, but our initial encounter was how I shall always remember him.

Ivan was hired to sedate me; he was a proper doctor. He was very good at his job, they said. They said he was the best. He would keep me just drugged enough to stop all those rebellious thoughts in my head from spilling out onto my tongue. The first day he came into the room, I could hear them all talking in muffles through the glass. His voice was new, his low tones stood out from the others. He made me strain to listen even though I knew I couldn't hear through the glass. He was shouting at the scientists. I couldn't hear his words. I turned my head and struggled to see the top of his graying head. He didn't come in that first day. Instead, they spent all day rotating the box. I felt a little queasy, but after the move, it was fine. My feet touched floor and would have given way if the chains on my wrists hadn't held me up. I could make out the figures of silhouettes working behind the lights, so they moved the lights again. The brightness was annoying but necessary, and the newly moved lights blocked out all the darkness and kept me safe. Before they moved the lights, I could see one figure in particular standing just behind the light—as close as he could without causing any danger. I knew it was the new doctor because who else could it be? Once everything had settled down again, Gary extended the tube from the open front of the box. I sipped on dinner and wondered about my curious turn in fortune. I liked the doctor before I even knew his name.

I slept on my feet, which was a bit awkward, but the scientists said they would learn how to make the box revolve permanently. I was so stupidly happy for that little bit of freedom. You know when people say that they "turned their lives around?" That was me in a much more literal sense. My shoulders ached the whole night through and for days afterwards; but the difference in my mental attitude was palpable. They brought in a half a sheet of glass the next day and moved all the lights to slide it into place across the front. It meant I could have my computer again; and again, I wondered why they were keeping me here like this. Why, if I was so dangerous, did they not just kill me? Why not end the threat once and for all? When the doctor came to see me, he talked through the open gap and put his torch on the floor. He was careful but not as careful as the scientists. He was not used to the threat yet. Perhaps he didn't fully understand it. He introduced himself as Doctor Ivan Korovich and apologized that he couldn't shake my hand. I liked him more when he spoke. His voice

was deep and accented, and his face matched what I
thought it would be. He had kind, gray eyes that crinkled
round the edges and salt-and-pepper hair. He had lines on
his face but not so many that he was an old man…just a
man who had lived a little. He leaned on the door with his
arms folded across his white jacket and asked me how I
was. I cried. My tears are normal, so he didn't run and
hide from me. I told him all about the ducks and bubbled
like the little girl in the story when her family dies, and
when he tried to wipe my eyes with a handkerchief, one of
the scientists risked his life to stop him. We didn't speak
anymore after that, but Doctor Ivan Korovich surprised me
because he came back the next day, and the next day, and
the next. Ivan came every day. He told me to call him Ivan,
so I did. Ivan was the first man I ever loved.

Ivan had been coming to see me for a very long
time before we were ever alone together. He asked me if I
knew who the "white-coats" were. I told him obviously
that he was one, and the scientists, and Gary. He laughed
at me. The white-coats were indeed scientists and doctors
and researchers — but they were not the same ones as the
men and women I knew of. There were a whole lot of
people out there who knew about me, he said. He said
they wanted to help me. I told him I had everything I
needed in the box. He looked a little sad. I understand why
now, of course, but hindsight is a wonderful thing. Ivan
was sad to see me in the box. At the time, I tried to tell a
joke or asked him a stupid question so that he would do
something else and not be sad. It hurt me that I had
disappointed him. I really, truly adored that man.

When he was gone that night, I searched on the
internet for the white-coats. My mind expanded in a criss-
cross of merging information. There were others like me —

others who were different and who we couldn't control or understand. The white-coats wanted to bring us out of our containment facilities. They wanted to learn how to use our special powers so that the world would be better for everyone. I thought that their requests sounded reasonable. It hit me like a hurricane that there were people out there who thought I should be *free of the box*. I wrestled with the concept. The box was necessary. The box kept everyone safe from me. The next day, I decided to tell Ivan what had happened to the little girl.

She was only eight. She was playing in the mud with her younger brother. They were making mud-pies. She was putting little black stones in for chocolate chips when the rain started to fall. The little girl led her brother under the cover of the trees for shelter. The family lived in the gap between three fields. On the fourth side was the forest. They were not to go into the forest, but the little girl thought it would be okay to take shelter on the edges. The little girl found a field mouse trying to get out of the rain, and the two chased it for a while. When the rain stopped, the little brother was gone from the shelter. The girl looked at the trees and then shouted for him. When the brother did not return, she followed into the trees and was quickly lost. The girl spent a cold, scary night lost in the darkness. She slept between the overgrown roots of a tree and woke up shaking. She dreamed that there was something crawling up her leg, but when she woke, the thing was still there. The thing was a shadow. It was a shadow. It clung to her, and she fought it, but it would not be brushed off because she could not touch it because it was a shadow. The little girl screamed, and when she next awoke, it was daylight. She did not know where the shadow had gone.

In the rainy gray of an overcast morning, her parents called for her through the drizzle. She answered weakly and spent the next few days in a fever. Her brother was already at home; he had come home the afternoon before. They had been looking for her all night. Someone had loved the little girl once.

Her mother died first. The night had risen, and the little girl had come out of her fever with a fierce anger in her. A rage so powerful there was not a thing she could do to stop it. The anger came with the night just like a shadow. Just like a shadow, it crept out from her feet in her temper. Just like a shadow, it wrapped its ethereal hands around her mother's throat and choked her to death. Her mother died slowly, the shadow having leapt from the girl in a fit of rage. The girl couldn't stop the mother dying. And then the father and the brother saw what happened to the mother, and they were scared and angry. The father knew she had done it. The father went for his shotgun. The brother cried on the floor for his mother, whose body was on the floor at the little girl's feet. Her skin was turning blacker and blacker... It got so black that it faded into the night around it. The lights went out when the father returned. He took aim at the little girl, but there was nothing he could do but wipe at his leaking eyes and shake. He dropped the gun when the darkness spread up his legs. He looked at the little girl like it was all her fault, and then the darkness took him away too. The little girl told the little brother to run, but the little brother was screaming and crying and not paying attention, and the darkness came for him too. The little girl clung to her brother and followed him into the unknown. She let it spread up her arms and legs too because if all the people who loved her were dead and it was all her fault, then she might as well be dead too. She let the darkness pull her in, and she opened her eyes to nothing but black. She couldn't see her hand in front of her face, but she scrabbled around in the endless night anyway. The people she loved were gone, and she found no trace of them ever again. When the little girl next woke up, someone had brought her here. And she became the woman in the box.

Doctor Ivan Korovich put down his pen halfway through and listened to the story. I think he understood in the end. I think he knew already what was going to happen. I think maybe you do too, reader.

The white-coats came in the night (they told me after). They came with guns. I never saw a scientist with a gun before then. For a long time, there was shouting in the corridors, and then after that, all the scientists ran away. I only knew because I couldn't hear the buzz of their machines any longer. It was a noise I had never noticed until it went quiet. I could smell smoke, and there were the loud, ear-drum piercing sounds of bullets being fired, scientists shooting at scientists. It was Ivan who came to rescue me...Ivan whom I loved. I like to think maybe he loved me too.

He came into the room in a flurry, all soot-stained and wearing a black jacket instead of a white one. He came towards me in a hurry and smiled. I smiled back at him with a stupid grin. He ran out of the box and did something I couldn't see with the lights on, and suddenly, my chains were free. I buckled to the floor of course. He came back for me, and I had to remind him not to touch me. He said he didn't care and put an arm under my shoulder. I tried to pull away, but he didn't let me. I knew he never really understood the danger he was in around me. I knew it. I should have made more of an effort.

"The lights—" I started.

"They're hitting the generator now—" he started. It was the last thing he ever said because somebody put the lights out.

Somebody put the lights out.

END

The Killer and the Clergyman By Kevin Hayman

The man in Seat 32A had a secret. He looked like any other passenger that morning, waiting patiently for the train to depart Plymouth Station. His eyes were drawn to the platform clock, his left hand gently tapping his knee. But people aren't always who they seem.

Wrapped in old newspapers and stuffed deep inside an old Army surplus store kit bag was enough Semtex to blow up a small country — or a very large city. He checked his wristwatch: 5:53 a.m. Just over three hours until detonation, or as Adam De Chant liked to call it, *payback!*

He switched his battered Rolex to stopwatch mode and started the countdown. He watched as the initial seconds and then minutes ticked away. Three hours…two hours and fifty-nine minutes…two hours and fifty-eight minutes…

The gentle vibration of the train's engine ran through the carriage. From somewhere outside, a whistle blew, and the train jerked slowly away from the platform. Adam watched the sign disappear into the distance and grinned. Two hours and fifty-two minutes.

"Tickets, please." The conductor's voice sent a scurry of panic through carriage seven like a Mexican Wave: Frantic pocket searches and wallet scuffles for travel tickets and railcards followed. Adam De Chant had booked his ticket months in advance, and they'd been in his left Parka pocket since 4 a.m. He had checked this five or six times. Nothing was left to chance.

"Tickets please, mister."

Adam stretched out his left arm and revealed his ticket. The conductor took it, punched it, and handed it back. That's when he seemed to notice the kit bag on the seat next to him.

"Bags go in the overhead lockers or in the luggage holdall at the front of the carriage, I'm afraid."

"Not this one," said Adam, holding the bag strap so tightly that his fist had turned white. It forced the letters H A T E that were tattooed across his knuckles to stand out even more prominently than usual. "This one stays with me."

The conductor swallowed, and Adam saw in his weary face that he wasn't up for an argument, certainly wasn't up for a fight. He didn't need to be a mind reader to know that. He didn't *need* to be, but he *was*, and sometimes, he just couldn't stop himself from tuning in, like earwigging in on a conversation you knew you shouldn't be listening to. That was part of the *gift*.

Adam knew the man's name was Nigel, that he'd been married more than thirty years, and that he was close to retirement. He knew these things without presumption or question. He knew things about people that even *they* had forgotten.

He listened as the old man tried to reassure himself. *Now don't be hasty here, Nigel. This one could be volatile. Just tell him that rules is rules.*

"I'm sorry, mister," he said eventually, "but rules is rules."

Adam lurched forward and growled, "Let's not make a scene here, Nigel. I don't want to have to hurt you so close to your retirement. But if you don't move on to the next passenger, I'll cut your face off and wear it around the train as a mask. The bag stays with me."

Though Nigel didn't say a word, in his head was a pulsating storm that hailed fear. He did the sensible thing and moved on to the next passenger. Maybe later when his hands stopped shaking and his heart slowed back to its usual sluggish pace, he would realise that Adam had called him Nigel despite his nametag reading N. REDFEARN—maybe not?

Two hours and forty-eight minutes.

"This just in," declared the sumptuous young newsreader, interrupting the regular morning broadcasts. "A bomb has reportedly gone off in London's Paddington Station at precisely 9:00 a.m. Although too early to confirm numbers, casualties are believed to be in the hundreds..."

The train braked suddenly, forcing an early end to Adam's fantasy, but a satisfied grin remained. He checked his watch again. Two hours and eight minutes. Damn, he'd been asleep for nearly forty minutes. Got to stay alert. Focus. He looked out of the window and saw a nearing station blemish the Devonshire countryside. He'd been here before, *hadn't he*, as a kid? Something seemed somehow familiar. A daytrip, perhaps, with Uncle Will? He used to love to watch the trains. "Put me on your shoulders, Uncle," he had begged, "so I can see the train coming in. I see it, Uncle, I see it." No. Focus, goddamn it.

Those were idle memories, and there was little point in going back.

"Next stop, Exeter St Davids."

The train stopped at the platform, and more passengers piled in like ushered cattle. It was quickly becoming congested, and still nobody approached Adam for the vacant seat. One young woman seemed to prefer to stand than sit with him. Maybe it was his skinhead haircut that put her off. He watched her in the middle of the aisle trying to stay balanced as the train set in motion again, surfing the vibrations in her stilettos as the carriage rocked side to side on the tracks. He knew she wanted a seat even before he confirmed it by invading her thoughts. There was no way she was going all the way to Paddington standing in those heels. He despised everything about her from her fake peroxide hair to the layers of slap she'd camouflaged herself with. She was a cold soul sleeping her way to the top—scum.

"Excuse me," said an elderly gentleman peering over Adam's shoulder. "I think this is my seat. Do you mind?"

Adam looked up at his cheery face.

"The bag, I mean. Would you mind moving it, please?"

The answer should have been no. He didn't want to move the bag. Didn't want to be trapped next to some yapping old pensioner for the rest of the trip. And he certainly didn't want anything to keep him from detonation—from payback. But for some reason, almost as if he didn't have a choice, he instinctively grabbed the bag.

"Thank you," said the man, pulling his black cloak up over his knees and sitting. "That's most kind of you."

Adam shrugged. He was still trying to come to terms with why he hadn't told the old man where to get off.

He watched him slide his black leather briefcase, with golden combination locks, under his seat, and fidget into a comfortable position. He must've noticed Adam gawping and extended his arm. "The name's Teddy Harper."

Adam didn't shake it; instead, he turned and faced the window.

"It's the collar, isn't it? A lot of people get nervous when I sit next to them. Think I'm going to start preaching or something."

Adam stared silently at a blur of passing trees.

"But don't concern yourself; I won't be doing that," Teddy added and leaned in closer to joke, "at least, not yet."

The driver called for Taunton Station and pulled up to the platform. A few passengers got off, and sure enough, the girl in the stilettos pounced for a vacant seat. Adam watched as a late passenger missed the handrail and went stumbling drunkenly across the carriage. Teddy had also seen this and chuffed out aloud. When he'd finished chuckling, he turned to Adam and asked if he was going all the way to Paddington. Adam's response was a mild grunt.

A pigeon tried keeping pace with the train for a while before admitting defeat, dipping its wings and flying off in the opposite direction. One hour and forty-two minutes.

"That's a nice watch," Teddy said, apparently noticing the Rolex. "On the conversation of time, did you know Plymouth to Paddington is around two hundred and twenty-five miles away? We're due to arrive at nine o'clock, although I doubt very much we'll keep to that. But let's assume we do. Do you know how fast that would mean we're traveling?"

Adam turned in a sudden frenzy and grabbed Teddy forcefully by the collar. "Old man," he snarled, "do I look like the talkative type? You want to sit here, fine by me. But if one more word leaves your lips, I'll throw you off this train before we get anywhere near Paddington."

Some spit shot through the air and landed on Teddy's nose. But Teddy didn't seem fazed by it. Instead, he calmly took a handkerchief and wiped it away, muttering, "Approximately seventy-five miles an hour, I think."

Adam pinned Teddy to the seat. "Did you hear what I said?"

"Oh, I heard, Adam. I just chose to ignore it."

Fury tightened his lips and the grip around Teddy's throat. Blood surged up his veins to his bulging eyes. He had it coming now. Adam clenched his left fist and pulled it back, ready to unleash on Teddy's wrinkly face. He'd provoked this and deserved the imminent consequences…

Wait a minute. He just called me Adam? Didn't he?

Maybe he knew him? That was possible, wasn't it? He had somewhat of a reputation, though if that were true, would he have taken the seat? He wasn't sure, but he guessed not.

"Who are you?" Adam demanded.

Teddy Harper, the man said. Only he didn't say it. He merely projected the thought into Adam's head.

No, it wasn't possible. Something about his telepathy was malfunctioning. He looked past the man's eyes, the way he had the conductor's earlier that morning, and concentrated. His telepathic streams deflected back like ricocheting hailstones. It was as if the man's thoughts were guarded by big, solid prison walls. Impenetrable. Impossible. He started to doubt his senses.

He cocked his head over to the now seated stiletto girl. She was trying to solve a crossword puzzle whilst nibbling the end of a ballpoint pen. The gateway to her thoughts was as open and as passable as the conductor's had been.

One hundred and thirty-four across: "JFK" director Oliver ___? Five spaces. "Reed?" No, not enough letters. How am I supposed to know directors?

No problem there. His telepathy was working fine. He looked back at Teddy, and now, something came. A word. *STONE.* He saw it as if he'd been allowed to see it, as if perhaps he'd been invited to see it.

Stone? What did it mean? *Who are you? Why can't I hear you? Why can't I hear your thoughts?*

Teddy stared calmly at Adam as if somehow, he had the situation in hand.

Stone, Teddy projected. *That's the word our crossword solver needs. As in the director, Oliver STONE.*

Adam felt his jaw drop.

And you can't hear me, Adam, because you asked me not to speak, wasn't that about right? I take it that goes for telepathy as well.

Now, it was Adam struggling to find the words.

"Who are you?"

"I told you," he said, raising his thick, greying eyebrows, "I'm Teddy Harper, a clergyman." He offered his hand for a second time. "Glad I've finally got your attention."

Adam slowly released his grip on Teddy and shook his hand, forcing a smile back; smiling was a weakness.

"I suppose I should confess," said Teddy with a wry satisfaction, "I've been listening to your thoughts since I stepped foot on the train. Actually, I heard your thoughts as you approached the station. I'll say this about you, Adam: You're one cynical son of a bitch. You remind me of myself many moons ago."

Adam wiped the sweat that had broken out across his forehead and suddenly remembered the bomb that was still ticking between his legs.

Oh, don't worry, Teddy conversed. *I know all about it. I'm not going to try and talk you out of it either. Damn waste of a good train, though, if you ask me.*

Adam grinned, and then Teddy said something that made it vanish almost instantly.

Looking at him with wide, condemning eyes, he asked, *There's blood on your hands, isn't there? You've killed before.*

There was no point in denying it. Adam knew this man possessed a form of telepathy far superior to his own. He could see the images snapping in Teddy's head like an animated sequence of still frames. The locations. The smells. The feelings. He could even taste burning sulphur in his mouth.

They were your foster parents, weren't they? You waited until late when they were tucked up in their bed asleep, and you squirted petrol through their letterbox with a children's Super Soaker water pistol. Quite ingenious that! Teddy smiled as if it had tickled him, but in reality, it must have appalled him.

Then you took a deep drag from your cigarette and thought about the years of torment you'd endured under them. They were sick people, Adam. I'm well aware of that too. So you flicked what remained of your cigarette through the letterbox. And as you walked away to the gradual murmur of roaring flames, you laughed. You laughed so hard and loud you nearly woke the neighbours, that about right?

Adam didn't answer. He didn't have to.

But, of course, you didn't wake the neighbours, Adam, did you? And the ten-year-old boy who lived next door, was burned to death.

"What do you want?" asked Adam, causing heads to turn in his direction.

"Shhhh," said Teddy, clearly aware of the unwanted attention. "I don't want anything." *It's you that wants to blow up Paddington.*

"How do you—" he changed to telepathy. *How do you know so much about me?*

Teddy smiled as if he'd been eagerly anticipating this question. "Your uncle Will told me."

My uncle Will? The shock of that possibility hit him so thoroughly he was glad he was sitting down. His hands hit his lap, strength sapped. Uncle Will was the only man, only person, who had ever loved him—a man whose thoughts were always clear and honest. Even when he had to smack Adam for being bad, his head and heart were always full of love for him. He desperately wanted Adam to achieve great things, like any doting father would, and had he not died so young, maybe he would have. Maybe. But he had died, hadn't he? And Adam had seen his uncle's crushed body amongst the debris, a shattered, golden Rolex watch the only surviving physical memory. Telepathy wasn't a gift, Adam knew; it was a curse.

Teddy had also seen the image of the train wreck. The bellowing smoke from the charred carriages splayed along the embankment walls, the carnage of dead bodies and shattered glass, the trawled countryside and rubble. He had seen it through Adam.

"You see my uncle Will through me, don't you?"

"On the contrary," said Teddy. "I see your uncle through *him*. You see, Adam, I don't just hear the living; I hear the dead too."

An afterlife?

"That's right."

No, this couldn't be true. He'd never heard the deceased and so assumed that dead was dead. It struck him that Teddy must be lying. But why should he? And after all, he was able to hear the living; how unfeasible was it that Teddy could hear the dead? He'd already proved his telepathy was far superior to his own. This was hard to take in.

It's all true, Teddy conveyed.

"Can you hear him now? Is he with us?" And as the words left his lips and because his image was so clear, he almost expected to see his uncle.

"He's always with you, Adam."

Now, Adam did smile. He felt it stretch his mouth so widely it hurt. He believed it too. He knew if his uncle Will's spirit really did live on, it would be by his side. *Yeah, by the side of a man who was about to create one of the biggest rail catastrophes in Britain.* He was hardly likely to get a pat on the back and be congratulated, was he? And what about all the other things he'd done? What about his foster parents? What about Justin Byrne, the boy who had been burnt to death?

Teddy brought the briefcase to his lap and opened it. Amongst the clutter was a pad of paper and a black calligraphy pen, which he pulled out and jotted something down.

"What's that?" said Adam. "You writing something about my uncle?"

"You'll see. I think what I'm writing will explain a lot."

Teddy hid his writing with his free hand. His thoughts were still locked behind a wall of secrecy.

"Next stop, Reading Station." Twenty-six minutes to go.

The train slowed, the brakes squeaking, the seats vibrating. A case in the luggage compartment fell onto its side as the train came to a stop. Teddy folded the paper in half and handed it to Adam then returned the notepad and pen to his briefcase.

"Whether you go through with this or not, won't affect me," said Teddy. "This is my stop, you see. And like I said, I'm not about to start preaching."

Adam nodded as he took the piece of paper.

Teddy put on his long, black cloak. "But remember, Adam, somewhere in the afterlife is a little boy who died because of you, and for what? Because your adopted parents abused you? These people aren't all bad, you know, and the telepathy's only a curse if you want it to be. So you see their fears and nightmares and carnal desires. So what? You only see them, Adam. You don't have to live with them as they do."

Adam looked at the paper slip.

"You do whatever you think right. But know this; life isn't a train ride. *You* have a choice. Be in charge of your own destiny. God be with you." He cocked him a wink, turned, and walked away down the carriageway.

More passengers boarded. The doors closed. The signal was given for the train to depart. Teddy waved Adam goodbye as it left the station, and at that moment, he slipped through the thick walls of Teddy's mind. The phrase repeatedly throbbed in his thoughts: *You remind me of myself many moons ago.*

He opened the folded note. Fifteen minutes to go.

Adam, it is with great regret that I write you this note. I haven't admitted these words to any living person since the event occurred. I want you to know that I was not always a man of the cloth – far from it. Before I found God (or perhaps you could say before God found me), I too thought my telepathy was a curse. I lived a life of crime and violence. I wanted to hit back at the very people who made me feel like I was nothing, like I was nobody. It was for these reasons that I too put a bomb on a train with the intention of blowing it up. For me, though, there was nobody to try and reason with me. The plan was a success. The train blew up and killed fifty-six passengers. Your uncle Will was a passenger that day, Adam. And for that, I'm truly sorry. Don't make the same mistake I did. You have a choice. And remember, your uncle Will is with you. Do the right thing. God be with you, Teddy.

Adam put his hand to his mouth in a futile attempt not to vomit. Fury overcame him. He wanted to get off the train, find Teddy, and kill him for the sick thing he'd done. Make it slow. Make it hurt. Then he remembered the sick thing he was about to do. Teddy was right; he had a choice. *To hell with people!* Uncle Will had gone in a train, and that was the way Adam De Chant was going to go. And he was taking these sickos with him. He grabbed the kit bag and made for the men's toilets. There, he would sort the bomb and blow this train to smithereens. Blow himself to smithereens. No more telepathy. No more pain.

He passed light-footed down the aisle. Nineteen minutes to go.

Don't do it, sir.

The small juvenile voice had come from his left—a bright-eyed boy looking eagerly up at him. *Don't hurt me and my daddy.*

The boy's lips had not moved.

"What did you just say, kid?"

You've got something bad in that bag, haven't you sir?

"In *this* bag?" Adam said, lifting it up.

The boy nodded slowly, scared.

"Well, there is one thing," Adam confirmed. He reached into the bag and smiled. "Here you go, kid."

"Wow, a water pistol—"

"A Super Soaker," Adam agreed. "Don't tell your dad it was from me when he wakes up, okay?"

Adam patted the boy's head and continued to the toilets, and as he did, he noticed the young girl with the stilettos get up and offer her seat to an elderly gentleman. Could he have been wrong about her?

Ten minutes to go.

In the toilets, Adam splashed cool water over his face and stood, watching the lines drip into the sink. *Are you with me, Uncle?* He took off his watch and hung it on the hot tap. *I wonder; could you be with me?* The answer did not present itself, but somehow, he knew it anyway.

Three minutes to go. Two minutes to go.

One minute to go.

END

One Last Conversation by Veronica Smith

Kim was at the grocery store the first time she noticed it; that shadow you see in your peripheral vision, out of the corner of your eye. When you try to turn your head to see it, it's gone. She didn't think anything of it until it seemed to happen all the time. People say that it happens to them occasionally. But this was happening to her twelve to fifteen times a day! "I don't know, Mom," she said on the phone a couple of days later, "isn't that supposed to be a sign of glaucoma or something?"

"You're thinking of cataracts, honey," her mom, Maggie, answered. "And that's *after* the surgery."

"Maybe some kind of brain disorder," Kim said. "I mean, this happens to me all day long." Maggie covered the phone with her hand, sighed, and shook her head. Her daughter was a mild hypochondriac, and it had been a while since she last had any "symptoms" to worry over.

"Then go see your eye doctor," Maggie suggested, knowing she would anyway. She just wanted someone else to confirm her worry.

"I already made the appointment," she replied. "I go tomorrow morning. Mom? Do we have a family history of brain cancer?"

Her appointment went smoothly, and the only thing she found out was that she might have a high level of cholesterol. Amazing that they can tell that from an eye exam! The thought of her arteries clogging and killing her panicked her, so she made a mental note to make a doctor's appointment to get it checked. As she was driving home, she again saw the shadow from the corner of her eye. She absently swatted at it and was shocked to feel something. She screamed and slammed on her brakes, swerving into the other lane. She quickly looked around and was relieved that no one was near her on the road. She pulled into the next parking lot and put the car in park then jumped out and peered in the windows, looking for an intruder in the back seat. After going in and out around the empty car, she got back in and continued driving home.

She thought to call her mom when she got home, but she didn't want to hear the condescending tone in her voice again. She knew what her mother really thought. But if she was nice enough not to bring it up, then Kim wouldn't either. She went to the bathroom mirror and stared at herself. Nothing looked wrong. Her blue eyes were bright as always, her blond hair needed brushing and maybe a trim, but she looked okay. She tried turning her head to the right and left but still looking ahead. She couldn't see any shadows. "Mom never did let me know about the brain cancer thing," she muttered as she turned away.

She sat down and turned on her television, patting her leg for her cat, Gremlin, to jump in her lap. As she was channel surfing, she stroked his silky fur; his purring was soothing to her, and she began to relax. She finally chose a show and had just put the remote down when her cell rang on the coffee table. She reached over Gremlin to get it, and she saw the shadow again out of the corner of her right eye. She reached up and swatted again, only this time closing her hand on something substantial. It felt like a snake or large worm but light and airy like a sponge. She tightened her grip and yanked. The worst pain she'd ever felt flared in her head as she yelped and passed out.

According to the clock, she'd been unconscious for almost fifteen minutes. *Now that can't be normal. First thing in the morning, I call the doctor and get a brain scan.* Her head still throbbed like she had a mild migraine. "Gremlin?" she called as she realized she didn't see him. She got up to look for him and found she was a little dizzy. "What the hell is wrong with me?"

Why would you think something is wrong with you? She twirled around to find where the voice had come from. Her heart raced as she ran to the kitchen to grab up her largest knife. *Ha ha! You don't need that.*

She held it out in front of her and backed up until she hit the counter. "Who said that?" she called out, her voice faltering.

Why can't I see you?

"What do you mean?" Kim asked.

I can't see you at all. The voice was quiet for a moment; then, it seemed to whisper indistinct words and giggle, and Kim couldn't figure out where it was coming from. Cautiously, she went out into the rest of the apartment and checked everywhere. The whispering continued but never changed pitch or volume. The last room to check was the bathroom. She went in and stood in front of her closed shower curtain, certain that her intruder was hiding in the bathtub. She held the knife at the ready and quickly pulled the curtain open. There was nothing there.

As she turned, she glanced at the mirror and kept turning. Suddenly in her peripheral vision, she saw a reflection in the mirror. Horrified, she turned to look, and the vision disappeared. She ran back to the living room and sat down, shaking. What she saw was unreal. It looked like her entire head was writhing with giant worms. They were black and almost opaque. It reminded her of a medusa or gorgon.

So that's what you look like.

She began crying. *I'm going crazy; that's what's happening to me.*

She stopped crying when she heard, *It's not crazy. It's just me, Kim; I'm here.*

Kim screamed and grabbed her head in her hands. "Stop it! Stop it!" she whispered. "Go away!"

But there's nowhere else to go.

Kim called in sick for two days in a row. She didn't know what to do or who to talk to. She couldn't get the voice in her head to shut up. Once it started, it never stopped. It barraged her with questions of what she was seeing and doing, but Kim wouldn't answer it.

I need to see. I need to know. Tell me!

Kim took to banging her head on the coffee table, but that only brought about more complaints from the other tenants in the building. They had already come to the door when she screamed the other day. She told them she was fine and had a nightmare; what else could she say? She could see them shake their heads and look at each other before they went back to their own apartments.

Just that crazy lady having another weird attack.

She couldn't confide in any of them. She couldn't tell her mother. She didn't have anyone she could tell. She needed to call the doctor and make that appointment, but every time she reached for the phone, the voice in her head screamed long and loud. She'd had a headache since the voice arrived, but that scream put her in unbearable pain — pain that almost knocked her out again.

Tell me what you see! Kim sobbed as she stubbornly refused, her head pounding more every time she refuted the voice. *I can make it stop hurting.* Kim stopped crying and for the first time replied to the voice.

"Truly? It hurts so bad. Please make it stop. What do you want?" Suddenly, the pain went away, and the voice came again yet soothing this time, calming and serene.

Tell me what you see.

"When? Where?" Kim asked, confused.

All the time. Everywhere. I want to know what you see.

"I see my apartment walls?" she said hesitantly. "Is that what you want to know?"

Yes! The voice seemed triumphant in its small victory over Kim. *Tell me more!* Kim walked around the apartment and described everything she saw. The voice demanded that she tell the past of any personal objects. Any time Kim balked, a pain spiked her head. After a time, she didn't refuse the voice anything.

"I have to go to work," Kim said the morning of the third day, "I've called in sick for two days, and I need to go back, or I could lose my job."

Why do you need a job? Why not just exist?

"It doesn't work that way," she replied. "If I don't have money, I can't stay in this apartment. I'd have to live on the streets."

What's wrong with that? We can live in the world out there. In here, all I know is all you tell me about. We'd be free. The voice's use of the word "we" wasn't lost on Kim.

"This is *my* life, and I like it this way," Kim replied, afraid the voice would cause her pain for her rebellious remark.

Then let's go to work. I want to know more.

"Are you sure you're feeling all right?" her boss, Mark, asked her. "You look a little pale, and you look like you haven't slept much."

"Sure," she replied. "I'm feeling much better. In a few more days, I'll be back to normal. I want to get caught up. I'm sure there's a huge pile of work on my desk." Mark patted her on the shoulder and told her to take it easy. She nodded and got herself a cup of tea before sitting down to her computer and logging in.

What are you doing, Kim?

"I'm working," she replied softly, looking around to make sure no one was around to hear her "talking to herself." The day went by slowly, and she didn't get near as caught up as she wanted since she had to explain everything she did in detail to the voice. The voice didn't seem to understand any kind of technology and needed repeated explanations. It kept telling her she needed to "see the world" instead.

By five o'clock, Kim was more than ready to go home.

When do we see the world?

"I'm tired," Kim said, muttering quietly so the others at the bus stop wouldn't hear her. "I'm going home."

We should walk around and see the world, Kim. We really should.

A pain began to increase in her head, and she shook her head. "No, I just want to go home!" The others waiting for the bus looked at her, and she ran off.

"You got a dollar?" the homeless man in the torn shirt asked her as she got closer to him. She didn't want anyone to hear her talking to herself, so she turned down the alley in a shortcut to the long walk home. She knew it was frequented by vagrants, but they never hurt anyone, so she felt safe. She stopped and reached into her purse for a loose dollar or two she knew was there.

Who's talking to you?

"He's just a guy down on his luck," Kim replied, not worried if the man heard her; they talked to themselves sometimes too.

Why are you giving him your money? You said you need that to live on. He's begging for your hard-earned money because he's useless.

"No, no," Kim said, shaking her head, starting to hand two dollars to his outstretched hand. "He's just having a hard life and needs a little help; I can help him."

No, you will not! Sudden pain flared up in her head again as she dropped the bills and fell to her knees, holding her head in her hands.

"Are you okay?" the man asked her, so concerned for her that he ignored and stepped on the bills as he helped her to her feet.

"I'm..." She screamed as another blinding pain shot through her head, and her vision wavered.

He's useless. He only takes. Kill him!

"No!" she yelled, and the man backed up in confusion.

Kill him now! The pain increased and she again dropped to her knees. *I can make the pain go away. Just do what I tell you.*

"No, I won't!" she sobbed between the waves of pain.

Kill him, or I'll make the pain so bad you will wish you were dead.

Kim leaned forward until her forehead was touching the dirty concrete. "Hurts," she muttered. The pain increased, and she slid onto her belly.

This pain can end, Kim. Kill him.

"Okay," she gave in weakly. "But make the pain stop."

The man looked around for help, but no one else around. He needed to get this nice lady to a hospital. He turned to go to the main street when he was struck from behind. He fell against the brick wall and turned to see the woman holding the tire iron he usually kept by him for protection. She was standing again and didn't seem to be hurting anymore, but her eyes seemed distant, and she hung her mouth open as if in horror.

"Lady…" he began as she hit him again on the side of the head.

His vision blurred, and he began seeing double. *What the hell?* It had to be the head injury. For a moment, it looked as though the woman had grown thick, black strands out of her head, and they were squirming around like snakes. "What are you?"

He sees me! Kill him now!

Kim swung the tire iron again, and he fell on his face. She stood over him and hit him over and over until he stopped moving. Then she kept hitting him until the voice told her to stop.

She walked into her apartment in a daze, barely remembering the trek home.

You did well, Kim. I'm proud of you.

"What's there to be proud of?" she asked sadly as she closed the door behind her.

You got rid of that useless beggar. The world is better off without him.

"What do you know of the world?" Kim said, raising her voice, "You know nothing of the world except what I tell you. You wanted me to 'live the world.' Well, that's what he was doing! That's what I'd be doing. Why did you make me do that?" she fell to the sofa and cried.

Meow. She looked up, startled. Gremlin hadn't been seen since the night the voice first appeared.

"Here, kitty."

She wiped her tears, smiling, then rubbed her finger and thumb together to call the cat to her. Gremlin looked at her warily and took two delicate steps forward before stopping. A low growl began to emanate from him. It increased in tone while the cat's hair stood up on his back and his ears laid back. He bared his teeth at her and backed up.

"Gremlin?" Kim asked, confused, "Come here, kitty."

Yeah, come here, kitty. We want to pet you.

Kim called in sick again the next day and spent the morning deciding whether or not to turn herself in to the police, especially after seeing the morning news; the main story was the homeless man beaten to death.

Let's go out and see the world. Let's take a walk, Kim.

"No," she replied. "I can't do this anymore. Why can't you go back to where you came from?"

Where I came from? But Kim, I've always been here. I want to see! I want to do! I want to live the world!

"But why didn't you ever say anything before?" Kim asked.

You brought me to awareness when you pulled on part of my head. You gave me quite a headache.

Kim was confused; the black snake-like things were part of its head?

"You can't keep threatening me with pain every time you want something," Kim said.

I know. It hurts me as well. But it's worth the pain to get what I want. And I always get what I want.

Kim got together a basket of clothes to wash and went into her kitchen. Her washer and dryer were in the closet at the end. She opened the folding doors and dropped the basket, screaming, "Gremlin!"

Her beloved cat lay half in half out of the open washing machine. Blood pooled into the tub from the stab wound that flayed his belly wide open. His sightless eyes stared past her, and she screamed hysterically as she backed off.

"What the hell is going on in here now?" Her neighbor from next door was banging on her door and yelling. She stopped crying and opened the door. He was red faced with anger.

"Look, I've been putting up with a lot of shit over the past week from you," he said, "but this time, I'm making a formal complaint with the landlord. You wake me in the middle of the night with your screaming, and now this."

She vaguely remembered being woken in the middle of the night to pounding on her bedroom wall but had fallen back asleep before it seemed clear.

"I'm really sorry," she said, realizing she didn't even know his name. "I've been going through some personal issues."

"Then go check yourself into a loony bin," he replied. "There's something so wrong with you."

Kill him!

"No," she replied quickly.

"What do you mean, 'No?'" the angry neighbor asked. "Are you talking to me or just a figment of your imagination like always? Freaking crazy lady."

Kill him now, Kim. He'll have you removed from this place. Kill him! Another blinding pain rent her head, and she grabbed it, stumbling back inside her apartment.

"Are you okay?" her neighbor asked, suddenly concerned as he saw the blood drain from her face. She backed into the kitchen, and he followed her. He saw her cell phone on the counter and picked it up. "I'm calling an ambulance."

Without warning, Kim grabbed a large knife from her knife block and swiped it across his throat. He dropped the phone and grabbed this throat, trying to stop the flow of blood that poured down his chest. He looked into Kim's vacant eyes as he seemed to float to the ground, splashing the blood around him when he landed.

Kim watched in horror and covered her mouth with a blood-covered hand until she noticed it. She grimaced and pulled it away, staring as his blood dripped from her hand to the floor. She ran to the front door and shut it quickly.

"I'm a monster," she whispered as she stood there with her back against the door. "I have to end this."

No, Kim. We are just getting started.

She had no idea how much time had passed as she sat on the sofa, ignoring the voice that constantly pestered her. But she could smell the decay and knew it was coming from Gremlin's body in the wash closet and the dead neighbor on her kitchen floor, so it had to be more than a day or two. Luckily for her, he must have lived alone because no one came looking for him.

She was teetering on the edge of insanity, and that didn't worry her at all anymore. It seemed that *this* was the only way to make the voice bearable. She sat alone and enjoyed the calm of nothing, pushing the voice to the background. But the voice was getting angry. Nothing it could do seemed to affect Kim at all. It was reluctant to cause too much pain to Kim because it did cause pain to itself. Now was the time. Before it was too late and Kim was completely unworkable. One last conversation.

Kim, wake up, and listen to me.

No response.

I want to live the world. I want to see the world. I will live the world. The pain I have unleashed on you so far will be nothing to what I will do to you if you don't do what I say right now.

That pain flashed through her head for a second or two, and Kim was beyond screaming. Her mouth opened so wide in a silent scream that her jaw seemed to crack. Her eyes were squeezed so tight that tears were leaking from the corners. Then the pain suddenly disappeared. She knew what she was supposed to do.

She cautiously stepped over the dead body to get to the knife rack again. This time, she picked the short paring knife. She slipped briefly in the pool of blood but caught her balance with a light hand on the counter.

Not in the kitchen. In the living room.

She walked to the sofa and sat down, leaving a trail of bloody footprints behind her.

Now, Kim! Kim plunged the knife into her right eye without flinching then twisted it, completely destroying her eyeball. Then she did the same to her left. A moment of clarity came to her along with the pain, and she fainted before she could make a sound. *Ahhhh!*

She woke an hour later and walked slowly to the bathroom, putting *her* hands out to steady *herself* along the walls. After turning on the light in the bathroom, *she* washed the blood from *her* face and smiled. *Her* reflection with bright, brown eyes and raven-black hair smiled back at *her*.

Kim woke in a dark haze. Her blue eyes weren't bright any longer. Her hair was flattened against her head as a strange pressure pushed against her from all directions. Even her nose felt flattened as if she was pressed up against a window.

Out of the corner of her eye, she saw a black-haired, brown-eyed version of herself admiring herself in her mirror. She screamed, but this time, she was the only one that could hear.

END

Normalcy by Kristi Brooks

The jolt of hitting the doorframe caused Layne's bladder to loosen just enough that a small trail of pee leaked down her thigh before dripping over the top of her kneecap.

Taking a moment to catch her breath, she leaned against the wall and stared at the digital clock that kept blinking 12:00. It had been days since she'd last been this coherent, so she had no idea what time it really was. Right now, waking up was proving to be a painful experience.

Once she'd finished going to the bathroom, she took a moment to look at herself in the mirror. It always startled her to see her reflection: a young woman with blond hair and crystal blue eyes. Her attractive face was unmarked by acne or wrinkles, and it was hard to pinpoint her age. However, she neither felt pretty nor young, and seeing this face in the mirror gave her a great sense of unease. Leaning in, she used her fingers to prod at the slight darkening under her eyes, the only indicator that she'd had a rough week.

Layne sighed, raked her hands roughly through her hair to smooth out any tangles, and trudged to the kitchen.

After rummaging through at least three different cabinets, she found a half-empty box of cereal that had been put on top of the plates. She held it over her head for a moment in victory and laughed a sharp, shrill sound that bit into the otherwise empty apartment. Sitting cross-legged on the dull pink couch one of her old roommates had left behind, she thoughtfully spooned the cereal into her mouth, trying to match the colorful swirls in each bite.

As she was tilting up the bowl to drink the last few drops of milk, she noticed that the clock on the bottom of the DVD player was also flashing 12:00. Layne tilted her head and got up, moving over to the window and pulling back the curtain.

Outside, the security bars on the apartment windows there was nothing. A pool as thick as the void of a black hole pressed itself against the glass panes. Placing her palm on the glass, Layne flinched at the steel cold sensation and jumped back, the curtain slipping back into place.

Shaking her head and chiding herself against childish thoughts and boogeyman images, she gathered up her bowl and carried it to the sink. The water ran in a light, water-fountain-like trickle instead of a steady hiss as she rinsed her breakfast bowl. The landlord had promised to fix the problem, but it'd been weeks now, and he hadn't come.

As she was walking back to the couch, the world became unsteady, and the floor wobbled beneath her feet. She'd been in an earthquake once when she was younger, and she remembered how the cool concrete floors had rolled beneath her feet as the surface of the world shifted around her.

That was what it felt like now, what it felt like every time they came for her. In an attempt to get somewhere safe, she lunged across the room, her body splaying out across the worn, pink cushions just as the vision closed in around her and the world dropped away.

The dark room was penetrated only by the dim moonlight filtering in through a partially shaded window. The person who had called Layne had been a man. She could feel his erection. Its primal sense of urgency overtook her, and she was aware of his obsession…or was it love?…for the girl beneath him. Grabbing a tube of KY Jelly, he primed her. Layne felt through his fingers, saw through his eyes, experienced everything with him. That was what she loved about the sessions: for a brief moment, she got to be anyone she wanted.

As he entered the girl, Layne noticed the porcelain-faced beauty never responded. Black hair framed her face in perfect disarray, complimenting her features and making her look like a discarded angel. She never opened her eyes, never moved her painted lips.

He kept thinking of her rejection of him and of this moment. He didn't feel triumph. He was triumph. Then he looked away from the girl's face and saw a deep Y cut surrounded by ugly, black stitches that stood out on the woman's chest. She was already dead.

Layne didn't want this session to continue, but she was powerless to stop it, stuck in this crazy man's head until he let her go. There was a reason she was here, but it eluded her. She had to force herself to stay receptive to his needs; otherwise, the entire experience would be wasted. Layne wanted to believe she was here for something even if it was only to observe him.

They never even knew they called to her, beckoning her mind and forcing her body to respond. She had lived her life according to their whims. She wasn't even sure what gave certain individuals the power to call out to her. They weren't all as unbalanced as this man, but lately, she had been seeing a lot more of the demented kind. Maybe it was something in the air, like the old wives' tales.

The man was through now, but he didn't immediately leave. Instead, he lay beside the corpse on the bed, stroking her hair and cheekbone. Gazing at the dead girl for several moments, Layne felt something else surging through him. Something she couldn't quite pin down, and that was unusual. Why was someone calling for her if they weren't willing to share? Focusing her energy, she searched his mind.

Regret. That was what it was: regret! He looked over at the white body bag, and Layne understood as daylight appeared and she found herself outside.

The girl was there, alive. She was wearing all black, and that made her pale face stand out with amazing contrast. Her hair was a deep brown, almost black, with maroon highlights. And she was smoking a cigarette, the gray, wispy circles briefly embracing her dark figure before dissipating in the sunlight. She was so beautiful, even in her torn fishnet stockings and her sour face. Lust and desire undiminished by time flowed through him as he watched her, leaving this memory just as fresh and sharp as reality.

Then he was gone, and Layne was alone in her empty apartment.

She blinked, her eyes refusing to focus. It happened every now and then; her body refused to believe she was back. She shook her tingling hands out in front of her. His desire and triumph had left her feeling dirty. He had been inside a corpse, fucking the goddamn thing, and…

"Shit," Layne mumbled as she fell back, her head lolling off to one side. Pain shot up from her neck and down her side as she moved. There was no telling how long she'd been lost in that crazy man's fantasy, her body limp and twisted in some unnatural position. She braced herself with her arm and then pulled herself upright, her free hand rubbing small circles on her neck and shoulder.

Over the years, she'd learned to deal with the muscle pain and the random blackouts as best she could, but the feeling of nausea that rolled over her now was something new. Getting up, she stumbled into the bathroom, heaving the contents of her morning bowl of cereal into the toilet. The broken bits of colorful circles now turned into bile-tinted, rainbow mush. Wiping her mouth with the back of her hand, she felt a sudden flare of unexpected pain along her jaw, and when she looked down, she noticed a few bright red flecks of blood.

Layne used the tip of her tongue to feel around in her mouth, and it didn't take long to find the sore. Her back tooth was throbbing, the pain suddenly intensifying from almost nonexistent to overwhelming in a very short period. She winced, and her body heaved once more, the pain so deep it was as if it was trying to purge itself of the tooth. However, her stomach was empty now, so nothing came up, but each time her muscles tightened, the pain in her mouth shot up another level until eventually, tears were streaming down her face.

She pushed her fingers into her mouth, over her tongue, and grabbed a hold of the tooth. It was fragmented but clearly still embedded in the gums. No amount of tugging on it would make it come out. Layne leaned back against the cool tile of the bathroom and took small breaths through her nose so as to not disturb the tooth or expose it to more air.

After a little bit, Layne was able to make her way over to the built-in drawers along the far wall of the bathroom. Opening the bottom one, she managed to rummage through it and pull out a flathead screwdriver. Her plumbing was shit, so she always kept a good assortment of tools handy for any emergency repairs. Eyeing the screwdriver, she didn't see any horrible buildup, and since the sink felt like it was an eternity away, she decided to worry about it later.

She held the top of the screwdriver and placed the metal against the root of her broken tooth, pushing it into her gum as tears rolled down her cheeks. Then, she put her feet up against the wall in front of her and made sure that her back was firmly planted against the wall, bracing her elbows on her bent knees for maximum leverage.

Opening her mouth, she took a large breath and held it tight in her lungs before pulling down on the handle and forcing the metal rod up into her tooth as she tried to pry it from her mouth. The pain was so intense that it shot through her entire body in large lightning bolts that pushed into her brain and almost made her black out. But just when she was about to give up hope, she felt the tooth give just a little.

The screwdriver slid into the opening as if it had always been intended for that purpose. Every muscle in her body was trembling, and she felt as if she might once more be pulled into another gagging fit. She dug her nails into the palm of her free hand as her right hand gripped the handle of the tool even tighter. With one last breath to steady herself, she pulled down with every ounce of strength she had in her, everything from her neck to her leg muscles burning in bright unison as her entire body was focused on this one central point of pain.

"Aaaaaaa!" she screamed into the empty air of the bathroom as the taut pull gave way, and the tooth released its hold on her gums with an audible pop.

Layne collapsed on the floor, blood pooling from her lips as she worked the diseased tooth from her mouth and spat it into the palm of her hand. The relief was wide and immediate, and she felt the tension seeping out of her body. There was no clock in the bathroom, but it wouldn't have mattered even if there had been because time seemed to stand completely still after that. Nothing moved, nothing mattered.

It might have been hours or even days later for all she knew, but eventually, she was able to pull her body upright and stumble to the sink. Turning on the hot water, she placed her hands under it and rinsed off the blood, scrubbing at it with gobs of soap until even her flesh burned, but the ghost of the blood remained.

In fact, it seemed that the crimson had spread now like a virus, infecting the flesh of her arms and across her abdomen. Her hands gripped the sides of the sink, and she took a couple of deep breaths, trying to regain her composure. Until now, she hadn't looked in the mirror. She wasn't sure why. Maybe she hadn't wanted to see her bloody face. Maybe she hadn't wanted to admit that she was so broken that she was pulling out her own teeth with screwdrivers.

However, when she looked at her hands again, she was holding a knife.

The blood had spread even further than before, and the bathroom seemed to shift around her as she continued to stare into the running water of the sink as it disappeared down the drain.

Layne closed her eyes tight and whispered to herself. "It's not real…it's not real…it's not real…"

When she opened her eyes again, however, things were far worse.

Clumps of hair and scalp now clung to the sink, bloody islands in a sea of white. Layne realized that this was not her reality but that she was in someone else's vision. She had to be. Even though she had never traveled twice in this short period of time, not to mention the fact that they were both bad trips. No peace and love in her future today.

This was not going to be good. The person's field of vision moved, startling Layne. The tiled wall was also covered with bits of debris, clinging like lost insects, creating random patterns on the slick green surface. Then, the mirror.

It was her face in the reflection. The bits of hair and skin had come from her head. Then the image changed, shimmering like a mirage, and it was no longer her in the mirror but someone else looking at her through Layne's dark, lost eyes.

It must have been my imagination.

Lifting her arm, the girl brought the knife to her head, cutting out a large chunk of scalp, patches of bone peeking out through the tangled, bloody mess. The piece of flesh and hair was flung off the knife and into the sink with a simple flick of the wrist, splatting angrily against the porcelain. The metallic smell of blood filled the air. Layne wanted to gag but couldn't, not here anyway. She thought she would feel pain, but the girl's body had already taken over. There was only a dull tingling, throbbing feeling where her head should have been.

The girl bent over and grabbed a flathead screwdriver in one hand and a hammer in the other. Looking in the mirror again, she positioned the screwdriver against her frontal lobe. Layne wanted to scream but couldn't. She was the watcher, the only witness to this poor girl's trephination attempt or worse, suicide.

"I have to get it out. Surely, you understand. I can't let it go on like this. I just want to be normal." The girl's voice cracked on the last note.

She couldn't be talking to Layne. Even though they conjured her presence, they were never aware of it. They just wanted to share a piece of their lives with someone and somehow summoned her. But she had never had one acknowledge her, let alone talk to her.

All I want is to go home and crawl back into bed, and this damn girl is holding me here. And now I'm going to have to interact with this grief-stricken creature. I'm not prepared for this.

"Oh, stop thinking of yourself. I thought you needed to see what I've become. Don't you understand?"

The girl stopped, an expectant look on her gore-streaked face, but Layne couldn't even manage a response. She could only focus on the poised screwdriver and the rush of fear that was now controlling her. What would happen when the girl hit the screwdriver? Could she die if her host died?

"I'm doing this to warn you. You have to know what will happen. I can't take it anymore. The black ooze that's causing this nightmare needs to come out. Once it's gone, I can be normal again. Normal, what a beautiful word, don't you think?"

And with that, the girl lifted the hammer and set its flat, metal surface against the plastic handle of the screwdriver. Screams, curses, and warnings filled Layne's head, but the girl wasn't listening anymore. She drew the hammer back and struck. The pain zigzagged across Layne's mind like black lightning bolts. Layne couldn't think, couldn't do anything but watch as the hammer once again drew back and came crashing down.

And then she was rolling on the floor, holding her head and weeping in anguish at the physical and mental torment. After a long time, Layne picked herself up and looked around through tear bleary eyes. She went to the sink and drank the cool water straight from the tap, avoiding the mirror.

Thank God I'm still myself, she thought. I'm sane and in my own house.

The cool tile smacked against her bare toes as she walked to the tub. But as she walked, the smacking sound ceased, and her feet now rose and fell on a floor so soft it felt like she was wearing fuzzy house slippers. Fear and dread began creeping back from the corners of her mind as she looked down. The rest of the floor was fine, but where she was standing, there was soft, white fabric. It reminded her of the padded cells that haunted her dreams. Horrible faces filled with doctors and needles that prodded her until she thought her brain would bust from the torment.

Her hand crept up to her head, her fingertips trailing across a soft gauze bandage. Except for a few tufts that poked out of the bandage at the nape of her neck, her thick, blond tresses were gone. Pain seared through her body as the memory of what had happened struck her and echoed through her like static electricity.

She wanted to scream but didn't. Concentrating on her home and the cool tile beneath her feet, she tried to forget about the incident, about the fact that it had been her face in the mirror. It hadn't been this morning, but not so long ago, it had been her bathroom, her skin, her hammer and screwdriver.

She visualized the tub, and as it came back into focus, she bent to turn on the water and thought instead about the hot bubble bath that awaited her. Maybe tomorrow, the sessions would be better.

END

Pure Soprano Of Death A Poem By Norbert Gora

Breaking through the
vastness of space,

admiration of alien stars
choked their hearts

beating quickly, the
minds bathed in
curiosity.

They sped away, fearless,

driven by the enormity of
questions,

uncontrollable hunger for
answers.

To the heart of the galaxy

brought them this
unknown voice,

an aria of delight for the
senses.

Seductive singing was
like a hook,

led them on a rod of
stellar ballad,

with every sigh
increasingly obsessed,

only attentive to this
flirtatious rhythm.

The storm of doubts
raged over their heads,

how is it possible that
sounds materialized

out of nowhere, carried
loosely on the ridge

of vacuum.

Pure soprano—heavenly
timbre,

soothing nerves as a taste
of sweetness,

enveloped them in a
shawl woven with tunes

of vocal paradise, they
were careless,

thoughtlessly.

Everyone has heard it in
the head,

immersed in the rapture,

intoxicated by the
extraordinary beauty.

Singing gradually took
over the captain's

control, cut off oxygen,
drained energy.

No one remembered
when soprano

gave place to the devil
groans,

sonatas of pain, bitter
tears, and death.

The last act of melody of
the space horror

covered soulless bodies
in a coat of oblivion.

Sandy By R. Judas Brown

The sound of a train blaring past woke me to the light filtering through the cracked window above the door. In my sleep-blurred vision, the door ran red and slick, a viscous barrier falling from the ceiling to the floor in an unending sheet. Shaking my head to clear the cobwebs, my eyes refocused, and it became its truth, a simple wood door painted glaringly red. I felt it inside me, the accusation of its glare.

Sandy whimpered softly up at me from the floor. She wanted out, but it would have to wait. I was already late, and I needed my job. We needed a roof over our heads. We needed food on the table. I took the door's glare, making it mine and focusing it toward her. The sound trailed off. That was better. Sounds made my head hurt, sharp spikes digging behind my eyes. Standing, I stretched, making my way to the bathroom.

Stumbling, I snaked my foot out in Sandy's direction. She flinched back, waiting for the kick, but I never meant it to land. I smiled as I made my way down the short hall. She knew who was dominant, and that was good. I flipped on the bathroom light, and the incandescent bulb snapped to life. Its orange glow showed everything in its place. That was important.

After making my nasties, I took my red pill. The Tylenol went next, going down easy; they were small, white, and oblong. Then the blue pill. I didn't take the scary green pill though. Two weeks without. This was good. I was pretty sure. Something said it wasn't, but that couldn't be right.

I looked at them for a minute, trying to decide, to be sure. Even there in the bathroom, alone with myself and my reflection, everything was so busy and jumbled. I tried to focus, just like the doctor said I should, on what I knew. I had a job. I was useful. I had people who depended on me. After that, everything seemed to get...busy again. I didn't have time to think, so I got dressed. Maybe I could think later.

Sandy curled in her corner, watching me with cautious eyes when I turned before leaving for work. I straightened my uniform in the mirror across from the door. The polyester polo shirt was itchy, and maybe a little wrinkled, but that would have to do. I smiled at my reflection, reassuring and friendly. I reached down to the doorknob before a last thought occurred, and I turned back.

"Be a good girl, Sandy. I have a short shift. Stay quiet."

I turned back to the door. The blood had slopped over my hand. I stepped back, angry. If it had run onto my pants, I would have to change. Then I would be really late, and I would be fired. But no, it was just a wooden door still, brass knob shining up at me. I opened the door a crack, slipped out, and shut it hurriedly behind me. Sandy had almost gotten out a week ago when the traffic was worse. I couldn't bear seeing her like that. Screeching tires and blood and jagged white bone in flashing lights and noise. So much noise.

The knob locked automatically. I took out my keys and locked the top and bottom deadbolts, checking each three times. As I walked down the steps, I paused, allowing a couple of young girls dressed far too provocatively to pass. There was no shame the way they walked, and I fought down a bit of anger.

They were going in the same direction as work, so I was forced to walk behind them. I ignored them, but it was hard. The way the heat of the sun made all their creamy, exposed skin faintly shimmer. Their round bottoms pressed their underwear into the tight, thin material of their shorts as I watched them move, swayed along by their hips. The tank tops they wore so thoughtlessly clung tight to their sweat-slick bodies, and if I were in front of them passing, I probably would see their tight, hard nipples pressed against the thin fabric. I began to get hard with my anger. I felt it threatening to boil over. Someone should do something.

They were heading toward the local college with its buildings full of naughty girls and mean boys. I reached into my pocket. It was daylight, but when someone makes you do something, you can't help it, can you? I felt my knife, laying heavy in my pocket against the other thing I wanted to use. It was heavy too; that was their fault.

The bells of a church rang three times, quarter 'til.

Already running behind and now a few blocks past the street my store was on, I turned back. Maybe later. Walking quickly, I made it just in time. Out of breath from hurrying, which made me angrier at those too-young sl—

But I was a professional. I clocked in and counted my register only twice because of time. That did nothing for my mood.

I could see out the window of the little convenience store to the church across the street. Men were loading a long box into a large, black car. Standing on the steps, a young man stood, his arm around a middle-aged blond woman. Even with the red, puffy eyes, she was as pretty as her daughter. Her hair was the same: blonde and long. Her breasts were large, and the way they pressed against the satin of the black dress, I'm sure they were as heavy. I doubted she was as nice though. She didn't look like the sort of person to give someone a ride home from their job when it was raining.

He helped her into a long limousine. Other people, reflecting the same features though removed to various degrees of attachment, piled into the car and the similar, stretched-out sedan directly behind it. With a flash of lights and a short whoop of a siren, the police car in the front pulled away, each car in line obediently following.

"Excuse me! Hello!"

The people in line at my register were staring. The lady in the front, with the petite waist and the mole on her left upper breast, was angry with me. My lips were dry and chapped from the breathing I was desperately trying to control. I could feel my heart racing, and sweat popped along my skin. Underneath the counter, I was straining against my pants. Her eyes flicked down, breaking contact, and she folded her arms, hugging herself, hiding what I know she wanted me to see. Behind her, the line shifted uncomfortably. I am a professional. I rang them out wordlessly until I was alone. Then, I went to the bathroom to take care of myself.

#

I juggled the brown bag with the leftover burritos, cooled from the leisurely walk I had taken by the college dorms, into the crook of my arm with the two sodas. Sometimes, the top deadbolt stuck and took some wiggling; best to be prepared. It turned with a click, and the rest of the locks followed. The sun was bright and shining, pounding onto the door and making the knob hot. I held it with my toe to keep it from opening too far as I sidled in. Closing it, I made sure none of the blood got on my clean hands. Sandy looked up from her corner expectantly. She was a good girl.

"No accidents today? Good girl, Sandy!"

I set the bag and drinks on the table. Everything in time. I hadn't always been as conscientious of that. This was Fourth Sandy. She was new but a quick learner. I missed Third Sandy. I hadn't realized how much until I had seen her mom. We had never met, but even with the crying eyes, I recognized the lady who had smiled with Third Sandy from a rail at the Grand Canyon in the pictures on Third Sandy's phone. I might train Sandy to do some of the same tricks, but no. Each Sandy is different, and that is part of being in their right place.

I shushed her gently as I loosened the gag enough that I could pull it out of her mouth. I never take it off; it helps her remember who is in charge. Easing my keys out of my pocket, I undid the padlock on the chains. They rattled some as she shifted.

"Burritos today, Sandy! Go make your nasties, and I will warm them up!"

"Please," she whimpered.

I have never tolerated insolence. I swung my hand in an arc, cracking it across her cheekbone hard enough to knock her back. Sandy crumpled to the floor and began to sob. It grated through me, and the lights in the apartment started to reach out with little halos. Too late, I realized I needed my blue pills; the extended trip home had taken too long. Her sobs became wails, and everything I looked at seemed to be melting.

Pain stabbed through my head. I didn't want to be mad at her, but I could not abide whining. The sound echoed through the apartment. It seemed to ricochet through my head. I pulled my hand back to hit her, balling my fist. The sharp spikes of light stabbed through me, and I felt myself falling, stumbling. Catching myself at the entry to the hallway, I bounced between walls, ending up eventually at the bathroom.

I couldn't see. I couldn't hear. Shreds of jagged fire arced through my head. I grabbed blindly at my bottles. Trying to concentrate enough to feel the shapes, I took pills. Pills and pills and pills. Finally, it ebbed, too much and too fast. Horrified, I looked at the bottle in my hands.

Too weak, I hadn't paid attention and took some greens.

A cloud rolled through me, through my head, and as it cleared, I saw. The pretty Sandys, all of them, begging me. Their arms up, pleading, shielding. I saw the way my hands fell, sometimes empty, sometimes not. The gentle arcs of blood, red and opulent, sliding through the air. I heard the last little rattle of their breaths. I watched their eyes fade and dry.

Horrified, I ran back down the hall. Sunlight shone through the open door. Outside, there were screams. Slamming the door, I latched it. My blood was pulsing, heavy in my ears. The walls were painted in splatters of rust. A hasp in the wall above a pallet fashioned from discarded women's clothes sat next to my own bed. The partial visions, no, memories floating to me through the haze made me shudder.

Outside, sirens stopped, and a man, loud and angry, came across a loudspeaker. It didn't matter what he said; I wasn't paying attention to him. All I could see — or hear — was them. I saw their signs as I walked back down the hall. The long, parallel scratches in the paint on the walls and the dry, brown footprints, so small and dainty, told the full story.

By the time I went back to the front door where the man was still calling for me, all my bottles were empty. Inside my head, inside my body, there were strange things going on. No matter how fast I breathed, I couldn't get any air. I felt tense, but my legs seemed to shift around under me while I fumbled with the latches, my fingers thick and fuzzy. My pulse was a drum beat in my temples, and my gasping sounded like a discordant sitar by the time I worked the last bolt open and stepped into the fading sun.

All the angry men in their blue suits with their long, black guns danced in front of me. One step, two steps, down the stairs they stared. Something hit my back;

I thought it was the whole world, but it was far away, and the sun was a red, angry thing.

My eyes hurt, but it's black now, and the cold black is creeping out to hide me.

I hear you, Sandy. I'm sorry. I'll see you soon…

END

Scarab By J. C. Michael

"Anything else I can do for you?"

Slim, blonde, and almost as attractive as his second wife, Felicity stood in the doorway waiting for an answer. For his part, Paul Nawton thought of the various things he would like her to do for — and to — him. He smiled. "Not right now; maybe later."

"Okay." She made to leave then stopped, one foot on either side of the office threshold. "Sorry, I nearly forgot. A Mr. Demdyke called for you. He asked that you ring him once you were free."

The name got his attention immediately, pulling his thoughts away from the body of the woman in front of him. "Demdyke? As in *the* Mr. Demdyke?"

"I-I don't know; he didn't say any more."

"And why would the owner of the company need to say any more? What the hell do they cover in induction these days? How to claim sick pay? The damn grievance procedure?" Felicity had edged fully through the door now, but he wasn't letting the little fishy get off the hook that easily. "Here's a quick history lesson for you. Mr. Demdyke — *the* Mr. Demdyke — is the grandson of Dagda Demdyke, founder of Scarab Industrial, who left the squalor of Victorian England to seek his fortune here in the New World. Since then, his family have built this corporation into what it is today: a global leader, a trendsetter, an innovator, and you can't even have the courtesy of knowing who pays your wages."

He'd half stood as he spoke, each raised inch forcing the young woman a foot further away. He sat. "Shut the door on your way out."

Gingerly, as though approaching a dangerous animal, Felicity moved forward and closed the door. It shut with the quiet yet assured thump of quality leaving him alone. Demdyke? Seriously? In five years as vice president, he'd only spoken to the old fool half a dozen times and only twice in person. The Demdykes may have built the business, but now, he held it together, not his co-V.P and certainly not the octogenarian old coot who sat by making a fortune out of everyone else's hard work.

Reaching under his desk, he pulled a small key from the magnetic plate that held it in reach yet out of sight and opened the top drawer of the right-hand pedestal. The oak slid out easily along well-worn grooves, and his hand hovered over the two matching silver flasks now revealed. To the right, the MacAllan single malt was worth more than Felicity would earn in a year. Perhaps he would have doubled her earnings if she'd played her cards right, but she'd irritated him now and would be sent back to the general secretarial pool like a minnow too small to bother taking home for the table. He'd handpick a replacement tomorrow, and if there was nothing suitable in the pond, he'd get onto recruitment and make sure a trout made way for a salmon. He took the flask and ignored its twin, the contents of which were less expensive yet more illicit, and poured a little into the crystal glass on his desk. The phone rang.

"Nawton?" The voice was dry and cracked.

"Mr. Demdyke? I've just this moment received your message and was about to call. What can I do for you?"

"Don't blame the damn girl, Nawton." It was the kind of curt response his limited experience of the man had led him to expect. "Suffice to say you were going to call but were beaten to the punch. I wouldn't expect you to drop everything, man. I'd rather you kept busy taking care of my business." There was a chuckle and then a cough. Both sounded phlegmy.

"I didn't mean to, and yes, I've been busy. The…"

"I read your weekly briefings, Nawton, and since the last one was sent at 10 a.m. this morning, I doubt much has changed in three hours. The girl's cleared your diary for the afternoon. I'll be with you in twenty minutes. We have much to discuss."

There was a click. Then a hum. Nawton put the phone down, picked it up again, and hit 0. "Felicity, what did Mr. Demdyke ask you to do about my meeting with Wharram and Percy this afternoon?"

"He said to get Mr. Hutton to deal with it. I suggested you could re-schedule, but he insisted, and I didn't think it my place to argue now I know who he is."

"No, that's fine. Don't worry about it. And forget about earlier."

"Thank you, Mr. Nawton."

He put the phone down. He'd keep her around for a while longer—at least until a suitable replacement took his eye. He'd been too quick to judge before and ended up with a secretary old enough to be his mother. She'd proven to be experienced, in quite a few ways, but he preferred his women like his shirts — wrinkle free.

***

"Mr. Demdyke, sir, a pleasure to meet you again."

Demdyke waved away the hand that was offered to him, and not wishing to lose face, Nawton quickly amended the gesture into an indication that the old man sit in the red leather chair in front of his desk. Ignoring him a second time, Demdyke instead took the larger chair behind the desk.

"Always liked this office. It was mine when Father still ran the show. Before your time."

Nawton sat down, the smile on his face a bandage covering the fury he felt. So what if the old bastard owned the company? Owned the building they were in, the desk between them, and the chairs they sat upon. It was *his* office now, and Demdyke's rudeness was in danger of inciting a response that may well have been justified but would be far from appropriate.

"You find me arrogant?" There was cunning in the old man's eyes, and his thin lips pulled up over a set of perfectly shaped yet nicotine-yellow teeth. Nawton liked to view himself to be cunning as a fox, but the fox now felt himself in the presence of a wolf. It was an uncomfortable feeling. "Forgotten what it's like to be the little man? Gotten used to answering to no one? A few emails here and there, and that's all the interaction you have with your betters, isn't it, Nawton? Unless you pray. Do you pray, Nawton? Are you answerable to God?"

Nawton had no idea what to say. So he said nothing.

"Cat got your tongue? Maybe a drink will help." He nodded toward the cabinet that ran along the side wall of the office and upon which sat a set of crystal glasses and a matching decanter. The whiskey wasn't as good as the MacAllan, but it was good enough. "You pour while I enjoy the view." Demdyke slowly stood and walked over to the corner of the office where the two glass walls met. The view out over the city was certainly impressive, even to Nawton, who had seen it almost every day for half a decade.

"Here you go, sir. I remember you prefer it straight."

Demdyke smiled. "Good man. I like that. Attention to detail. So, to business. You've been doing well. Costs down. Profits up. All I need to know is which of my vice presidents is the leader and which the follower."

"We both have our strengths, sir."

"And weaknesses?" The lupine smile was back as the glass reached the old man's lips, and he slowly sipped at his drink.

Nawton took a drink himself but only a slight one. He wanted as clear a head as possible when dealing with Demdyke as his intuition was screaming that one false move could prove to be exceptionally costly.

"It's time for me to fully step aside, Nawton. Hand over the reins. I had a son of my own once, but God saw fit to take him from me when but an infant. I never had the strength to risk putting myself through that despair again.

Had he lived, he would have taken this office and ultimately taken charge as I did from my father and he did from Granddaddy Dagda himself. But that isn't an option, Mr. Nawton, which leaves me with two: your good self and Mr. Hutton. Both long-term employees. Loyal employees. Employees who know how this business ticks and how I expect it to run. Men who know the rules and who know just how far to bend them. I like that, Nawton, pushing things to the edge. This is my business. Not the government's. Not the workers'. If I make a decision, that's how it should be for good or bad. My property. My rules." He turned to face the window, leaving Nawton to look at the back of his head, the close-cropped silver hair, the slightly worn collar of his shirt, and the golden scarab beetle attached to the skin between the two.

"I know you're looking at it." Demdyke turned and headed back to the chair behind the desk.

"It looks exquisitely made." It was the best response Nawton could come up with on the spot.

"Sit, and I shall tell you its secret. The scarab was found in the street in Whitechapel by my grandfather the week before he set sail for this great country of ours in 1888. Not long into the journey, he met a certain Mr. Stevenson, a curious man travelling with a cargo of even more curious items collected on his travels across Asia, Africa, and Europe and which he aimed to sell here in New York. To my mind, it was naïve of my grandfather to show this man the scarab, but I suppose he was intrigued to know if such a hawker of unusual artefacts could shed light upon its providence."

"Did he recognise it?"

Demdyke took a drink, his eyes narrowing. "Oh yes, he examined it, recognised it for what it was, and became obsessed with it. He tried to trade for it and tried to buy it, and when his advances were in vain, he tried to win it, for my grandfather never could refuse a bet. And so he gambled his way across the Atlantic with Stevenson, possessed with an almost insane desire for the scarab, gambling away his savings as he lost hand after hand after hand."

Demdyke paused for another drink, his voice having become increasingly coarse as he spoke. Nawton wondered if he had said as many words to his employees in the past year as he had today. "So that's where the money to set up business came from? And the company name?"

His drink gone and Nawton's question ignored, Demdyke continued. "Despite his fevered desire to obtain the scarab, Stevenson had always tried to gain it fairly, never once resorting to threats or violence, and when they eventually docked, my grandfather took pity on him. He offered Stevenson half of his money back in exchange for the reason he desired the scarab so much, an offer the now penniless Stevenson readily accepted. 'It will make you what you can be,' he said. 'Join with it, Dagda, for it will magnify your potential and bring you the rewards you deserve. You are a fair and good man, Dagda Demdyke. The scarab will serve you well so long as you listen to the advice it has to give.' And with that, he explained how the scarab could be used to attain such ends."

Nawton remained impassive. The scarab looked expensive and was an intriguing piece, as was the way Demdyke wore it, but the fairy story was testing his patience, which was gossamer-thin at the best of times. "So he used that thing how exactly?"

Demdyke bristled slightly at the question but pressed on with his tale. "Daddy said Grandfather was never sure how much of his success was down to the scarab, how much was down to him, and how much was simply down to the capital he won from Stevenson that gave him the start he needed. I think it was a combination of all three, but the key elements were he, the raw material, and the scarab—the catalyst, the symbiote. Eventually, the secret passed to my father and from him to me. I want you to try it on for size, Mr. Nawton. See what it tells you, where it takes you."

"I don't know what to say. Thank you, Mr. Demdyke, I won't let you…"

"Save it, Nawton. It's only a trial run. You have a month, so impress me. After that, your colleague, your *competition*, gets a shot. Mr. Hutton is as capable a man as you. I merely wish to know which is the greater."

With that, Demdyke reached behind his neck and pulled. There was a wet sound and a slight pop, like a suction cup coming loose, and then the scarab was on the desk. Nawton looked at it, looked at the blood smeared over it, and then jumped as what he had assumed to be a piece of jewellery scurried at him.

"What."

It was on his hand and running up his arm.

"The."

He shook his arm but to no avail as the scarab reached his shoulder.

"Fu—"

Pain stabbed into his neck as he felt what could only be a bite followed by a searing, burning pain that ran down his spine.

"Relax, man," said Demdyke through a wicked smile. "What did you think it was? A nice piece of decoration? It's alive, Nawton. The gold just a casing for the creature within. The pain will ease. Eventually."

Nawton tried to speak, tried to move, but all such actions were beyond him. He was paralyzed but not without feeling. That remained. Lightning strikes of pain rushed along his central nervous system, and he could feel a sucking and burrowing as the creature dug into his neck. He tried to move again but couldn't, the only part of his body seemingly capable of movement being his eyelids, which fluttered as he began to lose consciousness. Once, twice, three, four, five. Darker each time. Deeper each time. Then he was gone.

***

A flutter, then a flicker, and his eyelids were open, blinking in the light. He was back in his own chair with no sign of Demdyke but his empty glass on the desk. His head pounded, and he rubbed his temples before reaching around the back of his head. The scarab was there, lower than where it had been on Demdyke, but he guessed it needed to be secreted away beneath the collar line where it wouldn't be spotted day to day. Perhaps it had risen on Demdyke in preparation of leaving for a new host? *Details. Details. Don't worry about the details. Embrace what I bring to*

you. I know you now. I'm going to give you what you deserve.
Words in his head. Thought, not spoken, but alien to him.
Different. He rubbed at the scarab. There was a knock on
the office door.

"Come in."

It was Felicity. Nawton looked at her, the pain
forgotten.

"Mr. Demdyke told me to give you half an hour
and that then you'd need to see me?"

Need. Need. That's right. You need to see her. All of her.
"Yes." He almost stumbled over the word, but he was
starting to get a handle on things. There was a power. A
surge pumping through him. He felt energised, confident,
a coke-like hit that started as lapping waves but was
building, building to a tsunami of ability, a knowledge that
he could do whatever he pleased. The voice of the scarab
was within his head, a duality of thoughts replacing the
singular entity he had previously been.

"Are you okay, Mr. Nawton?" She walked toward
him, care and concern on her face. He stood and moved
towards her.

"I feel great. The meeting was a bit of a shock, but
yes, great." *Tell her. Impress her. Reel her in like a prize catch.*
"It appears you could be looking at the new president." A
broad smile. Another step closer.

"You look warm." She touched his cheek, and he
placed his hand over hers. Their bodies were almost
touching, then they were. His other hand moved around
the small of her back. Their eyes met first, then their lips.
His hand sank lower to the hem of her skirt, and then it

was beneath it, feeling the sheer pantyhose beneath and pulling her to him as her kisses intensified. She pulled away.

"Mr. Nawton." And then she was over his desk, pulling her skirt up in a way that could be nothing more than an invitation to take her right there and then. *She senses it. She wants you. To share in your power. Do it.*

He needed no encouragement from the thoughts that the scarab injected into his mind as this was his arena, and she was his reward. His first reward. For his was now destined to be a life of plenty.

He tore at the fabric covering her backside and ripped it aside. *That's it. Get it out, and put it in. Have her. Penetrate her. Fuck her so fucking hard she bleeds.* The sex was quick and rough. His hand slapping against her thighs as he thrust deeper and deeper into her, the scarab urging him on, applauding the virility which had been absent for so many years from its previous host. Demdyke had appetites once but never like this. *We will have fun together, you and I.* He reached over her motionless body.

Why isn't she moving? Nawton thought.

It doesn't matter. Keep going. He opened his desk drawer.

Why isn't it locked?

Don't worry; you just need what's inside. He took out the second of his silver flasks and poured a heap of cocaine onto the desk.

Where's Felicity?

She's knelt down, sucking on you. Can't you feel it? Wet. Warm. He felt it. He moved the coke into a thick line and ran his face along it. Then back again. Hoovering the particles up each nostril where it burnt and sent stinging snot around and to his throat. He stood. Staggered. *Look outside. See the city. King of the city now, aren't you? Look,* cajoled the parasite. *Look.*

He looked. He screamed.

***

"That's the last time you spoke to him?"

"Yes. Like I already told the officer, I went to see him about irregularities in the accounting for the past quarter. I told him that both he and Sydney, Mr. Hutton, were to work to the end of the day and then take leave until everything was independently audited. It was Sydney who had flagged up the issues alongside a few other concerns about Mr. Nawton's behaviour, but I had to be seen to be fair."

"So you suspended him?"

"As far as anyone would be aware, they would be out of the office working on a major deal. Their deputies would step in to look after the day to day while they concentrated on what would be portrayed as a potential game changer for the business. A bit of smoke and mirrors but less unsettling for all concerned than openly suspending two vice presidents."

"And what happened subsequently? It's all on tape?"

"Yes. It's a good few years back now, but that office was mine once, and I had cameras installed after a particularly ungrateful employee threatened me. I don't know if Mr. Nawton was even aware they existed. They certainly weren't in use. But he was fidgety, anxious, and it worried me. He'd been a long-term employee. A loyal employee as far as I knew, and regardless of the accusations, I was yet to see proof to the contrary."

"He was worried though?"

"Wouldn't you be if you were suspended from your job? Even if you were innocent? Look, he didn't say much. I told him we needed to investigate things, left the office, and out of concern for him, asked Security to turn the cameras back on. But I didn't ask anyone to monitor them, and they don't feed into the main control room. If only I'd had them watched, this whole bizarre nightmare could have been avoided."

"Mr. Demdyke, you expect me to believe that you were genuinely worried about him rather than keeping an eye on someone you suspected of defrauding your company whilst occupying a position of absolute trust?"

Demdyke shifted slightly in his chair. "Detective Persimmon, you can believe me or not. That isn't the issue here. I had a meeting with an employee, left, and asked for cameras in my building, placed in accordance with internal procedures and the presence of which, overt or covert, is accepted by all employees within their contracts to be turned on. The result is that what occurred following the meeting has been recorded, and I would expect that to be something which should make your job easier."

"Have you viewed the tape?"

"Yes, after Sydney had subdued him and while we waited for you to arrive. The man must have had a breakdown or some kind of psychotic episode. I can't excuse his alleged embezzlement, should it be proven, nor his treatment of some of the staff—again, only alleged at this point. And what he did to that girl." Demdyke shook his head and rubbed at the back of his neck. "But all the same, he had served the company well for many years even if things did fall apart at the end."

"I'm not sure I'd be quite so understanding, Mr. Demdyke, but I guess you knew him, and that makes a difference. Can I have the tape now?"

"Of course, Detective, although it's funny how we still say 'tape,' isn't it?" He passed over a USB stick and smiled. "Now if that's all, I'll bid you good day."

***

Detective Persimmon watched the tape, the *recording*, five times. The first time was straight through; the second was all stop, start, and take notes. Then straight through again. And then a couple more run-throughs with pauses, rewinding, and freeze frames to try and draw out anything that could be hiding behind the obvious.

He watched as Paul Nawton, 55, twice married, twice divorced, sits at his desk for twenty-five minutes doing nothing. He looks neither fully awake nor fully asleep but rather comatose. At twenty-five minutes, nineteen seconds into the recording, Felicity St. John, 23, single, been with the company nine months and working for Nawton just three days, comes in. Nawton stands. She places some papers on his desk. He grabs her from behind. She slaps him across the face and storms out. That's when things get weird. Nawton doesn't appear to realise he's been slapped, doesn't turn as she walks out of the door. Instead, he drops his trousers, places his penis on the desk, picks up a crystal glass, and smashes it down upon his manhood. On the fourth strike, the crystal smashes, but he keeps going until there's nothing left but a squashed, bloody stump. Seemingly oblivious to the pain, he then leans over the desk, opens a drawer, and removes what looks like a silver hip flask. From this, he pours a white powder, tested and confirmed as high-grade cocaine, over the desk before running his face back and forth across it. The action is repeated thirty-eight times, side to side, the friction burning two large patches of skin from his face. He stands. Walks over to the window, presumably sees his reflection, and screams. That's when Hutton, 57, been with the company 33 years, married, two children, and who recently approached the company board with concerns about Nawton's harassment of staff and certain financial irregularities, rushes in. Nawton attacks him but is wrestled to the floor. Demdyke is in the doorway with Miss. St John. Persimmon zooms in, but the picture loses definition. Hutton is there, pushing down on Nawton's neck. Demdyke is pointing with one hand, turning Miss. St. John's face away with the other. Hutton's fingers are grasping, squeezing, pulling. At what?

Persimmon leaned closer to the screen. Come on. Come on. Static. The recording ended. He leaned back and rewound the tape again.

END

Arbeit Macht Frei by Jeff Parsons

The voice inside his head had destroyed his life, his marriage, his job, and his sanity. It had literally led him down a dark road of depression and despair.

But at least he wasn't alone. He had the voice—a know-it-all, goody-two-shoes, pain-in-the-arse voice. Also, the voice seemed to know things before he did.

Not that its brilliance was useful.

"Useful" would have been to help with directions. He had been lost in the bramble-scratching woods since this morning, but now... He stood before an unusual obstruction, unsure of what to do.

<Something's definitely out of place here,> the voice said.

"Really? Ya think?" he quipped.

The "something" was a fence, about twenty feet high, built upon a concrete base, humming an electrified warning and topped with spiraled rolls of razor wire. In the night sky above, the splash of the Milky Way was obscured. The fence top also had glaring perimeter lights, starkly illuminating a grassy field contained within, about a half mile square. Essentially, the whole situation was completely alien to the northern Maine wilderness.

As his eyes adjusted to the harsh light, he noticed two buildings inside the enclosed area located on the opposite side.

"What in the—?" The experience was unnerving. He was so tired of being afraid. He had a fleeting thought about going home but quickly remembered that his home had been foreclosed upon and his job lost and his wife...

So where is my home? he asked himself.

To be honest, with his illness and his wife... They called it a separation, but really, she just couldn't deal with his constant problems. Maybe there was no going home.

<Trust me. Leave now.>

"Trust you?" His voice trembled. "To do what? Ruin my life?" *Damn... I can't take it anymore.*

<I've only wanted to help you. Speaking of which, try to remain as calm as possible. A jeep is approaching on the perimeter's path.>

The jeep pulled to an abrupt stop before him. The doors had Bureau of Strategic Defense logos on them, showing a lightning bolt zigzagging from the sky.

Two security personnel leapt from their vehicle, their eyes locked upon him like predators, tracking his position, monitoring his movements, calculating all possible responses. Their attitude, reinforced by pistols, tasers, and batons left no doubt that they were there to protect.

Their appearances were of diametrical opposites. One was tall and stocky and did not look too bright. The other was short and wiry with a clever, shifty expression. They were much like a bear and a fox. The first impressions stuck.

<Stay calm.>

"No kidding…" Too late, George realized that the guards had overheard him. He often got into trouble when he did that.

"Yes, sir," the Bear guard rumbled, "you're trespassing on federal land." The next words were carefully enunciated. "Who are you? Why are you here?"

"I'm George Donavon. I got lost in the woods. Saw your light and walked to it."

"Why were you in the woods?" Again, the Bear questioned while the Fox watched and waited, taking calm, measured breaths.

"I've been traveling." He pointed to his backpack. "Needed to camp for the night. Got turned around in the woods."

"Why were you traveling in this area?"

George had had enough of this.

<Don't! No, no, no…>

"Look. I'm sorry if I trespassed. I didn't see any signs about your property," he explained in anger, exasperation, and fatigue then blurted out, "I'm traveling because I've lost everything." His voice rose in increasing tones of distress. "I have…NOTHING!!! I'm *looking* for a job up north because *maybe* no one else thought to look up here. Last I checked, it was okay to travel in the US of A!!!"

The Fox guard had moved to a position behind him.

<Wow. That was over the top. They just need to know why you're here.>

"Okay, that's enough, buddy," the Bear guard said, pulling out his taser. "Lay down your backpack and…what…?"

George had gone into a Karate fighting stance. "I don't think so…"

He felt a whale of a blow on the back of his head. He fell in slow motion to the ground.

Did that little guy hit me?

<Yep.>

As his vision faded into blackness, he saw both guards looking down on him. Their bodies seemed to smear into the air around them.

Suddenly, George was out.

***

George awoke in a small lockup cell, lying on a cushioned bench underneath a woolen blanket. There was a shiny sink and toilet unit nearby. He looked around. His cell was at the end of a row of empty cells—twenty in all.

At the far end of the corridor was a security door.

<Welcome to the Hilton.>

"Not funny."

He sat up. His head hurt. He also felt weak and mildly disorientated.

How did that guy move so fast?

<We'll have company soon. Show some respect, and we'll be out of here.>

"We? Now, that's funny! This has never been a joint effort. You've always ridden me like a horse."

<You've always been in charge.>

The security door opened with a buzzing release of electronic locks. The two guards, Bear and Fox, strode down the corridor to his cell followed by an older man in an expensive suit.

The leader-type in the suit pressed up against the cell bars.

He had an earnest smile, slow in starting but wide in aspect, showing an amazing array of perfectly arranged, pearly white teeth. He continued to smile as he spoke in a hypnotically calm tempo.

"What brings you to visit us?" the leader asked.

<Don't be a smartass.>

"Looking for a job."

<Sigh.>

"You're aware that by traveling on these lands, you can be detained without cause?" George kept quiet. The leader continued, "Why didn't you cooperate with my security personnel?"

"They attacked me!"

<Careful, that won't help…>

"They subdued you while you were resisting arrest."

"I was hit…"

"Yes, I know. They chose not to use a taser. I would say that's a fortunate decision, considering your medical condition."

George was confused. "My what..."

"If I may, I made some discreet inquiries about you while you were resting. Life hasn't exactly been fair to you. A heart problem. Seizures. Psychological difficulties. Lost your job. And...other tragedies. I think...we can help you."

<These people are dangerous. Be careful.>

"You went through my wallet. Why should I trust you?"

<Good question.>

"The alternative, not trusting me, would be unpleasant for you. I'd rather avoid some embarrassing paperwork. Besides...we need help. Your engineering skills would be quite useful."

"You know about that?"

"We're thorough. I can also help get these refilled." He held up two empty prescription bottles.

"Those were in my backpack. You have no right to..."

George was extremely embarrassed about his ongoing difficulties. Several years ago, shortly after the seizures began, he started seeing things that others didn't. The voice also appeared during that time; a psychologist said it was a coping mechanism.

164 | The Voices Within Anthology

"I meant no disrespect. Medicine is extremely important. Judging from the dates on these bottles, it's been awhile since you've been on your meds. We can help with that." The sincere concern flowing from the leader was irresistible. "Would you like a construction job? Nearby, building houses, making good money, with room and board."

<You violated their security, and now, they want to help you? Don't you think that's *odd*?>

"Shut up," George muttered. The leader didn't seem to notice.

"I don't know what to say." The possibility of working again, making money, having food to eat, becoming stable, maybe getting the marriage rekindled... George was on the verge of elated tears. "Okay. Yes, please. Thank you."

"No...thank you! Gentlemen, secure some food and drink for George, and drive him over to the site. Good to have you on board!" He nodded and strode away down the corridor with the Fox guard.

The Bear guard opened the cell door and motioned for George to follow. They walked through the security door, which required a badge to open.

There was a cafeteria nearby, perfectly clean, with chairs stacked on tables. His backpack sat on a table.

The Fox guard was closing a refrigerator door—it was mostly filled with meat sealed in plastic wrapping. *Wow, they sure do get fed well around here.* He handed George a generic cola and a thick wedge of cheese.

"Thanks." George opened the soda and gulped it down while finishing off the cheese. Just then, he had a vision swimming across his altered senses: a man's arm writhing in agony, screams howling above the wet rumble of crunching noises. His senses returned him to the cafeteria.

The guards were staring at him.

"Wow. That was good. Hit the spot."

<That vision was a warning.>

About cheese? Not now...

George realized how peculiar his situation was; the voice inside his head was advising him on his visions.

"Come," said the Bear guard. "We'll escort you to the work site."

George was led down a bright corridor. On his left, bay windows overlooked a gleaming factory floor where two men—technicians—sat before control panels, watching George and the guards pass by. The control panels probably operated the two huge machine structures that dominated the area. At the end of the corridor, they exited a door to the outside.

The daytime sky was overcast with dark clouds. He was inside the fence. There was another building close by near an access gate.

The guards opened the rear double doors of a white van parked nearby. George stepped inside and sat down. It reminded him of a windowless paddy wagon. The door closed. An overhead light popped on. The van started moving.

***

Soon enough, the drive ended, and the door opened.

George stepped out into the worksite. There was the fresh smell of cut lumber, the shrill howl of power saws, and the staccato of hammers hitting nails.

The Fox guard watched George walk to the site's office building. The guard then got in the van and drove off.

What was he thinking?

<He was making sure there'd be no trouble.>

George hesitated at the office door. He understood why the guards would feel that way. It just made him feel sad. *When am I going to get better?*

<Don't worry. All you have to do is listen to me.>

"I have. And look where I am now. On the road. Alone." He glanced around. Nobody was nearby. "I hate you."

He tried to look interested, not anxious, as he opened the door.

The office had desks, bookshelves, a table covered with blueprints, and a man talking on a phone, waving him forward.

"Yes, I'll keep you notified." The man hung up abruptly as George approached.

"Hello, George. I'm the site supervisor, John."

They shook hands.

The overhead fluorescents snapped off. Then, their strobing resumed, revealing flickering, pale shadows moving throughout the room before the lights suddenly popped back on.

George had flinched. Not because he was startled by the power surge. He had seen something while the light was struggling to restore itself. The supervisor's image had fragmented, like a crude software pixilation backlighted by an infinite depth of darkness, momentarily pointillistic while his appearance reformed.

What the –

The supervisor chuckled. "They're doing electrical testing next door. One day, we'll get an independent power supply, but until then...it happens several times a day. So...have a seat, and tell me about yourself."

George forced himself to sit down and relax, casually rubbing his right hand—it was chilled to the bone from touching the supervisor.

They talked about his past. He had worked in the manufacturing field as a Quality Control Inspector. Times were tough with the economy's downturn. He got laid off—no reason given. Now, like millions of others, he wandered the roads, looking for whatever work he could find. He had left his marriage behind as well. He didn't tell the supervisor about that, nor did he talk about his anti-seizure and anti-psychotic medicines...

<They already know about your schizophrenia. Why they would hire you, knowing that, is a mystery...>

He almost told the voice to shut up.

The supervisor was sympathetic. "Hard times are upon us, but you needn't worry about that anymore. I've been authorized to offer you a job at twenty dollars an hour plus room and board."

"Yes, thank you, sir."

"Go find Elias. First building on your right as you leave. He'll get you started."

George left the room, astonished at his good fortune. He had a job!

<There's something very wrong about all this.>

"I don't care," he whispered. "They're helping me."

He entered the building on his right. The outside shell and internal framework were complete, and that was about it.

A young, stereotypical carpenter turned to greet him. "You're the newbie!"

<Word travels fast.>

"Uh, yeah. Elias?"

"That I am," Elias said. They shook hands. "Pleased to meet you. We'll get you a tool belt later. Are those safety boots?"

"Steel toe. They've seen a lot of road lately."

"I know the feeling. I was unemployed for a long time. Then, I answered a job club ad. Got an interview, and here I am. Most of us started out like that. Same for you?"

<Careful.>

"I was in the area and had nothing better to do," he laughed, surprised at his good mood. "I was going from town to town, camping along the way… I got lost in the woods. They found me. Gave me a job! Best luck I ever had."

"I'll say." Elias opened a storage container and handed George a hardhat, goggles, and gloves. "Here ya go… Okay, let's get to it. Today, it's drywall. Just follow my lead. I'll introduce you to some really colorful characters."

The work was hard but exhilarating. George had forgotten how much he loved to work with his hands.

He met about two dozen people, mostly during lunch break, which was held in one of the buildings. There was a good variety of lunch meats, breads, and beverages. He ate and drank until he was full and then some. His coworkers were amused but understanding. Everyone there had experienced hard times.

George didn't talk much about his past. No one seemed to notice. The voice was quiet. He also had no visions. He went through the whole day feeling normal, like he was living in a dream of who he used to be.

Just before dark, they quit working and went to the same building for dinner. Again, the buffet was simple but tasty. Hamburgers, hot dogs, potato salad, and so on. While George served himself, he had a disturbing vision: The food and drink were composed of human body parts and vile, disgusting fluids. He shrugged it off and enjoyed his meal.

Afterward, everyone split up, going to various unfinished homes, each apparently filled with plenty of cots, a stocked refrigerator, and a big-screen television. Soon enough, George was with Elias and four others, lounging comfortably, drinking beer, munching on snacks, and watching a football game. It was heaven.

After the game was over, Elias showed him where the cots were laid out. By then, he was exhausted. He was soon asleep.

***

The next day began with a mild buzz. George couldn't remember feeling this content in a long time. The morning spread of breakfast was great—he piled his plate high with eggs, pancakes, and sausages. He looked forward to putting on some weight. He ate quickly and left with Elias.

It was drywall again, but today, George was given his own tool belt. It felt reassuring to have one. Two others joined them: Jeremy, who almost never talked, and Ron, who talked virtually nonstop.

Ron was cheerful, friendly, and funny. He had a retro look about him: gold earring, mullet haircut, and a heavy metal band T-shirt. George liked him immediately, living vicariously through many of his interesting stories.

While they were working together, apart from the others, they had a long talk.

"Arbeit macht frei," Ron said. "Work sets you free."

"Yes, it does at that."

"That phrase was placed above the entrance of a concentration camp. Did you know that? We're also surrounded by a fence. All of us were drifters before we came to work here. But where do we go from here?"

"Dunno. Back to unemployment?"

"George, let me be direct; don't trust our employer," Ron said, looking at him closely.

"Uh…why not?"

"I've been here for five months. One by one, all of my coworkers have been taken away and replaced by new people… like you. Recently, I went looking for some information in our supervisor's office. It was strange… I wasn't able to hack into his computer. Yes, I have those skills, but…well…the computer zapped me really bad…and it seemed to move, like it was alive… I freaked out and left. Okay, you're giving me the crazy look, so tell me: What's inside that fence?"

"I was in a cell for a while. Then, I saw a factory floor, oh and two really big machines. Outside, I saw two buildings, both near the access gate."

"Anything else?"

"No, wait… The fence. It has transformers and huge lights on it."

"Hmmm… Tonight! I'm gonna sneak inside the fence tonight."

"Why!?! You could lose your job."

"The job! What good is money if you can't spend it? Did you know that we're never allowed outside the compound? They call it a security risk – ha! We all come in through the front gate, but there's only one way out – they take you away."

"I think you're mistaken…" George began to sweat. On his neck, it trickled, cold as a winter breeze, down his back.

<Don't get involved.>

"Like I said, I've been here awhile. Seen things. Lost my working buddies. I can't let it go. I need to know what happened to them."

George just nodded. They went on back to work. Nothing else was said about it.

***

He had a restless night of sleep.

***

After breakfast, there was an all-hands meeting held outside in the morning's cold air. They were informed that Ron had been fired and escorted offsite for violating company policies. Several people snickered derisively. Others were shocked and confused.

George was assigned to work with Jeremy. He knew how to set up drywall by now, so his mind wandered, wondering about what had happened to Ron. Finally he asked, "What did Ron do? Why'd he get fired?" Jeremy just shrugged and left, saying that he was going to get a soda.

<Leave it alone. You don't want something happening to you…>

Under his breath, George said, "Like what? Disappearing?"

<Oh no! Here come the guards.>

"Huh, where?" He turned and saw them just before they grabbed his arms and marched him backwards into the nearest building.

The Bear guard asked, "What did he tell you?"

"Who?"

The Fox guard stepped forward but stopped at a gesture from the Bear guard.

"Ron Russell."

<Not a word...>

"He said that you guys have no right to push people around."

"On the contrary. This site has special rules. We can do whatever we need to do. Now keep that in mind when I ask: Why was he inside the security area?"

"He was? Maybe he was curious about something? Sounds like a bad reason to get fired." George began to wonder if some of Ron's bizarre rantings were true.

<Well done.>

The Bear guard stepped close to George. "It would behoove you to avoid curious behavior." The guards left the house, presumably to shake down someone else.

"Why'd they do that? It's like they enjoyed it."

<Some secrets should be left alone.>

"I'm going back inside the security area."

<Are you crazy?>

George couldn't help chuckling. "I hope not. But being ignorant certainly didn't help everyone else before me."

<You don't know what happened to them...>

"Precisely. That's why I need to look for answers—before it happens to me."

<The perimeter is monitored. Hide in the back of the supervisor's truck. He drives in there at the end of the shift.>

"Hey, that's a good idea."

<You're welcome, says the figment of your imagination.>

    ***

The guard's interrogations had shaken everyone up; no one talked much until supper time. By then, George's coworkers were raving about that night's football game. He said that he wasn't feeling well and excused himself early in the meal.

He left the building. No one was outside. He climbed onto the truck bed and lay down beneath a paint-spattered drop cloth. It wasn't long before the supervisor arrived.

The truck started up and rumbled away. After several minutes, it passed through the automatic gate into the brightly lit fenced area.

The truck rolled to a stop, the engine turned off, and the supervisor got out, closing the door. George heard a door open and close somewhere nearby.

The hum of the fence grew loud while he waited, listening intently.

He lifted up the drop cloth and carefully looked around the area. No one was in sight.

Moving quietly, he eased out of the truck bed, walked to the nearby building, and opened a side door. The door was part of a short hall: an airlock. A loud, repetitive thumping vibrated from the door ahead.

He opened the second door and entered an area stacked with 55-gallon drum barrels. They were covered with biohazard symbols and Department of Transportation certification stickers. The barrels were used to transport something nasty—dangerous to human life.

Beyond the barrel area, there was a vast expanse of smooth cement floor, gleaming white beneath the overhead lights. He'd seen this before from the glass-enclosed walkway on the other side of the building. Dominating the open space were two mountain-sized machines, one of them currently operating, shaking everything with its thunderous grinding.

Metal container bins were forklifted to and from the shredding machine's conveyor ramps by the same two technicians he'd seen earlier. Pieces of meat were fed into the machine, and the ground up remains were taken away to a packaging machine that filled up the barrels.

"What are they doing?"

<Look inside one of the barrels.>

"Hell no. You want me to get a virus or something?"

<You'll be fine. There's an open one behind you.>

"Hmm… Someone forgot to close the lid." He pulled hard. It came off with a screech.

Inside, a polyurethane bag had been ripped open, exposing packages of raw meat, vacuum-sealed in clear plastic. He'd seen this before. In the cafeteria.

<Why would a meat processing plant need security?>

He edged closer to the front row of barrels, trying to get a better view of the shredders.

An unpleasant feeling began to overtake him, like he was tumbling in midair, even though he was standing absolutely still. Maybe it was another seizure…

His vision blurred, leaving him dizzy, and then as his eyes readjusted, he saw something startling. He watched it without being aware of himself, mentally retreating from the horror unfolding before him. He bumped into a barrel, jarring himself back into reality, even more terrified now.

He had seen…bodies going up the ramp into the shredder. Human bodies, twisted and broken into unnatural shapes.

<Oh my God.>

There was a noise at the airlock entrance.

He quickly looked around. Against the wall, closest to the barrel storage area, there was a metal grate stairway that went up about thirty feet to a door. He'd never make it up there in time. He didn't dare run out onto the floor's open space area. He decided to hide between the barrels.

The door opened. The two guards, Bear and Fox, came out and went up the stairway into a room beyond the door.

<Sheesh, don't these guys ever rest?>

George was so relieved. He thought he'd get caught for sure…

He looked out onto the floor area. The technicians were busy driving their forklifts around, oblivious to everything but their work.

"I have to do this. For Ron…" George's curiosity unraveled the paralyzing fear that threatened to overcome him.

<Just leave! Tell the authorities what's going on here.>

"The authorities probably work for these people."

He crept up the stairs. If a technician happened to look up, he'd be spotted immediately.

He made it to the door unseen.

<You're going to get us in trouble.>

"Nah, just me. The psychologists said you don't even exist unless I want you to."

<Ouch.>

The room was arranged with typical office equipment. There were electrical schematics posted on the walls along with various operations procedures with titles like "Loss of Offsite Power," "Emergency Diesel Generator," and so on. The grinder's roar was muffled after the entry door closed behind him.

He walked across the room to another door. He opened it a crack and peered into a control room. The leader, supervisor, and guards were looking out through a large window to the well-lit field. A technician, one he'd never seen before, also sat at a control panel near them, interacting with a kaleidoscope of shifting, liquid colors floating in mid-air.

George rubbed his eyes, but the vision refused to melt away.

Suddenly, lightning struck one of the blazing fence lights outside. Milliseconds after, all of the lights flared into painful intensity before shutting off.

He saw something.

When the lightning had flashed, something arrived with it, swallowing the field in unnatural Stygian blackness. The darkness then separated into many entities that oozed through the fence into the woods. When the lights went out, he also saw that the control room people were made from the same dark void.

He backed away and let the door close.

"Did that…darkness…come from outer space…an alternate reality…or…Hell?"

<That couldn't possibly be real.>

***

George left the building unobserved.

The fence, the lights…whatever it was, maybe a gateway… used a great deal of power. If he destroyed the power source, it would shut this place down at least for a while.

The other building was nearby. Maybe it held control circuits for the site's power. He ran over and opened the nearest door.

Inside the building, there were many rooms of electrical equipment — breakers, relays, switches, dials, and display monitors — but the most impressive equipment was the main fuse boxes, huge ones, the size of refrigerators. An enormous amount of power flowed through there.

<Sabotage won't help your story.>

He opened an exit door.

The light shining from behind him lit up the immediate area of the mysterious field before him. On his right, there was a diesel engine and fuel storage tank.

He let the door close.

If he opened the tank's relief valve on top, he might be able to get the diesel fumes to explode eventually. He could also disable the main fuses; it might overload some circuits.

Hopefully, he could then get away and alert the authorities.

<You can't trust the authorities, remember?>

"Shut up!"

Grabbing an insulated screwdriver from a tool cart, he went outside and climbed up the ladder on the side of the storage tank. The relief valve looked simple enough. Using the screwdriver, he adjusted it to remain fully open. A fierce hissing noise indicated that the dangerous vapor was being quickly released. He carefully climbed down the ladder, making sure that the screwdriver didn't touch anything; one spark could set off an explosion.

He entered the building and went to the first main fuse. They each had a shutdown lever encased behind a key-locked glass cover. He started to unscrew the first cover when —

"George." Spoken from behind him.

He leapt away from the sound, his back now touching the exit door.

They were all there: the leader, supervisor, guards, and technicians. Observing him — silent and devoid of emotion.

Then, the leader smiled. His hands lifted in heartfelt supplication.

"Please don't. We're here to help you and..."

"I was in the control room. I know what you do here."

"Did you see our test of the fence lights? Did that frighten you? I was scared. A lightning strike almost destroyed our plant's electrical system. George, I have to admit that I'm a little confused by your behavior," he murmured. "What do you think we're doing here?"

"Bodies! You grind up bodies. Those were human beings once."

The leader glanced at the supervisor behind him, who shrugged.

"It seems that you've discovered something you weren't meant to see. We destroy electronic parts, top secret ones, and disperse the fragments in the landfill field. But we also process biological specimens."

"Specimens? Is that what people are to you?"

"We process rabbits, monkeys, pigs, and cows. We reduce the bodies, seal the parts, store them, and then batch incinerate them. They are biological test specimens. Not people..."

"That's not what I saw..."

<Leave while you can.>

George pressed his hands against the door.

"I can only assure you that you were mistaken. Please... Come with us." George watched in horror as the leader transformed into a vision of his wife. "We can talk this out."

At that overwhelming moment, George bolted through the door, unknowingly creating a tiny spark that ignited the diesel fumes. It was like the sun suddenly picked him up and launched his crumpled body through the air.

He was lying on the ground. He didn't know why. The nearby building was collapsed and engulfed in flames.

As his vision faded, it seemed to be moving…restructuring itself.

<That's my boy. Go to sleep now.>

The last thing he saw in his life was the fuzzy shapes of people looking down upon him.

As he passed away, the leader said, "Pity. It must've been difficult having hallucinations."

They all laughed as their images dissolved into swirling motes of fading light…

END

Watch Out! Jeffrey K. Blevins

Boris the Burglar, with his black, pointed fedora and indistinguishable facial features, covered by the collar of an overshadowing black trench coat, is the name and image attributed with most Neighborhood Watch signs. His sinister scowl is veiled by darkness, allowing only white eyes to breach through the layers of black.

According to the National Sherriffs' Association, he is a fictitious character whose primary purpose is to fit the general description of many cartoonish villains—sneaking around in the shadows, unwilling to wear bright colors during the twilight hours. He has become an iconic representative of all "suspicious characters," though most successful career criminals don't make it a habit of strolling down a potential victim's street wearing any of the items worn by the comically illustrated character.

Boris the Burglar, aiding the formation of neighborhood watch groups in 1972 as a symbol of insidious intentions, will be remembered throughout history. The National Sheriffs' Association, as a result of the Kitty Genovese murder in Queens, New York, gave birth to the "Mascot of Misdoings" in an effort to raise public awareness—to bring vigilance to the community's watchful members.

By most law enforcement personnel's testimony, Boris was conjured and created to warn would-be delinquents that a watch group was actively in effect and that they should vacate the immediate area on the promise that a swift arrest would ensue should they pursue the perpetration of illicit activities. Thus, in all technicality, motivating the potential crook to lurk within the darkness of any non-participating Neighborhood Watch streets. Every noble program has its flaws however.

Boris is merely a distinct representation of the Justice Department's war against wrongdoers. Outlaws and sinners should twirl on their heels when seeing the sign that displays Boris the Burglar's fabricated appearance, knowing a barrage of police-calling eyes would fall upon them should they cross the street's threshold.

But is Boris simply be a cartoon-like figure that denotes an area of observing citizens? Or is he more than made-up? Could there have been an insidious conspiracy that manifested as a result of determined police officers who tried desperately to apprehend something evil? Something unnatural?

In the fall of 1971, one year prior to the announcement of official "Neighborhood Watches," an anonymous artist received a particularly disturbing request. One that included the illustration of an unreported serial killer's likeness. Reading the unsettling, top-secret document, he painted an image matching that of the following year's Boris the Burglar.

In short, the mysterious manuscript that detailed the department's frantic need disappeared into the tomes of rumor and speculation amounting to that of many infamous U.F.O. reports.

Today, nearly fifty years later, this artist reveals his illegally copied documents of a demonic visitor who ... wasn't what he appeared to be.

One thing has become clear: The Susanville Sinner was and will forever remain at large, embodying a baffled police force's inadequacy when attempting to apprehend the unknown.

Susanville, California ... October 11, 1971

Autumn leaves swirl beneath the feet of frolicking children, forming artistic blends of reds and oranges as they wisp through the chilly air. Recess is a popular time amongst fall-faring students—rambunctious youngsters who are set on depleting their energy before returning to class for the final announcement of "See you tomorrow."

The afternoon sky is covered with its traditional cloudy plumes, promising a particularly cold night.

"Mrs. Bales?" Jimmy Dominguez asks with childish charm, "Will you marry me?"

The first-grader's friends snicker and run away sporadically when the attractive twenty-nine-year-old schoolteacher casts a loving glance.

"I'm sorry, Jimmy, though I believe you will grow up to be quite the catch, the Mrs. Portion of my name symbolizes that I'm already married."

She smiles as the young boy's innocent eyes watch her intently, yearning to absorb knowledge. "Don't worry though; all the girls better watch out for when you bloom."

Jimmy gains a sudden infliction known as embarrassment, whereupon he likewise scampers away across the yellowing lawn, presumably retaining the useful information.

Charish Bales enjoys teaching the first grade; it's a time when the youthful pupils are blameless, and the Cooty stage hasn't taken full effect.

She smiles as Jimmy reunites with his young following, and they march in step towards the classroom building—no doubt pretending to be soldiers.

A gust of wind kicks up around her long and elegantly floral-printed dress. With it comes the troubling sensation that she's being watched.

Scanning the playground, everything is exactly as it should be. Stationary vehicles line the chain-link fence that separates the town's main road from the school; leaves fall from the trees just as they should in accordance with the calendar's date; an ordinary citizen crosses the empty intersection paralleling the establishment's east end, undoubtedly returning to a boring cubicle in his routinely dull office space.

Nothing is out of the ordinary.

"You're being silly." She whispers as not to gain notoriety as "the teacher who speaks to herself" (a child's scorn can outlast that of a woman's).

Yet in light of the media's constant articles regarding Charles Manson and his three cult followers receiving the death penalty, everybody remains in a perpetual state of unease. News only becomes just that when it is broadcasted relentlessly.

Moments before returning to the facility's academic building, she again feels watchful eyes glaring behind her — call it, a woman's intuition, call it a sixth sense, or call it a third eye of instinct...whatever it's called, it is real.

Against her better judgement, she turns to face the area of suspected scrutiny. Her body momentarily turns rigid with apprehension. From behind a hundred foot sycamore tree that stands along Main Street, a man (seemingly so) grins before lurching back behind the tree's cover.

Disbelievingly, she approaches the tree until reaching a cautious distance away from its looming branches.

Nobody stands behind the Sycamore.

Her imagination couldn't have been that overwhelming. The man's eyes had been a glowing blaze of yellow, masked beneath a pointed black fedora and mostly covered with a body-length trench coat.

She vividly recalls seeing the man's quick flash of jagged teeth and wonders if it was all imagined. How can a stalker disappear without a trace? Unless he was contrived by her media-enhanced excitement. It's the only reasonable answer. Just because she's versed in the first-grade teaching requirements doesn't mean she has a first-grade level of intelligence. Human beings don't vanish into the wind, and a paranormal explanation certainly isn't a route she's willing to pursue.

To her, ghosts and goblins are strictly saved for the entertainment purposes that are often exploited by Hollywood, holding no more tangible merit than The Tooth Fairy, Santa Claus, and The Boogeyman (the stalker displaying more of a physical description to the latter). Regardless, intelligent people don't see spectral apparitions. Perhaps it was a teenage prankster who discreetly fled out of her line of sight.

In the end, the distant encounter isn't of significant importance. Frightening, yes. Alarming? Certainly.

But worthy of informing the police department? Hardly. They have far more valuable calls to answer and wouldn't want to be burdened by her report.

Detective Lance Kenzy arrives on scene.

"This is horrible," he mutters to another investigator while analyzing the gruesome scene. "When is it going to end?"

Junior investigator Michael Christie frowns, shaking his head from side to side. "I don't know, Lance. It doesn't look good. Following the pattern of the other six, it seems as if it won't stop until we physically stop it."

The U.C.L.A graduate is likely correct.

The small (and nearly forgotten) town of Susanville, California has been under the gruesome assault of a bizarre serial killer. Six days ago, excluding today, an unorthodox string of occult slayings had begun. Mrs.

Charish Bales is merely the seventh victim of an already horrifying ordeal.

"Notify the principle," Detective Kenzy begins. "Inform him that school is to be cancelled until our investigation is finished." A dreary look seizes his heavily-burdened brows. "We don't need the town panicking more than they already are. Especially not the children. Issue a state of caution and have the radio announce that individuals shouldn't venture out alone."

"Will do, Detective."

Charish Bales, lovely from the day she was born, swings from the tetherball pole, strangled by the neck as if condemned to the ancient gallows. Identical to the other six victims, the words, "WATCH OUT!" are deeply etched into her forehead.

The town's respected detective completes his preliminary reports before returning to his humble homestead atop Cherry Hill. He sighs upon entrance into his house, a look of residual grief painted across his every expression. He's tired and hasn't slept well in the last week. The grisly murders are taking their toll.

Five-year-old Kevin Kenzy barrels into the room after hearing the door open. "Daddy!" he shouts with merriment.

"Hello, son," Lance whispers, forcing a smile.

He can't help but admire a child's innocence. At five years old, a young child couldn't comprehend the cruelties and many abominations that lay in the world before them. To Kevin, his father's presence is simply enough, never knowing that some people refuse to differentiate between right and wrong. In the case of The Susanville Sinner, wrong is the only action that is right.

"Where's your mother?" the detective questions, desperately trying to hide the week's fatigue that burrows beneath his eyes.

"She's in her room sleeping!" he yells excitedly, illustrating either a lack of concern towards his slumbering mother or a genuinely enthusiastic response towards his father's return. Being a child, it's likely due to a father's return.

With the front door open wide, both the detective and his son feel a cool breeze reach the nape of their necks.

Curious, Kevin strolls toward the opening, always awestruck by the beauty of mountain living. "Daddy, are you going to leave right now?" he asks in a saddened tone. "You just got home."

Lance grins while turning to face his son with a downward smile. "No, I'm here for a while. What makes you think I'm leaving?"

Naturally, the boy's years in life have been spent watching his father come and go at a moment's notice. He's waited through long hours without his dad and has had many nights without a bedtime story to comfort him into the world of dreams.

These are all answers Detective Lance Kenzy is expecting.

His son is full of many surprises.

"Because you didn't take that man to jail," he speaks innocently. "You never bring bad guys home with you."

His small finger points to the unmarked patrol car sitting in the slightly slanted driveway.

Lance freezes instantly, horrifically gazing upon the nearly featureless man who grins menacingly behind the safety bars in the back seat. His black fedora pokes at the side window, sharp teeth glimmering in contrast to his blackened face. Long eerie nails tap on the window in an alternating pattern, as if to taunt.

He is the essence of evil … and unlike any "man" Lance has ever seen — if he's a man at all.

"Get inside!" he shouts while turning around to shove his son inside, "Lock the door, and tell Mom to notify Officer Christie down at the station!"

While circling back toward the motionless patrol vehicle, he draws his pistol and points at the window, fully prepared to unload sixteen .40 caliber rounds into the strange intruder.

But nobody is there.

He investigates the back seat and quickly scans around the mountainous terrain.

Still, nobody is there. Not a single indication of what one might expect when dealing with a person breaking out of a patrol car: no broken glass, no footprints, not even a sign of forced entry/exit.

"What on Earth is happening?" he whispers in a state of disbelief.

To describe the experience as a hallucination would mean that his son was likewise being hysterical. The event couldn't have been caused by exhaustion, else Kevin would have to be exhausted too. They both saw him. Whatever he was.

Lance proceeds back up the steps to the front door with absolute vigilance. He'll never forget the way those teeth ground together maniacally or how those elongated, pointed fingers rapped threateningly against his window.

But after too many years of seeing the evils of men, how is he really supposed to consider a more supernatural explanation? When the world is full of murderous thieves and lawless crooks, how can he be willing to contemplate something that isn't believed to be real?

The answer lies within his soul, knowing that his own son saw the man as well.

He unlocks the door to find his wife whirling a frying pan directly at his head. If it wasn't for an instinctive ducking movement, he would've been knocked to the ground with a lump the size of the mountain he lives on.

"Whoa, Honey!" he exclaims while grabbing her wrist,. "It's me!"

She subsides and calms herself after clasping both arms around him. "Kevin told me there was a man outside. I didn't know what he was talking about. I didn't even have time to call the station. Is everything okay?"

"Yes," he lies, not wanting to cause unnecessary alarm. "Everything is fine."

But is it? He wonders if perhaps there is need for alarm.

Still, he strokes her hair with the conclusion that telling her specific details will only enflame the fire of concern. Apart from a demonic scare, the vanishing perpetrator didn't cause any physical harm. Not yet at any rate.

The day's events settle down as another autumn evening courses throughout the detective's home. His wife munches on a bag of microwavable popcorn while watching a television show, and his son is presumably playing with a box full of toys inside his room.

But as the evening promises to transform into a restful night, the landline phone rings with its usual sharp pitches, and the silence's tranquility is broken.

"I got it!" Lance's voice echoes throughout the house.

After seven rings, he answers the phone friendly enough, "The Kenzy residence, how can I help you?"

His heart stops beating, and a cold chill tightens its grip around his spine when he hears the caller's voice. "Do you know who I am Detective?"

Not a single man on this planet could mimic the voice of Satan himself. There was too much malevolence lacing the stranger's tone. Too much hatred and wickedness, like that of a Hell-born entity.

"What do you want? Who are you? If you come near my family, I swear to God I will shoot you in the head!" Anger replaces Lance's distress.

"Swear to God all you want, but it isn't God you are dealing with," laughs the hellish voice. "I've called to sing you a verse from a song I'm creating. Kenzy, would you care to hear it?"

Before Lance can respond with an aggressive promise regarding the consequential retaliation should his family be attacked, the stranger interjects, "I'm going to sing it anyways, and I suggest you listen."

With cold, calloused annunciations, he sings ominously, "In a town where goodness grows, a monster comes, he'll cut off toes. Where women sleep atop their beds, he'll sever their hands, their feet and their heads. A detective tries but can't protect. Many more will hang by their neck. He leaves no times for a single shout; his only message is to simply WATCH OUT! Now rest assured I'm your Susanville Sinner. Perhaps one day, I will join you, your wife, and Kevin for dinner."

The phone disconnects, and the buzz of nothingness sounds through the cold device.

The stranger's foreboding song spoke everything of his insidious intent but nothing of his motive. What was his agenda with a mostly non-historical town? Susanville wasn't out-of-the-ordinary by anybody's standards.

The ole Police Force spirit fills the detective as he rushes into the living room where his wife responds rigidly to his sudden alarm.

"What are you doing?" she questions as he unlocks the gun case that holds both his spare service revolver and his department-issued shotgun.

"Take this," he demands while placing the loaded revolver in her delicate palms. "Make sure all the doors are locked, and don't stand near the windows!"

"What's wrong? Is something happening?" she manages weakly as he pumps the seven-shot 12 gauge.

"Just be alert; it's probably nothing," he states distractedly before shouting up the stairs toward his son's second story bedroom. "Kevin, get down here immediately please! We need to be in the kitchen right now!"

The urgency in his voice carries into the small child's ears. Kevin bounds down the steps and scampers into the kitchen.

Both Lance and his wife gasp as they see their son enter. In bold red letters, his forehead reads, "WATCH OUT!"

"Why did you write that on yourself?" Lance questions with a cocktail mixture of anger, frustration, and worry.

"I didn't, Daddy!" Kevin explains cheerfully. "The man with the black pointy hat in my bedroom did it. He said he was invited for dinner."

END

What the Heart Wants – Frank Martin

The following are excerpts taken from the personal reports of Dr. Henry Eastman, former director of the now defunct experimental donor program.

Time logged: Post-op + 1 hour

I'm happy to state the surgery was a success. The patient, Jonathan Cross, exited the operating room roughly three hours after entering, near record time for a heart transplant. He currently sits in the recovery room, where he will began the slow and, some say, torturous process of adjusting to literally having his heart cut out of his chest and replaced with a new one. But at fifty-eight, Mr. Cross still has a full chapter of his life ahead of him.

During the procedure, his wife, Jane, sat nervously in the waiting room, where I periodically gave her updates on her husband's progress. I'm not usually one for small talk, but I engaged Mrs. Cross to distract her mind from the inevitable anxiousness that comes with being a helpless spouse. John has been my patient for several months now, ever since I approached him to be the first candidate in the new donor program, but I learned more about his life in those few minutes with his wife than I ever had from him directly. I was surprised to hear he and Jane had four children together, two of whom had children of their own. And that was just the tip of the iceberg poor Jane unloaded onto me about their life. It seemed with the frightening possibility John might not leave that operating room alive. Jane felt like she had to give her husband an impromptu eulogy, and I was more than happy to listen.

Unmarried and with no kids, it's hard for me to imagine how it feels to watch a loved one suffer and cling to life when there's nothing you can do but hope and pray. But the worst part of it was over now. John's old, failing heart was gone, and now, he had a new one, a healthy one, to live out his life with. To play golf with. To go on cruises with. To watch his grandchildren grow up with.

When put into that perspective, it's hardly surprising why he agreed to the program so rapidly. When I first approached the organ donor board with my proposal, they were understandably hesitant. The legality surrounding medical protocol and privacy acts made running the program a peculiar situation. I had to inform patients, volunteers of the program, they would be receiving their transplant from an unlikely pool of candidates but wasn't allowed to disclose who these candidates were or why their organs had become available.

I was concerned some patients would balk at the secrecy, which was why I approached someone low on the donor list to receive the rarest of organs: a heart. Some might say I was taking advantage of someone's time of need. Using their desperation to further my own ambitions. But I was saving lives. With over a hundred thousand people on the donor list, seven thousand of those die every year waiting for a new organ. Someone had to do something. So I did.

And yes, I did ask Jonathan if he felt taken advantage of. In fact, it was the last question I again asked him on the bed of the operating table right before he went under the anesthesia. And he answered by calling me his savior.

But John wasn't done yet, and I wouldn't rest easy until he was out of the hospital and safe at home. He still has a week of recovery ahead of him. I'll be there monitoring him every step of the way.

***

Time logged: Post-op + 14 hours

After several hours unconscious in the recovery room, Jonathan was moved to the intensive care unit. Another several hours after that, he slowly came out of the anesthetic with a sore throat. Other than periodically poking my head in to check his condition, I left John's general post-op care to the hospital nursing staff and his surgeon. I was here strictly in an observational capacity to monitor his progress as the first participant of the program. And so far, there wasn't much for me to do other than record his vitals until he had recovered enough for me to question him.

I had to wait until the next day for that time to arrive. From the moment John entered his room at the ICU, Jane hadn't left his side, and I relied upon her to let me know how he made it through the night. She said he slowly but surely became more and more alert until he reached the state where he was able to greet me when I entered the room that morning. He was already off the IV and eating solid foods, well ahead of a normal post-op schedule for a heart transplant.

Besides the normal aches and pains that come from a major procedure, it physically appeared as though John was doing just fine, and the report I received from his surgeon reflected as much. But his recovery wasn't without its hiccups. Much to his wife's surprise, John told me his hearing was acting up. Jane laughed it off, thought he was making a joke as an excuse to stop listening to her. However, he was serious. John said he could hear a faint rustling in either ear but never both at the same time. The noise was very reminiscent of a man's voice, almost like a whisper. It wasn't constant and would only last for a couple seconds at a time but was bothering him enough that he felt I should know.

John couldn't tell who the voice was or what he was saying. The words were too low and muffled to discern. In fact, there was a good chance they were gibberish and spoken by nobody in particular.

But the what wasn't as concerning to me as the how and why. It was hard to pinpoint an exact cause so early after surgery. Even though he wasn't necessarily operating near the brain or spinal cord, there was still a slim chance the surgeon caused some kind of neurological damage while he was operating. More likely was the whispers were an uncommon side effect of the anesthesia.

But I couldn't rule out, in fact I had to consider, John's symptom was actually an unforeseen consequence of the donor program. It was still too early to tell, and John wasn't displaying or reporting any serious discomfort just yet, but the voices he was hearing had to be closely monitored in the coming hours if not days. Hopefully, they went away in time. But if not, it would certainly be an obstacle I would have to overcome if the program were to continue beyond Mr. Cross.

***

Time logged: Post-op + 22 hours

By noon of the next day, John was surprisingly more active than the last time I saw him. So much so that his surgeon was growing concerned by his speedy recovery. Not even twenty-four hours after he left the operating table and John was already insisting that his catheter be removed. Once again, I left the direction of his care to the hospital staff. He was their patient, after all. But I admittedly felt sorry for the nurses who were tasked with keeping him in bed.

Despite the continuous pleas from his wife, John repeatedly tried to get up and go to the bathroom. Several doctors, including members of his surgery team, had to come in and explain to John why he was on bed rest. His body just wasn't ready for any kind of physical activity. Needless to say, he wasn't happy with their orders and considered them merely suggestions.

Not surprisingly, Jane was growing worried by her husband's behavior. Privately, she expressed to me that she was concerned her husband was acting out of character. He was becoming snippy and irritable. Short-tempered and quick to judgment. Granted people are often uncomfortable following a major surgery. She was with him all the time and therefore more sensitive to his periodic outbursts of frustration. But based on my brief interactions with her husband, I would concur with her assessment. John did not seem like the well-mannered man I knew in the months leading up to his surgery. It wasn't until I was alone with him I had an indication as to why.

John revealed to me the voice had gotten worse. Louder and clearer. More frequent too. He still didn't recognize who it was, but he understood it now. And there was no way to turn it off.

At first, John didn't want to share with me what the voice was telling him. He felt embarrassed and scared. Maybe even ashamed. Like the voice was some manifestation of his own feelings. But I assured him that wasn't the case, and the best way for me to help was to fully understand the problem.

Only then did he open up about the paranoia and anxiety the voice expressed. Everyone who entered the room was subject to its judgment and told John exactly how it felt. How the nurses taking care of him were incompetent. How the doctors were more interested in billing his insurance than healing him. Even the cafeteria staff was apparently plotting against him, poisoning his food in small doses to avoid detection.

John knew none of these things were true. He told me himself. But there was only so much a man could take before it started to eat away at him. He wanted to get out of the hospital. He wanted to go home. But he just wasn't physically ready. And now I was beginning to think mentally as well.

The surgery team was still concerned about his unnatural recovery and ordered blood drawn to test for any anomalies, which the nursing staff reluctantly performed while being berated for their incompetence by the patient. I, on the other hand, was more interested in what was going on inside John's head. The psychosomatic auditory hallucinations he described could've been those of a paranoid schizophrenic. Yet he was much too old for a late onset of the disease, and it would've been pretty coincidental, and unlikely, it developed following a heart transplant.

Either way, it was too soon after surgery for an MRI. I will just have to wait and see how his condition progresses. Hopefully, it will get better with time.

***

Time logged: Post-op + 27 hours

It was around dusk when I again went to check on John, and this time, I could hear him shouting from down the hall. Upon hearing his voice, the slow walk I took out of the elevator turned into a brisk jog towards his room. What I found inside were two nurses backed up against a wall in fear while John argued loudly with the surgeon by his side. I needed a moment to take in the scene, and only then did I see Jane was also in the room, cowering in the corner, fearful of what her husband had become.

He was screaming at the man and refusing to take his immunosuppressants. The drugs were a necessary part of recovery. In fact, he, like all transplant patients, would have to take them for the rest of his life to prevent his own body from rejecting the foreign heart now inside him.

The surgeon was there to explain that to him, but John wasn't listening—if he was ever listening to begin with. Now he was just shouting at the top of his lungs, throwing insult after insult in the man's face, none of which had anything to do with the situation at hand.

By just standing in the doorway, I couldn't tell how long the standoff had been going on, but the look of frustrated defeat written on the surgeon's face was a troubling sign. So shocked by the whole ordeal, it took a moment for everyone to notice I'd entered the room. Even the surgeon, lost in his own head, seemed utterly discontented and stared right through me in disbelief.

And he had a right to be. Why would a patient refuse to take a routine post-op medication he agreed to before the surgery? One that was designed to keep him from dying.

At this point, John was simply screaming for everyone to get out, and although they did so with the bedside manner of saints, the hospital staff was grateful to escape Jonathan's verbal assaults.

On his way towards the door, the surgeon gave a brief nod in my direction, communicating he wanted to speak with me. Jane actually picked up on the subtle gesture as well and followed us to a position outside the room where John's incessant shouting had become nothing more than background noise.

The surgeon began by reporting the results of John's blood work, which showed elevated levels of adrenaline and testosterone. While it certainly offered some sort of cause for John's aggressive behavior, the surgeon had no idea how or why the hormones became so high in his body. Completely at a loss, the surgeon then turned to me for an explanation, assuming the donor program had to be the culprit.

I immediately froze at the accusation. If a rumor began circulating that the program's first participant became abnormally hostile, then it would surely be shut down. So I abruptly deflected the issue to a more probable link to John's irritability: the voice.

Jane and the surgeon were both shocked by the revelation. The surgeon for medical reasons and Jane because she felt hurt her husband of thirty years had been keeping such an important secret from her. Although the surgeon was perturbed I never informed him of such a vital detail, he was too troubled by the development to focus his attention on my withholding the information. His recommendation was an immediate mental evaluation along with a transfer to the psychiatric wing of the hospital. I was about to disagree when Jane beat me to it. She refused to believe that her husband was crazy.

Ultimately we decided to monitor John's situation closely to see if he improved. If he didn't, or God forbid grew worse, then there was no doubt what had to be done. We were all in agreement to wait until morning before addressing the behavior issue.

It quickly became apparent to me I wasn't going to be getting much sleep tonight. The next couple hours would dictate the donor program's future, and my eyes would surely be glued to John's room, hoping and praying he could somehow defeat the mysterious voice that ailed him.

***

Time logged: Post-op + 42 hours

This will be my final entry regarding the progress of Jonathan Cross' case. Before beginning, I must apologize if any of my details are off or erroneous when compared to the hospital's official incident report. Unlike my previous entries, which were penned while the facts were still fresh in my mind, this account is being retold several hours after the event in question. I had been speaking with the police all night (or morning depending on how you look at it) and only just have time to write it down.

I remained outside John's room for several hours after meeting with his wife and surgeon. There was no change at first, and I could hear his voice booming out from within the room. Anyone who walked through the door, from nurses to administrators, was met with resistance and insults.

For the majority of time, I was either going through paperwork or keeping a close eye on John's volatile vitals through a monitor. Occasionally I stopped by to make my presence known, and it was becoming increasingly clear John was experiencing some kind of delirium. Wide-eyed and sneering, a visible anger radiated from the patient's face. It was a disturbing rage that could only be interrupted by what I assumed to be the strange voice bellowing in his ear. Amidst his tantrums, John would suddenly stop and turn his head up as if listening intently to something only he could hear. It was hard for anyone who witnessed the man's manic behavior not to think he was under the deranged spell of psychosis.

The reality was beginning to look like John's downward spiral into madness wouldn't stop on its own. It was actually getting worse. The surgeon was now insisting we speed up our timeframe for his transfer, but Jane was adamant about holding out hope. And since John had yet to shows signs that he was a danger to himself or others, the surgeon was unable to force his involuntarily admittance as a psychiatric patient.

As much I tried to deny it though, there was no improvement in John's well-being that would allow me to argue with the surgeon's order. I was just about ready to accept that inevitable truth when I noticed I wasn't hearing John's loud, hawkish voice as often as I had earlier. His screams were becoming shallower and shallower, and nurses were leaving his room less and less aggravated. His blood pressure and heart rate were still elevated, but it seemed that his overall demeanor had leveled out. For the first time since I heard his surgery had been a success, I was starting to feel relief that everything was going to be okay.

And that's when it happened.

I was sitting at a nurse's station, parked myself right in front of a monitor of John's vitals. No noise, John or otherwise, had come out of the room, and so I was caught by surprise when the steady rhythm of John's heart rate suddenly flat lined. I quickly looked up in shock, holding my breath while staring at the monitor. Even the nurse beside me had frozen in place, confused by the noise. Normally, such an abrupt and unexpected reading was a glitch that would quickly correct itself. But then the nurse and I realized at about the same time John was indeed a heart transplant patient who refused his medication. He'd been doing so well physically, yelling and refusing to sit still, that we were lulled into a false sense of compliance, forgetting he could indeed crash at any moment.

The nurse and I pushed up out of our seats to rush toward the patient when we both balked again from an unexpected noise. This time, it was a blood-curdling scream echoing from inside the room. Our brief hesitation ended almost as quickly as it came about; except now, our urgency to move forward was for a different reason.

What we found upon turning the corner was a blood-spattered room and an empty bed. Only after a quick scan did we find the source of the blood, which came from John pinning Jane into the corner and repeatedly stabbing her in the neck with a syringe.

The nurse screamed out in terror while I sprang forward to grab onto the manic man killing his wife. I tried to pull him off, but John's muscles had clenched up into a deathly grip, also reflected by the vicious glare in his eyes. Blood continually shot out in every direction, soaking me, John, and his poor wife, who could only whimper out a weak cry for help.

I was later told I was only clutched onto John for a few seconds, but it seemed like an eternity before an army of men and women collapsed on us in a gigantic pileup. Even with our combined strength, we struggled to fight off John's bloodthirsty ferocity and wrestle him off of his wife. And when we finally did, he wouldn't stop screaming about the hounding voice in his head that told him she had to die, ordering him to kill her over and over again like a perpetual mantra of death.

Eventually, John was restrained and handed over to the police, arguing with the imaginary voice in his head about who was at fault for Jane's murder. At this point, nobody at the hospital debated or even suggested John should be kept under medical supervision, which seemed strange given he had a heart transplant less than forty-eight hours earlier. But then again, he seemed to be doing just fine on his own. Physically, at least.

Before the hammer comes down, I've decided to voluntarily cancel the donor program. I'm sure there will be backlash from the participants already scheduled to have their transplants. But given the incident with Jonathan Cross, I don't believe I'm left with much of a choice. I could always tell the potential recipients about what happened to Jonathan and make them understand the severity of the issue. There is a good chance they will accept the risks regardless. They are desperate, after all. But ultimately, I believe the truth isn't worth the risk.

Instead, I believe I will use the word "postponed" rather than "cancelled" when describing the program's status. With millions of patients awaiting organs, there's no sense stopping it altogether. Perhaps a change in criteria for donor selection is in order. The previous owner of Mr. Cross's heart did have a particularly high body count attributed to him. Even for that of a death row inmate.

END

The Voice of Absolution Ash Hartwell

Joseph stood a little way down the street from the burning building. The fire had taken hold rapidly, and the flames were already spewing from the upstairs windows and shooting into the night sky from the yawning hole in the roof. The roof had collapsed surprisingly quickly, a sight that had elicited a delighted snort of laughter from Joseph. From his vantage point in the shadows, he watched the flames with the awed expression of a child on bonfire night. His eyes were alive with the blaze's reflected fire, his mouth torn between an excited grin and the healthy grimace of fear.

The distant sirens tore him from the flame's mesmeric charm, the flashing blue lights dancing on the buildings at the far end of the street telling him it was time to leave. He hung his head, momentarily disappointed. No one had stumbled from the blazing house choking, burnt, screaming for help, or wailing for family members still inside. But having seen how quickly the raging fire engulfed the building, Joseph knew they'd never stood a chance.

Joseph turned away from the onrushing emergency vehicles. He pulled his hood up to protect him from the cold and calmly walked away, his attention already turning to what take-away to get, the delightful suburban family of four he'd just incinerated already banished from his thoughts.

The next morning dawned cold and bright, a light frost turning the landscape into an old photographic negative, but the weak sun had long since burnt this away when Joseph finally crawled from his bed. After a breakfast of Jim Beam and coke, the latter snorted from the surface of his cluttered coffee table, and a few plastic forkfuls of cold chow mein, he flicked the television on. The local station carried the dramatic news of a fire that ripped through a family home in a quiet neighbourhood, killing all four occupants. The newscaster went on to fill in the details of the deceased, but Joseph had lost interest and began channel hopping, finally settling on a low-budget afternoon game show.

The programme ended and another replaced it, but Joseph hardly noticed. He was wired. The rush of reliving the fire, the thrill of hearing the reassuring whoomp as the accelerant caught, flooded his system with adrenaline, heightening the cocaine's assault on his senses. He watched the game show contestants struggle with a steady stream of pointless questions with disinterested eyes until one question, written large across the bottom of the screen, piqued his involvement.

What is a pyromaniac?

"I am. I'm a fuckin' pyromaniac!" Joseph shouted triumphantly, struggling to his feet and knocking over the coffee table. He stood alone in his outdated living room, swaying gently from side to side, pointing an accusatory finger at the television as if daring it to disagree then added almost sheepishly, "and I need a piss."

Having relieved himself, he dressed, opting for a smart yet casual outfit of shirt and jeans. He took another line of his dwindling supply of coke, making a mental note to acquire some more before the night was out and then left his house. It once belonged to his parents, but he inherited it following their timely death because of a faulty boiler spewing carbon monoxide into the house while he was conveniently away on a school trip. With the house, Joseph also received a significant inheritance, which he squandered in a little over two years of holding drug-fuelled parties for his friends. When the money dried up so did his friends. And now he was alone, and if he were truthful, he preferred it. He was free to come and go as he pleased with no one expecting anything from him or asking awkward questions.

It was already dark when Joseph, his senses buzzing with the high-octane mix of Charlie, Jim Beam, and fresh air, set off toward the invitingly bright lights of the city centre. He wanted some fun, the sort of fun you wouldn't find reviewed on Trip Advisor, and he was going to hurt some fucker. That was always the highlight of a good night—hurting some innocent bystander just out for a pleasant evening. Taking their cash and jewellery or stealing their car for a meaningless joyride was always incidental to inflicting pain although he did get a kick out of torching the car when he'd finished with it.

Enjoying the invigorating sensation of the cold evening air on his face, Joseph cut across the park, ignoring the twisting path and taking a direct route from one gate to the other. This would take him through the children's play area, deserted of kids at this late hour but usually frequented by a motley crew of winos and smackheads who often, surprisingly, proved to be rich pickings. Today was no exception. A couple of local wasters sat on the swings smoking. Joseph could smell the rich, heavy aroma of their chosen joint, the pinpoint of light as they inhaled providing their exact location, and he was on them before they realised he was even there.

"Hello, gents. What have we here?" he said, looming out of the darkness and taking the roach from one of the teenagers before he had time to react. His companion made to slide from the swing on which he sat, but a stern look from Joseph persuaded him to stay put. They were aware of whom they were dealing with and would've preferred to be face to face with the local police or even a rabid dog at that moment—anyone apart from an obviously high Joseph.

"J … Just a little s … skank," stammered Roach Boy. "Nothing else, Joe." No one in their right mind who knew Joseph ever called him anything but Joe. Even so, the boy uttered the name timidly, as if even knowing his name would lead to further trouble.

"I don't fuckin' believe you, Skank! Hows about you empty your pockets for me?" The two teenagers glanced at each other nervously, the only signal Joseph needed. He launched a vicious right hook, his fist connecting with the second young man's face, breaking his nose and knocking him backwards off the swing.

"Oh s … shit," stammered Roach Boy glancing at his friend, who sprawled on the ground, clutching his bloodied face, before staring wide-eyed at his assailant.

Joseph smiled. "Pockets?" he reminded the teenager, who quickly pulled a small roll of banknotes and a few baggies from his jacket pocket.

"That's it; I swear." Roach Boy handed the bundle of cash and drugs to Joseph with trembling hands.

"That's all right. I believe you." Joseph patted the youth's shoulder almost paternally then turned and walked away. He shouted over his shoulder as he left the play area, "If I hear you've told anyone about our little transaction, there'll be consequences." He was gone before they could reply.

As he left the park, a voice, so close it could have been the wind whispering in his ear, said, *You showed those two who's boss. He swung round, ready to confront the voice's owner, but there was nobody there.*

He laughed. "Damned right I did." As he turned back to resume his journey, he made a note to cut back on Charlie. He didn't want to get paranoid; it would cloud his judgement, lead to mistakes. And Joseph couldn't afford to make mistakes.

Joseph stopped for a bucket of chicken at one of his usual haunts, flirted harmlessly with the bored-looking woman behind the counter before heading across the street to the busy Phoenix Pub a little after nine. He exchanged pleasant nods with the doorman before pushing his way through the door and up to the bar.

The barmaid, her breasts straining to free themselves from the confines of her two-sizes-too-small shirt, hurried over to serve him, ignoring several other punters in the process. She ran her fingers down the nearest pump handle seductively as she spoke. "What will it be?" He could only just hear her over the music thumping out from the array of overhead speakers.

He smiled at her, the comforting smile of a friend, the smile that put people at ease in his presence. "I'll have a pint, please." He pointed to the nearby pump, indicating his choice of beer.

Is that all? You can have something stronger than that.

"Sorry?" He looked at the barmaid, but she'd already moved away to find him a glass. Casually, he propped himself up on a barstool and scanned the crowded bar. He couldn't see anyone who could've spoken to him as everyone around him seemed engaged in their own revelry. It was close to Christmas, and the bar was full of partygoers dressed to impress or wearing fancy dress. At a nearby table, a smartly dressed middle-aged woman was sitting provocatively on a much younger-looking elf's knee, brandishing a sprig of mistletoe much to the amusement of the other people gathered around the table.

Strangely romantic, isn't it? Although I doubt they'll be able to look each other in the face tomorrow morning.

"What the fuck," Joseph murmured, shaking his head slightly.

"What was that?" The barmaid stood next to him, his pint on the bar between them.

"Nothing, Babe. Keep the change." He flashed a smile and handed over a note pulled from the roll he'd stolen from Roach Boy. She smiled back, tucking a stray strand of hair back behind her ear, and he knew he could have her if he wanted. He was blessed with such devilishly good looks even a nun would find it hard to resist and the arrogant confidence women find so compellingly attractive, a potent mix that meant he was never short of lovers … or victims.

"Let me know if you want anything else." Her words hung in the air, their meaning clear.

"I'll be sure to." Joseph watched her slink to the other end of the bar to serve an overweight executive who openly leered at her breasts as she pulled him a fresh pint.

She's such a whore, Joseph. Look at her flaunting herself to that disgusting creep. Doesn't that make you angry?

This time, the voice was loud inside his head, drowning out the cheesy Christmas anthem playing in the bar, and he knew whose voice it was. It was a voice he would never, could never, forget. It was a voice so deeply entrenched in his psyche he found it hard to separate it from his own internal monologue. It was the voice that haunted his nightmares, the voice that drove him on whenever he faltered, the voice that persuaded him to seek solace in the comforting embrace of his addiction and the brief respite offered by oblivion.

It was the voice of Janice Webster, the attractive teenaged girl from across the street whom his parents trusted to look after him and his younger brother while they partied the night away. She would invite her boyfriend over so they could have sex in his parents' front room while Joseph watched through the crack in the door. She knew he was there; she would look at him and smile like it was their private joke.

That's what she was doing when his three-year-old brother, Jonathon, accidentally set himself alight while playing with their father's cigarettes in bed. When Janice finally heard his screams and rushed half-naked up the stairs, his burns where so severe he died before the ambulance arrived. It was then that Joseph's fascination with fire began, and he would proudly tell everyone he was going to be a fireman when he grew up.

Unfortunately, it was also the time he took the first steps toward his lifelong dependency on alcohol before moving on to ever harder drugs. His eventual expulsion from school left him both physically and mentally unqualified for a career in the Fire Brigade, a fact he blamed on everyone apart from himself.

It was also the Janice Webster who, with her husband and teenage kids, he had burnt to death the previous night. She'd deserved it just like his parents before her. Between them, they had ruined his life.

Between them, they were responsible for Jonathon's death.

What's the matter, Joseph, cat got your tongue?

He gripped his glass, his knuckles turning white. "Don't call me Joseph! No one calls me that anymore."

Ahhh, so you can hear me then … Joseph. The voice was now quiet, calm, two old friends reminiscing.

Joseph shut his eyes, tightly screwing up his face. Clutching his head with both hands, he covered his ears. "Go away! Fuckin' leave me alone!" he hissed loudly, momentarily forgetting where he was.

"You all right?" He felt a comforting hand on his shoulder. Raising his head, he looked into the barmaid's deep brown eyes.

She actually looks as if she cares. That's so sweet.

He nodded, turning on his reassuring smile, Yeah, just a little stressed, that's all."

Why don't you take her home to meet mother ... Oh that's right, I forgot ... she's dead!

"I know how that feels ..."

Empathy. She's good. The voice spoke over the barmaid.

"... end of the bar offered me a tenner to go to his car with him, the dirty bastard!"

And she's got morals ... or maybe just higher price expectations.

"Tell the thug on the door; get him thrown out." Joseph said helpfully, ignoring Janice's commentary running through his head.

"They won't. Not while he's putting money across the bar." She shrugged, gave him a resigned smile, and moved away to serve a man in a reindeer costume.

Why don't you teach him some respect? A girl like that could be good for you, Joseph.

Joseph took a long pull on his beer, wiping his mouth with the back of his hand when he'd finished. He looked down the bar at the executive who was waving a note at the barmaid, trying to attract her attention as she finished serving reindeer man. The man was overweight and balding, his suit cheap and ill-fitting, and he had obviously already consumed far more alcohol than he should have. He slouched against the bar, his eyes drooping, a sheen of sweat shining on his bald pate, his arm languidly sweeping back and forth with no real enthusiasm.

Look at him; he's an easy target, and you did want to fuck someone up! The skank in the park was kids' play, an overture to the main show.

That was true. The kid was petty cash, his ATM for the night. This guy was different. Roach Boy and his mate were locals, pushing dope to survive in this deprived, dog-eat-dog town. Joseph was a lone wolf, a mean, independent mother fucker who was further up the food chain than them. Shit happens. But this jumped-up, out-of-town lapdog was trying to shit in his front yard.

I bet she'll be grateful, Joseph. You could screw her on the couch like I showed you. Maybe this time, I could watch from behind the door.

Joseph watched as the barmaid served the executive. He tried to snatch the money away from her when she put his drink down, but she was too quick for him. She gave him a forced smile then turned away, winking at Joseph as she moved to the till.

You know what? I'm actually getting to like her. She might be good for you, help you find the redemption and salvation you so obviously crave.

"You don't know shit." Joseph looked at the middle-aged woman who now sat astride the elf, wearing his hat. They were kissing passionately to the noticeable embarrassment of their colleagues around the table.

Why else did you meddle with your parents' boiler? Letting them die in their sleep was such a cowardly way for you to kill them. But I got to hand it to you; the fire, burning down my house, and standing around to watch us burn — now that took balls.

"I did it for Jonathon, for revenge," Joseph whispered into his drink before taking another sip.

He was aware that to people around him, he must look like the local nutter, sitting in a bar mumbling to himself. He reached into his pocket and took out his phone. Untangling the headphones, he put one in his ear and placed the phone on the bar. At least people would think him engaged in conversation with someone tangible, not with a voice in his head.

Maybe he was going insane. He'd never given it much thought. He'd always enjoyed violence and never felt at ease in normal society, but wasn't that the same for everyone, wasn't that normal?

No, you didn't. Look deeper into your soul. This is about your guilt.

Joseph laughed out loud then looked around to see if anyone had noticed, but the pub was packed, and everyone was too busy enjoying themselves to care.

"I'm not sure I have a soul, and I certainly don't feel guilt."

You blame yourself for his death.

"I blame you for his death. You and my neglectful parents who happily left a cheap slut to look after their children."

I never heard you complain when you were watching. But that's just it; you were watching. If you'd stayed upstairs with little Jonny, then you could've stopped him. But you chose to watch me getting fucked instead of staying in bed like a good boy.

Joseph could feel his anger threatening to boil over. It had simmered quietly under the surface almost since his arrival at the pub, but he'd managed to keep a lid on it despite Janice's deliberate provocation.

Through clenched teeth, he hissed, "It was your job to look after us. It wasn't my fault."

I never said it was your fault — just that you blame yourself.

The drunken executive slid down from his seat at the far end of the bar and staggered toward the back door. The barmaid watched him go then turned to Joseph with a relieved half-smile before puffing her cheeks out and raising her eyebrows as if sharing an unspoken bond.

It's show time, Joseph!

Stuffing his phone into his pocket, Joseph negotiated his way through the crowded pub and out into the darkness of the rear car park. The bald man stood next to a dark saloon at the far end of the car park, fumbling through his pockets, his face turned away.

You gonna burn him, Joseph?

He could almost see Janice clapping with enthusiasm as he closed the distance between himself and the executive. He was within a few yards when the man, aware of his presence, began to turn. Closing quickly, Joseph launched himself at the man, grabbing his exposed head and slamming it against the car's unforgiving steel. The overweight executive slumped to the ground, a deep gash splitting his forehead open.

Good night, Vienna!

Joseph stood over the man's unconscious body and looked back anxiously toward pub. His anger had caused him to be careless. The barmaid, her body outlined by the pub's bright lights, stood watching him, her hand clasped across her mouth.

Ignore her, Joseph. You don't need her anymore. She won't understand you the way I do.

"But ..."

Joe! Listen to me, Joe. It's me, not her you want. I can offer you redemption, salvation ... freedom.

The antagonism and excitement in Janice's disembodied voice had gone, replaced by a cajoling, seductive tone. Joseph looked from the barmaid to the man spread-eagled at his feet and for the first time cared about what someone else thought.

There's nothing left for you here. You've got your revenge, Joe. Me, your parents, we're dead. Just you and your guilt left, nothing else, nobody else to blame.

Joseph bolted as the barmaid's first scream rent the night sky. He sprinted from the car park and took off down the road, eager to put distance between himself and the Phoenix Pub. He knew where he was going—and it wasn't prison.

Come to me, Joe. It's nearly over. All those years of hurt and resentment will be a thing of the past. Absolve your guilt! Clear your conscience!

Rounding a corner, he saw his destination lit up like a beacon, and he increased his pace, the voice in his head cheering him on like a marathon runner in the final straight.

Come on, Joe, you can do it!

He ran on to the forecourt, heading for the nearest car. The woman at the pump froze in fear as he rushed toward her. In a second, he'd pushed her aside, pulling the pump's nozzle free.

Do it, Joe. Fucking do it now!

He put the nozzle above his head and squeezed the trigger, dousing himself in the clear, clean-smelling liquid, letting it soak his hair, his clothes, and taking it into his mouth.

Do it for Jonathon! You were as much to blame for his death as me, as your parents. Cleanse yourself in the fire.

Joseph fumbled in his pocket, desperately searching for his lighter. The fuel was stinging his eyes, and he couldn't see properly. Finding it, he held it up in front of his face before flicking the wheel with his thumb.

There was a brief spark but then nothing.

Try again!

Janice's voice screamed in his head as he spun the flint wheel a second time. Through half-closed eyes, he saw the lighter flicker to life. He looked at his reflection in the car's darkened windows but saw only his brother's charred and twisted body.

Burn in Hell, you bastard!

Joseph heard the reassuring *Whoomp* as the accelerant caught!

END

Cutting Lies By Briana Robertson

"I don't want to do this."

"Did anyone ask you what you want?"

"No, but I…"

"Then shut up! Move!"

"Please…"

The slap was unexpected, the vertebrae in her neck snapping as her head whipped around. Her teeth cracked. Her cheek burned.

"I said move!"

She glanced around, searching for her assailant, but there was no one. Then who …? As though they had a will of their own, her feet shuffled across the carpet. Silently, she ordered herself to stop, but apparently, her body was no longer under her control. Reaching the end of the hallway, she faced the door on the left.

"Open it."

She watched her left hand lift, grasp the knob, turn. With a gentle push, the door swung open, the shaft of light from the hall stretching wide to illuminate what lay within. The form in the bed was small, still, the gentle rise and fall of peaceful breathing a deceptive indication that all was well.

"Quit stalling, bitch. Do it!"

All was not well.

She didn't want to do it. She couldn't do it. Yet she knew — with a rising horror and abrupt surety — she would do it. But not yet. She had to try. One last time, she had to try.

"Please, I'm begging you. Don't make me do this!"

"Make you? Make you? I'm not making you do anything. Deep down, this is what you want, and you know it. This is what you need. You regret him. You resent him. You always have. You're just too weak to admit it. You know this is what has to happen for you to be free. So shut the fuck up, and get it done!"

Unable to combat the compulsion, she slid farther into the room. One step, then another, she slipped across the floor, light glinting off the butcher's knife in her right hand. Reaching the bed, she gazed down. Her eyes pricked, stinging with tears. But there was no stopping the lift of her hand, the settling of her blade against the fragile, exposed throat.

Her fingers tightened. Her muscles tensed.

"Do it!"

She inhaled, preparing to jerk her arm, anticipating the swift splatter of hot blood. Green eyes drifted open, dazed and cloudy with sleep.

"Mama?"

**

She jerked awake, clammy with cold sweat, the yelp catching in her throat. Her breath sawed through her chest. Her gaze bounced frantically around. Her dresser. Her nightstand. The glow outlining her cracked bathroom door. This was her bed, her room. She pried a deep breath into her lungs, glanced down. No knife. Holding the breath in, she listened, her ears straining.

"Hello? Who's there?"

No answer. No movement. Nothing.

Just a dream.

A glance at the alarm clock. 5:30 am. Too early to be up, but sleep wasn't coming back. Not after that.

Rising on shaky legs, she shuffled into the bathroom, flipped on the faucet. The splash of frigid water against her face helped but not much. Not enough. With a great deal of hesitation, she finally forced herself to meet her own gaze in the mirror. The eyes looking back were her own: glazed and red-rimmed from an obviously ineffective sleep but her own nonetheless.

Her exhale was a whoosh of relief. But what had she expected, honestly? To see the fiery glare of some evil demon? Actually, that wasn't too far off the mark. She shivered at the realization. With another douse of water, she gave herself a good, hard, mental shake. It was just a nightmare. Nothing more.

Leaving the bathroom, she passed through her own room then paused by Cory's. She reached out, stopped. No. He was fine. There was absolutely no reason to open the door, risk waking her light sleeper of a six-year-old just because her brain had decided to take a nighttime stroll with the likes of Freddie, Jason, and Michael.

She headed down the hall towards the kitchen. Coffee. Coffee would chase away the cobwebs. And hopefully the last, lingering vestiges of that horrifying dream. What on earth had conjured that shit? What had she eaten last night, anyway? No. It didn't matter. It was over, and she'd do best to just forget it.

The drip of the brewing joe was strangely comforting; her nerves settled, and her body relaxed. Before long, the sun was peeking through the lacy curtains, the coffee warming her belly. With the light came a clearer head; she moved around the room, gathering the necessities for blueberry pancakes.

She popped the first batch into the oven to keep warm and was pouring more batter when the soft pitter-patter of footsteps sounded behind her.

"Morning, Mama." The greeting was punctuated by a yawn.

She turned with a smile, stepping over to ruffle her son's hair. "Morning, baby. How'd you sleep?"

"Good."

"Good. You hungry? I made your favorite."

His eyes lit up. "Pancakes?"

"Yup."

"With blueberries?"

"Are there any other kind?"

"Can I have syrup?"

She laughed. "Yes, Cory, you can absolutely have syrup."

"Okay."

As she turned to flip the bubbling batter, the perfectly normal, sharp squeak of chair leg on tile grated. She shook it off, picturing his blonde curls popping over the table's edge as he climbed onto his knees, propped himself up on his elbows. An anticipatory grin would show off the gap where he was missing one of his two front teeth.

Flipping the piping hot pancakes onto a plate, she shifted.

"You ready?"

Kill him!

"Mama, are you okay? Mama? Mama!"

Cory's voice finally registered. "Wh-what?"

"You dropped my pancakes."

She looked down dumbly. Shattered plate. Scattered pancakes, syrup-side down. What ...? She shook herself.

"Sorry, baby. I must have butterfingers this morning."

He giggled, convinced by her dismissive tone. She was nearly convinced herself. It must have been nothing more than a slip of the hand. What else could it have been?

With movements she hoped looked smoother than they felt, she opened the oven, threw together another plate, and slid it over to him. As he wolfed his breakfast down, she knelt to deal with the mess. Now she moved with deliberate care, picking up the larger shards, stacking them in her palm.

Slit his fucking throat!

"Cory Matthew! What did you say?"

"Mama?" His face ducked beneath the table to peer at her.

"Did you just say something?"

"No … Mama, you're bleeding."

"Huh?"

"Your hand." He gestured, fork in hand.

Crimson drops welled from a jagged slash across her palm, stretching from the base of her pinkie to her inner wrist.

"Oh. Ow …"

"I can help!"

"No! No, sweetie, stay back. I appreciate it, but there are still pieces of broken plate down here, and I don't want you to get cut too."

Reaching for the sink, she snagged a dish towel and wrapped it tightly around her hand. Red immediately seeped through the cotton strands.

"Are you finished with your pancakes?"

"Well, I've finished these. I'd like some more, but I can wait. You need to fix your hand."

Her heart swelled with love and pride. "Thank you, Cory. That's very big boy of you. Why don't you go into the living room and turn on cartoons for a little bit?

Just until I take care of my hand and finish cleaning up this mess. Then we'll have more pancakes. Sound good?"

"Sure, Mama." He watched her for a short moment, his gaze seeing more, she feared, than any six-year-old should be capable of, then slid off the chair and disappeared through the doorway.

Slowly unwrapping the towel, she inspected the wound. It was long, but fairly shallow, thank God. It wouldn't require stitches. Some triple antibiotic, gauze, tape. Give it a few days, it would heal well enough. She'd be lucky if she didn't end up with a decent scar though. Whatever. Rewrapping her palm, she headed back to the bathroom.

At least it was her left hand; being right-handed, she managed to rummage through the medicine cabinet with a fair amount of ease. With the necessities gathered, she flicked the faucet, hissed as the warm water sluiced over the open wound. She watched the water run red, wincing. Damn, that stung.

Give me blood.

Her hand jerked, her knuckles scraping the underbelly of the faucet.

"Fuck!" She spun in a quick circle, cradling her hand. "Who's there? Who said that?"

"Spill his blood!"

She flung herself around again, searching wildly. She yanked the shower curtain back. Nothing. Jumped back as she swung the closet door open. No one. Peered around the doorjamb into her bedroom. Empty. Insanely, she even opened the tiny medicine cabinet.

She was alone.

She must be going crazy.

You're not crazy. I'm here.

Who? And where? Heart racing, she investigated again. Still, she found nothing out of place. The slice in her palm forgotten, she thrust her hands into her hair, fisted them, pulled.

Kill him!

"No!" The scream ricocheted in the small bathroom. She slapped a hand over her mouth, ran to the hallway to see if Cory had heard. Giggles and the theme song of Thomas and Friends drifted down from the living room. He was fine.

She snuck back into the bathroom, shut the door. Forearms locked as she braced herself on the sink. This was ridiculous; it was nothing more than her mind playing tricks on her, unwilling to let that nightmare go. She needed to chill, get it together. This was all in her head.

Guess again, bitch.

Her gaze shot up, meeting its twin in the mirror. She recoiled. Her eyes. No, no, not her eyes. Her eyes didn't glow. They weren't red. Green. They were supposed to be green. This wasn't right.

Don't you like the change?

Maniacal laughter echoed in her head. She closed her eyes, shook her head. This wasn't real. She was still dreaming.

She had to be. But when she opened them again, the eyes in her face that weren't hers still stared back at her.

Kill him.

No.

Slit his throat.

She shook her head.

Spill his blood.

Not. Her. Son.

Do it.

No. She wouldn't. It — whatever it was — couldn't make her.

Wanna bet?

And she was moving, heading out of the bathroom, into the bedroom. Past the bed, to the nightstand. With the drawer where she kept a number of random things. Sliding the drawer out. Reaching inside.

The scissors felt right in her hand. Wait. No. That was wrong. Put them back. Let them go.

Her grip only tightened, reaffirming her lack of control. Her other hand came up, the tips of her fingers caressing the sharp edges, her blood staining them.

Not staining. Anointing. That's it. Rub them. Stroke them. Love them.

She went wet beneath the knees. Horror and shame washed over her, heat burning her cheeks. She clenched her legs, rejecting the response, but she could not stop the seductive slide of skin over metal.

Yes. Yes! You want this. You know it's right.

"It's not."

It is. You've never been complete with him. Never been allowed to be who you truly want to be. He holds you back.

"No. I love him."

That's the point. Loving him keeps you from loving yourself. Isn't that right?

"No ..."

Liar.

"No. I do love myself. I just ... sometimes ..."

Kill him.

"But ..."

Do it now.

"I ..."

It's the only way. You know it. Quit being a weak excuse of a woman.

"I'm not weak."

Then slit the little whelp's throat, bitch!

This wasn't right. It couldn't be. Could it? Did she really resent her son? Had she seriously given up on herself? Given up on her life to ensure his?

No. Not really. Well, maybe. Yes ...

234 | The Voices Within Anthology

But that wasn't his fault. Not her sweet Cory's. He couldn't help who his father was. Even when everyone around her had told her she had every right—that she'd be better off, even—to get rid of him, she rejected the thought. She didn't blame Cory, didn't hold him responsible.

Don't you?

"Shut up!"

You had such plans, such dreams. They all went up in smoke the second that brat slid out from between your legs, all red and squalling. Think of everything you lost.

Yes. She'd lost it all. But she'd gained so much in Cory. The joy of being a mother. The unconditional love he showed her in every kiss, grin, and giggle. He was perfect. He was. Sure, he had bursts of temper, but … but not very often, and only when …when …

He's his father's seed.

No. No! Cory would never do something like that. He wouldn't grow up to be his father. She wouldn't let that happen.

The apple never falls far from the tree. You can't stop nature from taking its course …

"I can, if I love him enough, I …"

No. You can't. But you can interrupt it. You failed to keep the seed from taking root. Dig it up now. Cut it off from life. Keep it from growing tall.

"But …"

Would you have him do to another girl what his father did to you?

Tears pricked her eyes as memories flooded her mind. So much fear. So much pain. So much self-hatred. She'd never felt more alone, more abandoned. People who knew looked at her differently. Her parents. Her friends. They didn't come to see her in the hospital. Were unwilling to even look at the child she carried for nine months then fought to bring into the world.

They hadn't come. Just like the man who'd taken her innocence, they'd left her alone, broken and battered and deserted.

Would she—could she—risk it? If there was even the slightest chance her Cory could stride down that road... Was the life of a potential stranger worth more than her son's?

What if his mother had been given the chance?

She should have murdered the bastard!

Wait, no. It was wrong to think like that. It was. Except ... what if none of it had ever happened? What if he hadn't existed? If she'd never crossed his path?

The room spun around her, shimmered, changed. She stood on a stage, the lights above shining bright and hot, both blinding and illuminating. Her arms were flung wide, her breath coming fast, beads of sweat dotting her forehead. Exhilaration flooded her; she wasn't sure her feet weren't ten feet off the stage.

She couldn't see the audience. But she could hear them. The applause was thunderous, threatening to blow open the doors. Flowers were being thrown at her feet, shouts of "encore" ringing above and beyond the slap of skin against skin. Laughter bubbled from her throat, a loud burst of triumph. They adored her. She'd made it. She was a star.

This. This is what could have been. This is what would have been had it not been for him and then the brat. It is what could still be if you still want it. Do you? Still want it?

God, yes. Yes. She wanted it.

You can have it. It's yours for the taking. You know what you have to do.

"Kill him."

Broadway fell away, leaving her in the bedroom she'd always secretly hated. It was so small, so fucking cramped, and much too plain. But things could be different. She could have more. Dammit, she would have more.

She marched through the doorway, scissors in hand, turned down the hall. Thomas and Friends had given way to Sesame Street. Fuck, she hated that show. Everything about it grated her nerves. Especially that little red annoyance, Elmo. Every time that screechy voice came on the screen, she wanted to chuck something at it. When he'd been younger, Cory had run around singing that dumb "la la la la, Elmo's world" over and over and over again. How did she stand it? More importantly, why?

No. More.

Reaching the living room, she paused. Took stock. Cory stood in front of the TV, bouncing in time with the music. His back to her, he was as yet unaware. That was fine.

She took a slow, quiet step. Then another. Closer. Glancing up, she caught a glimpse of her reflection in one of the small mirrors mounted on either side of the television. The bloody gaze didn't faze her now; red wasn't such a bad color after all. She grinned and wasn't surprised to see her teeth had sharpened into fangs. She ran her tongue over them, leaving them glossy. Maybe she'd use them instead of the scissors. But no. She wanted to feel the blistering rush of fresh blood on her hands.

Kill him. Yes, yes, she would. Stab. Slice. Rip. Tear. Her fingers dug into the scissors' handle. She could hear him screaming, his voice high-pitched and wailing, asking her why, begging her to stop. Just as she'd done the night that bastard had planted this one into her. He hadn't listened. Neither would she.

Kill the spawn.

Do it.

Now.

A scarlet haze flooded her vision, washing everything away but her prey. Each step brought her closer, each breath took her higher, every heartbeat pumped hot and heady. She was so close now. So close. Just another step. Just one more. And now she stood just behind him, so innocent and unaware of the crimson-eyed Grim Reaper standing just behind him, ready to cut off his life in one fell swoop. Her arm lifted, the scissors' blades flashing in a stray ray of sunlight. His neck was exposed, the pale, flawless skin such a convenient target. And the blood that would gush forth. So much blood. She grinned in anticipation. She opened her mouth, ready to say the brat's name. She wanted him to know. Wanted him to fear.

I want to hear him scream!

She inhaled.

Mama?

Abruptly, everything fell away, shattering both around and within her. The scarlet haze faded. The bloodlust vanished. The well of cynical hatred ran dry, leaving her empty. And lost.

What …?

What was she doing? What was going on? And who had just spoken in that creepy, distorted voice?

Her gaze swung down. Was caught. By the eyes of Hell.

No. No, it couldn't be.

"Nooooo!"

Her scream was strangled by the impact, morphing into the pitiful gurgle of one taken by surprise. Wha …? Her knees gave way, thudding into the carpet. She glanced down. What was … was that …? The handle of the butcher knife protruded from her gut, the blade buried to the hilt. Blood surged around the wound, spewed out and down.

Pain washed over her, turning her brain fuzzy. But she didn't pass out. She couldn't. Horror kept her grounded as she stared at her son, her beautiful Cory, standing before her, his eyes gleaming, his cherubic features distorted by the vile malevolence in the erroneous grin.

"Wh … why?"

"Because I hate you! You're a terrible mama! You're mean. You make me do chores. You never let me ride on the carousel at the mall. I never get my way. I always have to do what you say, and I hate it! I hate you! I don't love you; I've never loved you! I want a new mama! A better mama than you!"

No. This … this wasn't her Cory. This wasn't her son. He would never say these things to her. He did love her. Just like she loved him. She didn't resent him; she'd never resented him. Never regretted her decision to keep him, to want him, to love him.

He did love her. He did. This … this wasn't him. This was … that thing … that voice …

She couldn't leave her son in its clutches. She had to save him … had to save … Cory …

While it continued to rant at her, to scream obscenities, to gloat in her fast-approaching demise, she gathered what little strength she had left. Forced her fingers to grip the scissors now lying limp against her palm.

"I … I love you … Cory …"

She swung, hard, the momentum careening her off-balance, leaving her in a gory heap. But before she fell …

Thwunk!

The scissors hit home, lodging themselves in the delicate expanse of the boy's neck, finding the fragile artery. Blood gushed forth, burning her as it splattered her face. She'd … she'd done it … She'd set her son … free.

Her vision was fading, but she could hear … coughing. It was coughing, trying to breathe through an airway that no longer existed. And something else … what was …? Was that … laughter?

No … no, it couldn't be. She'd hit it. She'd hurt it. She had …

I win, bitch.

The laughter faded, leaving nothing but her own weak gasps and the ineffective wheezing of her son. What … what in God's name had she done?

The single word was plaintive, every nuance of its tragic perplexity ripping her heart to pieces before a final silence descended.

"Mama?"

END

Lullaby and Goodnight A Poem By C.S Anderson

The child cried

Mother oh Mother do you
not see it

Beyond the window a
gibbering shade of the night

The Mother replied

Hush now child

It is naught but a trick of
the moonlight

The child cried

Mother oh Mother do you
not hear it

A banshee wail mourning
every tear ever shed

The Mother replied

Hush now child

It is naught but the wind in
the trees instead

The child cried

Mother oh Mother do you
not feel it

An icy shiver of dread
inching down your spine

The Mother replied

Hush now child

Any such thing is merely all
in your tired mind

Enough nonsense now

Quickly now say your
evening prayers

Enough nonsense now

Slide beneath the quilt's
comforting layers

Enough nonsense now

All your fears will seem
silly come the morning's
light

Pleasant dreams my child I
bid you goodnight

The child listened to naught
but the wind in the trees

The child stared at naught
but a trick of the moonlight

*The child fearfully hugged
her little knees*

*And in the morning when
her mother came to wake her*

*The child has vanished from
sight*

Lullaby

Lullaby

Lullaby

And

Goodnight

BRATTLEBORO: Battle Cry of Lizzy By Michael S. Freeman

1949 Vermont – Brattleboro Retreat
(Vermont Asylum for the Insane)

Lizzy, 19 and frail, leans her head against the cold glass of the '49 Studebaker. Fall decorates the forest in a sort of Technicolor array that flashes past, blending and swirling, bending the light just enough to add the hazy glow of a Saturday morning cartoon.

Off, in the distance a rooftop emerges, growing from the treetops to the sky. The car pulls in a dirt driveway to at the front of a masterpiece of architecture. Two orderlies and a nurse dressed all in white with a little paper hat emerge from the building.

Lizzy watches as the strangers approach the car, then looks at her father in the front seat, his hands gripping the wheel, head down. "Daddy, please don't make me stay here," she pleads.

"Liz, you need to be here. Your mother and I feel all the fornication and the smoking and booze, well, there just has to be something wrong in your head. These people will find it and get it out." he offers with no eye contact.

Lizzy opens the door, taking her suitcase from the seat. Before she can even get the door closed completely, her father speeds away, throwing gravel and snow from the Goodyear radials. One of the orderlies snatches the suitcase from her hand while the nurse puts an arm across Lizzy's shoulders.

"Come on dear, we have your room all set up for you."

Lizzy reluctantly allows the nurse to lead her up the meager stairs to a pair of enormous doors laden with four by six panes of yellow encrusted glass.

The halls are cold and white with large metal doors embedded within the walls. In the middle of each hall sprawls a nurses' station, where more of the nurses are, clad in the same outfit as the woman leading her. The first door to the right of the station looks to be that of a frat house. Trash, paper, and broken down furniture are strewn about. A man shuts the door in Lizzy's face. A placard on the door reads, "ORDERLY LOUNGE."

Lizzy giggles under her breath as she thinks, "Figures. Men are disgusting."

The last room at the end of the hall has Lizzy's suitcase in front of it. "This is your room, young Miss," the nurse states as she unlocks and opens the door.

Lizzy looks inside only to see nothing but a broken down bed with a thin mattress, paint chips peeling from the drab, mint green walls, and one small window eight feet from the floor. The window is offering a limited amount of light, but the bars make a nice contrast on the cement floor.

The nurse flips up the wool blanket edge. "Now put your things away in this storage, then come join us for breakfast in the cafeteria."

The nurse leaves the room as Lizzy begins to put her things in the makeshift wooden storage. She pulls her shoes off and places her bare feet on the cold, but rather smooth floor. A comforting feeling sweeps over her, memories of Christmas morning and the hardwood of her bedroom at home.

A sharp rap on the door brings her back to reality. The orderly who brought her bag in, is standing at her door in all his chubbiness, looking like a marshmallow that rolled in the dirt. Sweat stains yellowed the pits of his pristine white shirt.

"Time to eat girl," He barks.

Lizzy makes her way through the maze of halls to the cafeteria. She is given a tray with a paper cup. Inside is a beige pill.

"What is this?" She asks the woman handing out the trays.

The woman looks up from her task. "It's your fucking medicine, dearie; now move your ass along."

Moving down the line, a blob of either oatmeal or already chewed bread is slopped on Lizzy's tray. The mass oozes, spreading into the slot on her tray, settling into a weird textured pond, confined by the walls of the tray. The next stop offers a large glass of room temperature milk that may or may not have curdled slightly on top, too questionable to be able to tell for sure.

Lizzy finds a seat alone. While she sits for her meal, the chubby orderly continues to eye her and not in a comfortable way. It feels more like the way dog looks at a bone. Uncomfortable by the situation, Lizzy gets up and goes back to her room.

Night comes; Lizzy is settling into her bed. Most of the staff is gone for the day except Chubby and a nurse for her wing. Just as she drifts off to sleep, the door to her room flings open, slamming hard into the block wall. It's Chubby. He enters the room, closing the door behind him.

"Now, you fine little bitch, now we are alone," He mutters as he moves towards the bed.

Lizzy looks for anything to protect herself, but there is nothing. She begins to kick at him, catching him in the testicles. Chubby hits the floor, doubled over in pain. Lizzy attempts to run past him, only to have him grab her by the leg. He pulls a syringe from his back pocket with his free hand. As he stabs the needle deep into her upper thigh, Lizzy screams out.

"Scream all you want; no one is going to hear ya," He says as he tosses her back on the bed.

Chubby straddles Lizzy as he opens his pocket knife. Lizzy falls limp while he begins to cut open her gown. The sweat drips from his nose onto her face. He slowly cuts down the gown until he reaches the hem, then opens it, exposing Lizzy's astonishing ivory-white frame to the moonlight seeping in the window.

Too busy trying to fumble his little pecker out, Chubby never notices the glowing smoke that comes up from a crack in the floor and enters Lizzy's nose. Just as he penetrates her, Lizzy's now soulless eyes pop open.

The nurse returns from her break. Hearing the commotion from Lizzy's room, she calls for the orderly. No response. The nurse begins to walk to the room, still

hearing sounds as if someone is tearing down the walls.
She gets to the door and fumbles for the key.

The tumblers click in the door, and she starts to
open it only to have the door slammed back shut, sending
her across the hall, and bouncing off the adjacent wall. The
nurse gets back to her feet and runs at the door, but it
opens and she slides into the room.

Inside, the lights flicker illuminating a bloodbath
from the walls to the floor. On the bed lays
Chubby, gutted, intestines still dropping to the floor from
his body cavity.

The light flickers enough for the nurse to get back
up and realize she is covered in blood. In complete shock,
she looks around the room for Lizzy or any sign of her, to
no avail. The light goes dark for a few seconds then all the
lights in the wing begin to flicker. Scared, the nurse makes
her way to the door, slipping and sliding from the blood
on her shoes. She makes it to the desk at the nurses' station
and picks up the phone.

"I need police … at Brattleboro," she sputters into
the phone.

A noise from Lizzy's room catches her attention.
The nurse peeks over the desk, but nothing is there.
"Please hurry."

The nurse lays the phone on the floor then eases
back to the side of the desk. She closes her eyes, but when
she opens them, Lizzy is crawling across the ceiling
towards her in a twisted, contortionist manner. Jerking
and popping, she clicks closer and closer. Backtracking, the
nurse tries to crawl away, but the blood made the floor too

slick. An ear- piercing wail comes from Lizzy causing the nurse to turn. Just as she faces Lizzy, the nurse sees her leap from the ceiling toward her face, then everything goes black.

Dawn arrives, bringing with it a mass of police and coroners parked in front of Brattleboro.

Inside is a horrific scene. The halls are flooded with a crimson river of blood from all the occupants inside. Dismembered bodies laid to waste throughout. Off in the corner is a rookie puking in a trash can.

2. PRESENT DAY

Journal Entry: December 22, 2015

My therapist tells me I need to write this down, so I figured no better time than the present.

I was sent to Brattleboro back in 2000 because of my suicidal tendencies. What I didn't tell anyone, not even my therapist, is when I was around ten years old, my parents had a party at our house.

Yes, there were drugs before you ask, and no, I was in bed for the night.

While I laid in my bed with my Hello Kitty blankets tucked tight to me, my door creaked open. It was Stan, dad's best friend and business partner. He crept into my room and did unspeakable things to me that night. When he finished, Stan told me if I told anyone he would kill my mom and dad in front of me then move on to my little brother before doing me in.

At ten I was terrified of this asshole's empty threats. I truly believed if I told anyone about the things he did to me on every occasion he could get me alone, I would in fact witness the murder of my entire family.

A few years passed, taking with it my childhood innocence. I changed to a dark version of myself at sixteen, and everyone took notice. I would find myself stealing, doing drugs, breaking into friends' houses, anything just to feel something but numbness. I picked up a razor blade and began cutting myself that year. I guess that is how I ended up in Brattleboro. Too deep one night. Who would have thought?

That is not what this is about though. To move forward, I need to get what happened at Brattleboro out if I can.

My parents took me from the hospital the night I cut too deep and brought me to Brattleboro. The nurses all seemed chill and the orderlies where pretty cool too. I mean, they smoked weed with me in the boiler room, and it was more like a party than being locked away in some nut house.

Being there felt more like home to me, more than any place I had ever been. Mom and Dad came to visit, and once in a while that prick Stan would stop in; only I refused to see him. Days blurred to weeks, and the weeks blurred to months. My friends would swing by from time to time and toke it up with me and the ords in the basement. But you know that old saying, "Give 'em an inch, and they will take a mile." That applied to my sitch that night. I was in my room, the last on the left from the nurse station. I had just gotten out of the shower, and was still in my towel. There was a knock on my door. It was Frank, the orderly that I loved keeping company with the most.

I invited him in, not really thinking I was just in the towel. Once I realized it, I dropped the terry to the floor, exposing all of me to him. A shy grin spread across his face as he closed and locked my door behind him. I bent over the metal footboard of the bed and allowed him to plunge his huge cock inside me. Oh my God, he was good at it. The power of his thrusts as his thighs hit my ass made we shiver in pure ecstasy. It was like nothing I had ever felt before. He pulled out just as his orgasm spurt from the tip of his dick. The warm fluid ran up my back from my ass crack to between my shoulders.

I stood up to a hazy room. I thought, "Man that was great fucking." Accidently, I blurted that it was so great I was left in a fog. He laughed at my observation then agreed that he was a little in a fog as well. A loud knock on my door sent us both rushing for clothes. He dressed first and stood by the door while I slipped on my sweatshirt and pants. I perched on the bed waiting for him to open the door. Frank turned the knob and BLAM! All four of my friends flooded into my room.

It was after visiting hours, and they needed to get baked, so Frank took us to the boiler room. Jules pulled out a nug of weed and a grinder, and then proceeded to make up the confection for the mind.

After a few minutes of smoking, I felt strange. Almost as if someone had taken me over. I blacked out. I remember bits and pieces of that night, like moving about in the dark, looking down on my friends and other people in the asylum from the ceiling, but nothing concrete.

I woke up the next morning completely naked and covered in blood. I was laying in the middle of the cafeteria kitchen, body parts in the pans and blood everywhere. I remember the panic as I tried to get up, but the warm to the touch blood was so slick I kept falling.

I got up and made it through the halls of the dead and dismembered people of the hospital, but there was no one there. I grabbed my clothes and dressed as I made my way to the boiler room; I found them. My friends scattered everywhere, ripped to bits with entrails and blood everywhere.

Frank hung from one of the pipes in the ceiling, his intestines hanging in his face, leaking his body fluids and blood onto my face and hair. I puked as I dropped to my knees in tears. I struggled to my feet, making my way to the huge double doors. I took one more look back at the massacre then a hard push and sunlight flooded in. I put my hand up to shield the sun when this jerk tackled me. It was a fucking cop. He cuffed me and threw me in a van built more like a steel cage for animals.

The trial was short and sweet with all the witnesses dead, and I was the only person alive in the whole facility. I was found guilty of 236 murders by insanity because I could not remember what happened. I was sentenced to life at Bridgewater State Hospital in the criminally insane ward.

So that is my story and the therapist was right. I do feel better, but I have to go. Company is coming and I need to visit them.

Best,
Elizabeth

Elizabeth waits patiently in the patient lounge for her guest to arrive. A man walks in and looks over the room, catching her eyes. It's Stan. He approaches the table, a somber look on his face. Elizabeth kicks out the chair across from her in a weak gesture allowing him to sit. Stan sits and leans forward.

"Elizabeth, I know I am not who you thought was coming today, but I have to tell you. Your parents, their plane went down last night on the way here." He sits back in his chair. "There were no survivors."

Elizabeth bursts into hysterical laughter at the news. A guard arrives at the table. "Everything okay here?"

Stan nods and whispers into the guard's ear what he told Elizabeth. The guard puts on Elizabeth's restraints and leads her and Stan off to a private room. Inside the room, Elizabeth stands, her back to the door. Stan enters, arms open as the guard shuts the door. "Elizabeth … Sweetie …"

Elizabeth's head snaps around, a soulless look to her eyes. "THE NAME IS LIZZY!"

The lights go out as Stan screams.

END

A Mirror Never Lies by David Owain Hughes

She caught a glimpse of the body on her bed as she cleaned her face in front of her vanity mirror. It was tangled in the sheets, which had become saturated with blood and small chunks of flesh and guts.

Blood could be seen rolling down the arm in the dim light cast by the bedside lamp. It gathered at the wrist and slid down to the fingertips. Where the blood spread out over the forearm reminded her of a grizzly roadmap — a roadmap where all roads led to butchery.

She could hear the drops hit the carpet, which kept in sync with her heart; it beat fast with crazy joy, causing a fire to rise from her crotch.

A neat pool was gathered.

They deserved it, Porsche, please remember that.

"Yes, they did," she answered the voice from within, which sounded nothing like her at all. It was passive, weak, and pathetic.

It belonged to a person who could bend like straw.

No weight. No conviction. She smiled.

With the blood removed from her face, Porsche smiled at herself. Miniscule flecks of blood could be seen on her perfect teeth.

"Damn!" she snapped, plucking a tissue from a box close at hand. Delicately, she rubbed and polished them clean. "I'll have to brush them later."

After running her fingers through her hair, she grabbed her bottle of foundation and applied some of the cream to her fingertips. Content, she started to rub it into her face, giving herself a light coat.

I don't want to end up looking like a hooker; that's not the impression I want to give. I'm sugary and sweet! she thought, again looking at the body on her bed. The haft of the butcher knife caught her attention. Part of it was missing.

Then she remembered.

The knife had been rammed into her victim so hard some of the handle had snapped off in her hand.

"Delicious," she uttered.

We need to hide the body, Porsche ... the voice bleated.

"Quiet!" she insisted, slamming her hand down on the desk in front of her. "First, I want to make myself look pretty. I never had the chance to ..." Letting her words trail off, she looked down at her lap. "They made me weak and took all my confidence! I was never allowed makeup or pretty dresses."

It's not like that now, Porsche ...

"Shut up! Shut up! Shut up!" she snapped once again. Standing up, she turned around and spat on the body. "You won't keep me as a trophy any longer!" Screaming at the body made her feel vindicated for her actions. "Fucking controlling *pig!*"

Porsche…

"I won't tell you again!" She slapped her face once, twice, three times before collapsing into her chair with force.

Looking at herself in the mirror, she could see her eyes glaze with tears.

"No, stop it. We're not *that* kind of person anymore. I *won't* cry. Too many tears have been shed in the past …"

You're a strong, sexy, and confident woman, Porsche, the voice whispered.

"That's right!" she said, looking at her cheek. The redness was starting to peter out.

Happy, she pushed her foundation to one side and gathered a collection of lipsticks in front of her: pink, red, purple, nude …

"Choices, choices, choices!" Giggling, she whipped the cap off the purple one and eased it up the tube. After lightly coating her lips, she pouted at her reflection. All the while, she checked to see how the purple matched her skin tone and eye colour.

"Hmm, it's nice but a bit too radical."

Plucking another tissue free from its box, she rubbed at the lipstick, causing some of it to smear across her right cheek.

Tutting, she replaced the cap to the purple lipstick and put it back where it belonged. Before moving on to the red, the body caught her attention once again. Her gaze was drawn to a deep, lengthy slash across its stomach.

The sight made her gag, then titter, as she turned away.

Looking back, she could see the intestines had slipped out of the large gash and currently lay on the floor in a neatly coiled pile.

"*Sausages!*" she cried.

The laugh inside her head was not her own.

Looking up from the mess on the floor, Porsche studied the body. It was her first real look at it. In her frenzy, she hadn't counted the stab and bite marks.

Starting at the neck, she worked her way down. The face was hidden out of sight, covered by a pillow that had once been white.

Having opted out of being a full-blown doctor, Porsche could tell the neck was broken due to the decolourisation of the skin, bruising, and the way in which the neck flopped at an awkward angle.

"The oesophagus is probably crushed too …" she uttered in a sing-song tone. A wry, maniacal smile parted her thin lips as she stared into space.

Refocusing, she continued down the body — the chest was pulverised. A rib was protruding through the flesh close to the heart. "It probably pierced the once-beating organ."

A hacked off nipple lay on the opposite pillow, sending a shiver of delight down her spine.

"How did I manage to cause such devastation?"

Before she could answer her own question, she glanced upon the evidence.

Scattered about the bed were the remains of the second bedside lamp.

It had served as her reading light before she'd use it as a blunt trauma instrument. She'd beat the head with it, which had redecorated the headboard.

Bloody, snail-like trails had splashed up the walls. Through drying, they had turned a brownish colour, which carried with it a hint of sickly yellow in the dim light.

After caving the face in, the body had been battered beyond repair.

She put a hand to her genitals.

Yes! The voice moaned.

This caused her to pull her hand away. "My, you are eager to be pleased!" Grinning, she could see the face that belonged to the voice inside her head, and it was pouting, the bottom lip quivering. "*Aw,* are you going to cry?" she hissed.

The voice remained silent, much like it had its whole life. Before Porsche had taken over, the previous occupier had been cowed. But not now. Now, the body had its rightful owner in place. It felt good.

She felt empowered.

The old persona knew this moment would come, but it never knew it would come tonight. And in such an explosive fashion.

Continuing her gaze down the body, Porsche again saw the abdomen was slashed apart—the privates were mangled. The inner and outer thighs had slices and deep cuts on them.

"I'm sure the subject endured much pain!" A throb of pleasure raced up her insides and nestled in her stomach. It felt warm, cosy, and welcoming. "Mm, yes … much pain. *Great* pain."

The whole scene came across as a hideous diorama.

"Diorama of Death!" she said, finally turning back to her makeup.

After trying and disliking the red lipstick, Porsche moved on to the pink one, which she found fitting.

Blowing a kiss in the mirror, she then winked at herself.

"Oh, I'm going to look ravishing tonight!" she squealed.

*Oh, yes …*the voice concurred. *You will be attending the ball?*

"Yes!" she said, clapping her hands together. Unclasping them, she plucked up the gold envelope that lay on the dresser. Opening it, she took the card out.

As a thank you for joining our online community,
you are invited to partake in the fun, games
and pleasure at Kinks – the only club
to offer such a variety of sexual bliss.

Flipping it over, she found a note inscribed there.

Note: For a good time, ask for Simone

She didn't know if that was a man or a woman, but the gesture produced a wave of fresh pleasure.

She ran her fingers over the grooves caused by the lettering; they had a sexy red hue to them, which brought to mind the word danger.

"Yes, danger. Such a rousing word. Oh, I will enjoy myself—a party to celebrate my rebirth."

The honour is all mine.

"You've had your time. Now, it's my time to shine. To glow. To be the person we *both* know we should be!"

Agreed. And I'll be here to help guide and assist you as much as possible.

Porsche smiled her pink-lipped smile.

"This *bitch* has attitude! Not like the old me. What word would you say best described the way you were?"

Stifled.

No, more oppressed.

"Yes, *oppressed.* That's a good word. You weren't allowed to express yourself. Not like I can. It's a good thing for both of us, as I will be able to look after us now."

Porsche could see the face inside her again. This time, it was smiling along with her. "That's what I like to see!" she told her reflection.

Finished with the lipstick, she put it away, along with the red and nude colours. Picking up her eyeshadow, she proceeded to paint them a light pink, which matched her lipstick and painted fingernails.

"Now for a bit of mascara ..." she said, grabbing the mascara wand and applying it to her eyelashes.

Sexy! This is how we should have looked years ago, but no.

"No. Because you held us back!"

They held us back!

"Don't you argue with me, or I'll put you into a dark and dusty corner of my brain and never speak to you again!"

The inner voice stayed silent.

Blissfully silent.

For now, anyway.

Happy that her makeup was perfect, Porsche stood up and eyed her wigs. *It's time for a colour change,* she thought. Taking the red one off, she put it in her drawer and took out a brunette, black, blonde, and silver wig.

They varied in length and style, not just colour.

"A girl is so, so spoilt for choice!"

She firstly tried the silver one, followed by the blonde and then brunette.

Unhappy, she lastly tried the black one.

Looking at herself in the mirror, she gasped. *"Perfect!"*

Yes, perfect, the voice chirped.

Taking a hold of her paddle brush, she raked it through her hair before adding pink ribbons to it, which she tied in big, looping bows.

She then took a new packet of stockings out of her drawer. After ripping them out of the box, she rubbed them against her face. She loved the smell of new, fresh nylon. It excited her.

Setting them to one side, she then crossed her left leg over her right in readiness. Wrapping her hands around her ankle, she drew them up her leg.

"So smooth!" she uttered.

Picking one of the sheer, black stockings up, she bunched the material together, much like a sock, and then slipped her toes into it. Pulling it up slowly, she looked at herself in the mirror.

With the one hold-up on, she looked at her long, curvy leg.

Amazing, she mouthed. "Never was or would I have been allowed such luxuries with them around! We certainly were oppressed."

Yes. It was always, "You can't be seen like that!" Or, "What would the neighbours think?" The thought of us wearing skirts above the knee or stockings … Damn. They would have gone berserk!

"Oh, I agree. They even tried to tell us what the people we work with would think?!"

A slut whore! That's what they would have called us.

Porsche smiled. "Well, there's nobody around to tell us what to do any longer."

With the second stocking in place, she then put her suspenders on, followed by a frilly maid's skirt and apron, which barely covered her privates. Turning, she lifted the back of her skirt and flashed her arse.

This caused her to giggle coyly.

Plucking a pair of pretty pink panties out of her drawer followed by a matching bra, Porsche set them on top of the dresser.

"Now, what am I forgetting?"

The body? the voice said, trying not to sound sarcastic.

"Oh, I've not forgotten *that!*"

And that?

Porsche knew what the voice was talking about. How could she not? The *thing* had been in her view all evening. Not only that, it had been on her person for the best part of fifteen years.

She looked at it now.

A Circle of Trust.

That's the name they liked to bandy around.

Lifting her hand to her face, she looked at the little gold ring. Her wedding band.

"Circle of Trust my arse!" Grabbing it, she tore it off her ring finger and tossed it over her shoulder. In the mirror, she watched it bounce off the headboard and land in among the mangled privates, where it sank into the pulpy mess.

"*Quicksand!*" she blurted.

She and the voice within both laughed.

They laughed together like best friends.

Like lovers.

Like childish schoolchildren.

Like the free birds they now were.

Free and ready to start living life.

They were indeed reborn and ready to lose their virginity.

"Look out, world. Porsche's coming to tear a hole through your fucking heart!"

Behind her, the clock on the wall struck midnight. The taxi was booked for quarter-past.

We should think about…

"*Quiet*! It's a lady's prerogative to be late, you know! Had they not come home and caught us in the act, none of this would be happening. They'd probably still be breathing too."

They'd been so mad …

"I know. All that rage and anger because I want to be pretty and playful."

Getting up from her chair, she walked over to the body and accidentally stood in the pool of blood, which had coagulated.

"*Ugh!*" she gasped. But unperturbed, she bent over and plucked the pillow off the body's face.

Not a drop of remorse coursed through her.

"This is what all your efforts led to, you dumb fuck. Your death. Had you listened to me, had you believed in the voice. The inner me. The Porsche …" Her words trailed off.

Shaking her head, she started to laugh at the sight of the smashed face before her.

"Well, now I'm free of you, *Gloria*! My pathetic, dead fucking wife. I can now be Porsche without you trying to keep me at bay. Your fucking husband was as pathetic as you for taking all the shit he did for all those years!"

I … the voice tried, but Porsche was in full swing.

"*Wife*?! That's a fucking joke. Captor, more like." Throwing the pillow back down on top of her wife's face, Porsche turned and plucked the tablets up off the nightstand. "If you knew I was taking these, why didn't you question it sooner? Didn't you think something was up when I couldn't get my dick hard? When I couldn't fuck you? When my hair stopped growing? Fuck, woman! I was starting to look like a little boy. A pre-teen!"

Turning, Porsche looked at her semi-naked body in the mirror – she'd always had a slim, athletic build. Many people had told her in the past that she looked "girly."

"I'll be back for my knife, sugar!" she said, walking over to the mirror.

Snatching the panties off the dressing table, she slipped them up her legs, which shone in the hold-ups. Before covering her sissy dick with her knickers, she again opened a drawer to her dresser.

Putting her hand inside, she pulled out her male chastity device, which was made up of rings, cords, and padlocks. Gently, she grabbed her shrivelled dick and put it into the hardened plastic chamber. She then slipped the rings down the shaft and over her balls – this helped keep the package in place.

Padlocking the last of *his* manhood away, she snapped the key in the lock and smiled.

The voice inside, even though loving every degraded second of the situation, crumbled to the power of the person he had finally become.

"With that whore Gloria dead, I can finally get my tits done!" she said, putting her bra on, which she then padded with socks. "If *you'd* remained in control, we would have turned into a sissy slave! We'd have become a Come Dumpster for *real* men. You wouldn't have wanted to be a cock-swallowing nancy-boy, would you? A drinker of jism and piss?"

No, the voice pouted.

"This way, we get to be a ballsy dominatrix bitch from hell." She could almost hear the crack of her imaginary whip. "When I do have one, it will flay the flesh from their depraved buttocks!"

With the bra in place, Porsche put the top half of her maid's outfit on.

"Good enough to eat!" Winking at her reflection, she again giggled. "A mirror never lies!"

Going to her side of the bed, she opened the drawer to the cupboard there and produced a small handbag; it wasn't quite a clutch but close.

"Don't wait up!" she told Gloria as she tore the knife out of the body. It made a squirty-squashy sound as it came free. "God, that sounded like a spent, soggy dick being sucked free of a sticky, over-pleasured pussy."

The simile brought a fresh smile.

Filing the knife away in her purse, Porsche took her leather jacket off the back of the bedroom door and slipped it on. She then put her Fuck-Me boots on, which were hidden at the back of her wardrobe.

"Now you're dead, I won't have to fucking hide everything!"

With her boots on, she blew Gloria a kiss. "I'll be home with the milkman!" Outside, she heard a horn blast. "Looks like my ride is here."

Before heading out the door, she took one last look at herself in the mirror. "Mrs. Bates. Eat. Your. Fucking. Heart. Out!"

You're a Goddess, the voice said.

orsche smiled. "Oh, I know that. Just look at how gorgeous I am! It's true, you know … A mirror never lies."

END

Cult of the Angel Eaters Mark E. Deloy

The prison psychiatrist sits across the table from me, twirling his pencil between his fingers and staring at me over his glasses like a school teacher. I glance over his right shoulder and smile.

"Yes, I'll tell you my story," I say, still smiling. "I'll tell you where it all began..."

I was serving time upstate for armed robbery, and a guy named Willy Sanchez was my cellmate. I thought from the get-go he was a strange dude. He wore a full, scraggly beard and had these crazy eyes that seemed to look everywhere at once like a chameleon. I was just a kid back then, barely twenty and scared shitless. Willy kind of took me in, protected me on the yard, shit like that.

So anyway, like I said, I always thought he was a strange guy. But when he started talking about angels and demons and "the other side," I thought he had really lost it. He told me he and I were destined to lead others in a place far from there.

I kind of laughed at him. I didn't mean to, but he was talking some crazy shit, telling me all about the astral plane and the veil between humans and ethereal beings. He told me the old myth about God and Satan being at war was just a bunch of bullshit and the real war was between humanity and anything spiritual. He told me angels and demons were just flip sides on the same coin, all working together to bring about the downfall of humanity. The angels just pretended to take care of us but were really influencing our decisions, messing with our heads and shit.

I went to sleep that night thinking my friend had lost his mind, and I'd better start sleeping with one eye open, or I'd wake up with a shank sticking out of my gut. But in the end, I went to sleep anyway, figuring whatever happened, happened, and there was nothing I could do about it.

I woke early the next morning. Willy was crouching down real close to the cell bars, staring out at the catwalk just beyond them. He was rocking back and forth. His lips were moving, but I couldn't quite make out what he was saying. It sounded a bit like a chant. I was a little pissed off and very weirded out. I almost said something to let him know he had woken me up, but I decided to keep quiet and see what he was up to.

The chanting, or whatever it was, went on for a few more minutes. Then all of a sudden, Willy got real still and just stared out into the corridor. I couldn't see anything out there, just a bunch of shadows. Willy's hand shot out through the bars and grabbed a hold of something. I could sort of see something, but it was like it didn't have a form—or a body. It was just a shimmery thing, like heat off the asphalt in summertime. Whatever it was put up a hell of a fight, slamming Willy against the cell door until his nose was broken and his face was a bloody mess, but Old Willy never stopped smiling. He reached his other arm through the bars, braced his feet against them, and pulled with all his might.

I thought about helping him. That was my natural first reaction, but I still couldn't see anything solid on the other side of our cell. It was like he was struggling against the very air itself. I sat up and stared harder into the gloom beyond our cage, but there was still nothing. I almost yelled out for a guard, but something told me to be still, so I just sat up on my bunk, my sheet pulled up to my chin like a little kid, and watched.

Whatever Willy had gotten a hold of was still fighting like a king-sized catfish. My cellmate was still grinning as his body was bashed against the steel bars over and over. Still, I had to give him credit; he wasn't letting go. I expected the guard on duty to come running, but he never did.

After about ten minutes the struggle started going Willy's way. The thing beyond the bars seemed to tire, and Willy started reeling it in an inch at a time. I heard the thing let out an agonized scream that echoed through my brain. Willy finally turned to me. It was the first time he acknowledged I was even awake since the struggle started.

"You hear that?" he asked me. "You did, didn't you? There's hope for you yet, boy."

Then Willy gave one final jerk and heaved himself backwards. Whatever he had been fighting against slid through the bars, and I saw it shimmer like Christmas tinsel. Willy pounced on it, tearing at the creature like an animal, growling and cursing. I sat back against the wall, amazed and horrified. As Willy bit and clawed at the sparkling air, it began to materialize. I saw golden wings and a child-like body. Its eyes were black, like pools of ink, and it had short fangs. The creature tried to bite back at Willy, but he crashed a tattooed forearm into the thing's face. The creature was stunned and hung its head across my friend's lap like a sleeping dog. Willy ripped one of its wings off, and the creature let out another ghostly howl.

Its blood spilled onto the dirty floor of our cell. The stuff looked like liquid mercury, silver and wet. Willy licked some of the goo off his fingers as if it were chicken grease. As Willy turned back toward me, I saw his eyes were now coated with it, and I could see myself reflected in them.

The creature never stopped struggling, never stopped moving, until Willy tore its head from its body. He raised it and stared into its beautiful face.

"W…Willy. What was that?" I asked although I already knew.

"An angel. Just a small one. It'll serve though. Good enough to get us out of this shithole."

Willy then began to devour the headless being. I could hear him slurping and chewing as if this was Thanksgiving dinner. When he finished, he threw the bones and the wings into the corner where they rattled like castanets on clouds. Then he wiped the silvery blood, which smeared around his mouth, onto his sleeve and began gathering up his possessions. He wrapped everything in a sheet from his bunk and slung it over his shoulder.

"You comin' or not?" he asked me. His eyes still shone, and I felt a shiver go through me. I couldn't answer his question, couldn't speak at all. He might have just killed and ate an angel, but we were still surrounded by concrete, steel, and barbed wire. We weren't going anywhere.

Willy shrugged and then turned toward the cell door. He waved a hand like a magician, and the locking mechanism began to smoke. I heard a soft click, and the door swung open. Willy stepped out onto the catwalk and looked both ways before deciding to go right toward the guard shack at the end of our cellblock.

I cautiously poked my head out of our cell and watched through the large picture window as Willy fearlessly walked into the guardhouse. The uniformed men inside seemed stunned at first and quickly scrambled to their feet, grabbing their aerosol cans of pepper spray.

Willy took his time, gave them a Jedi mind trick with that same wave of his hand that he had used to open our cell. The guards just stood there like apes, slack-jawed with glazed eyes and hunched shoulders. He gave one of them a command, and the guard retrieved his keys and handed them over. That was when I decided to follow him wherever he was going.

***

That turned out to be the desert. Eventually, Willy's power faded, but before it did, he'd gotten us a new Corvette, a sack full of cash, and more pussy than a rock star could ever hope for.

Soon enough, Willy said it was time to get back to business. He told me we had a mission, and we had to go to Arizona. He had a plan, and that was good enough for me. I'd seen what he could do, and I was with him all the way. Turned out he was planning on starting a family, and he wanted me to be the first member.

We settled twenty miles south of Sedona. Willy used his cash to buy an old horse ranch. There was plenty of room in the house as well as bunk houses for everyone who Willy said would soon follow.

We spent the next few weeks preparing for the others. I didn't argue. I woke every morning to the smell of fresh air and saguaro instead of shit, sweat, and pain.

Willy explained that angels were all around us, but they were fast. The bigger ones had more power but were harder to catch. You had to be patient, and when the time came, you couldn't hesitate because once you threaten an angel, they could turn on you like a cobra.

The fallen angels, what most people called demons, were another story altogether. They were the most dangerous but held the most power. Willy told me he'd once caught a demon and stayed high from its power for a full year. When Willy was high, he could do all kinds of things. He could push people's minds, move objects without touching them, and even levitate over short distances. He promised to show me how to sight the ethereal beings and eventually capture them. He told me he would show us all.

***

The others came one by one. Men and women lost to the world, eager to learn, eager for power. We gave them food and a place to stay, and in return, they joined our family.

First we were two, then six, then twenty, then sixty. I took several wives, and so did Willy. He led us in meditation and exercise, honed our minds and our bodies. We bought guns and trained for the coming war with men, angels, demons, or whoever came for us first. We dug tunnels under the house and set traps along the walls. Willy taught us that when angels or demons came, they could come in human form, cased in flesh and bone to protect them from our hunger.

And we were hungry. I led hunting parties into town every month. Like a pride of lions, we roamed the desert cities, searching for Seraphim and Nephilim. Most of the time, we caught nothing. But occasionally, we would spot a lone, minor angel who had strayed from its host or a lesser demon on its own, trying to corrupt one weak mind among many.

We would track the creatures following the angels' glowing footprints on cracked sidewalks or the demons' black slime trails along the sugary sand.

When we caught them, we pounced and fed, always saving the head for Willy, who said he could sometimes see the future in their dark eyes.

Life was good for a while. The power was good, but the sense of family, of belonging,, was better.

***

The final battle began on a windy day in May. We had been preparing for it for almost a year, but none of us were ready when it came. We never imagined they would come with such force from both sides. Willy said they had teamed up, just this once, to destroy a common enemy. Us.

We saw them for what they were when they came: a mighty mass of angelic warriors and demonic hordes. They wore their human hosts like clothing. We gunned down the bodies, but the spirits kept coming, pulling themselves out of the skin, bone, and Kevlar like butterflies from steel cocoons.

We dropped our weapons and stood at the ready. They flowed through the walls of our compound like water, snatching our children up first, eating them in front of us as if they were Christmas turkeys.

Then they came for us. We fought well, feeding as we killed and gaining strength. But in the end, their numbers were too great, and they had billions more in reserve. We retreated as our numbers shrank. Family members were torn apart one after another until only Willy and I were left. We ran down into the basement and hid in the tunnels. A legion of demons followed, armed with spears and teeth, climbing the walls and the ceiling like spiders after two flies.

"You've got to survive," Willy said as we cowered in the darkness, waiting to die. "You've got to rebuild it all."

I just stared at him, seeing only his outline in the gloom. The demons were right behind us, screaming for our blood.

"Take this tunnel," Willy said. "It'll lead you to the surface. I'll keep them off your trail."

"Thank you, Father," I said and hugged him tightly. As I ran down the tunnel, I heard the demons tear Willy apart. He never screamed, not once.

The tunnel came to an end just outside the compound walls. Armed men were waiting and surprisingly took me into custody. I surmised they were real law enforcement, uncorrupted and drawn in when they heard the compound was under fire. That was ten years ago.

***

"So you expect me to recommend that you be transferred from general population and be placed in psychiatric care?" the psychiatrist says.

"No. I know you don't believe me, but your disbelief doesn't change anything. You will never see what I've seen."

"I glance over the doctor's shoulder again. The angel had entered with him, and now, after hearing my story, looked eager to leave. It was, however, a guardian and thus linked to the man by a silvery umbilical cord.

I stood up and clamped a hand over the man's mouth before he could cry out for a guard, but it wasn't him I was after.

The cord felt wet and slippery in my calloused hands as I reeled in my fish. The angel struggled, but my mouth was watering now, and I would not be denied.

END

Jacob's Mind by Ty Schwamberger

A cool burst of sea-drenched air flowed over his
face while Chaabi played on a transistor radio sitting close
by in the sand. It was a typical day on the shores of
Tarfaya in mid-January. It was around 67 degrees, which
was perfect weather as far as he was concerned and
nothing like the weather would be in his native city in the
United States: Cleveland, Ohio.

,Jacob recently started working in Tarfaya,
Morocco, but in his free time, he did little more than sit for
endless hours on the gold-encrusted sands of the beach,
drink cheap beer, and try to play his interpretation of the
local music on his guitar. Jacob almost always bought his
beer on the beach from a local, who would push a rusty
metal cart stocked with a string of doughnuts and cheap
ale. The only beer this particular vendor had in his
inventory was Flag Special, which Jacob thought tasted
more like a homeless guy's piss more than anything else.
But he drank it — a lot of it — especially during the past few
months.

Jacob was naturally dark skinned but always
seemed to apply more sunscreen than was needed during
this particular season. The sun wasn't hot as you might

think it would be this close to the equator but more like the sun on a fall day on the shores of Lake Erie, near Cleveland — warm and inviting. He loved the beach and would do almost anything to be close to his passion of parasailing. He longed for this time each year for The Dash, which was a spectacular and challenging endurance event racing from the Canary Islands to Tarfaya, Shara Morocco, seventy-two nautical miles. He spent many hours a day just dreaming about what it would be like to parasail around the world. If only that were possible in this day and age.

As Jacob stretched his legs and stuck his feet in the sand, contemplating on whether to go back in the ocean, he heard a strange popping sound. He looked north up the beach and then south. Nothing. He proceeded to turn his head around to look behind him, his long locks of braided and beaded hair whipping against the side of his sunscreen-pasted cheeks. Again, he saw nothing. He thought maybe it was the ocean liner in the distance dumping medical sewage into the water again, but upon inspection with his telescope, he saw nothing. Nothing. Perplexed by this, he stood up, his lean and muscular six-foot-two frame casting a formidable shadow on the sands beside him. He had his shirt off, which made him look even more ripped, especially because he had been darkened even more by the Moroccan sun over the past few months. He looked around once more, seeing nothing, picked up his radio, blanket, and guitar, and decided it was time to get something to eat. The beer was starting to give him a little buzz, and after last night, he wasn't going to fall back into the drunken stupor that got him into trouble only a few hours before.

* * *

After jumping up the front steps and opening the door, Jacob entered his ocean-view condo. He was starting to get a headache again, and because he wasn't sure whether it was from the beer he drank on the beach or the night before, he walked into the bathroom, opened up the medicine cabinet, and took out a bottle of aspirin. Popping three pills in his mouth and taking a handful of water from the faucet, Jacob swallowed, dried his mouth, and walked out into the living room. He plopped down onto the couch and flicked on the television.

Only black and white lines buzzed on the screen.

He pressed the channel button on the remote with his thumb but still came up with nothing.

Dammit.

He turned off the television and walked over to the kitchen, which was adjacent to the living room. He pulled open the refrigerator and took out a cold brew and some leftover egg salad then made himself a sandwich on rye bread. He twisted the metal cap off his beer and took a few small gulps.

The popping sound went off again in his ears. Thinking it was his headache trying to get worse, he shook it off and went out on the balcony overlooking the ocean. It was beautiful. But it also reminded him how even beautiful things can turn ugly in only a small amount of time, especially when alcohol is involved.

He took a bite of his sandwich and another gulp of cold beer. He could feel everything slide down the inside of his throat, esophagus, and into his stomach. He thought it was strange he could feel the inside of his body and couldn't remember a time that had happened before. Hoping the night before had nothing to do with it, he took another sip of beer and sat down on his white wicker recliner. He put his feet up on the balcony railing, took a pack of Horn cigarettes out of his pocket, struck a match on his teeth, and inhaled deeply. Sweet, warm smoke filled his mouth and lungs. He held it in for a few moments and let it out through his nose.

* * *

As his eyes fluttered open, Jacob realized he wasn't on the cozy confines of his condo balcony. Not that it surprised him any; he just hoped it wouldn't happen again so soon. Not when it happened the previous night.

Pushing himself off the forest floor, he brushed a few leaves and sticks off his naked body and began walking. He knew the area well and how to get back home. The only unfortunate part this time was it was daytime, and he was naked. Hell, he was always naked, especially after the change, but it normally happened in the early morning hours when the sun was just beginning to rise and not many people were out and about. Jacob knew during the afternoon hours there would be plenty of people walking the streets, and they would be sure to notice a naked man strolling along even if he looked to be a normal person.

But Jacob knew he wasn't a normal person—not after meeting Dr. Jim Stevenson six months before.

Something was wrong with him; he just couldn't put a finger on what it was.

To many, Jacob was a regular guy. He held a desk job during the week and was the type of hunky guy ladies see on the beach and want to talk to. He knew he was good looking and often used that to his advantage to get the women he wanted. He just had to remember to put makeup on his face in the mornings, and he was good to go. He wished he had some makeup on him now, but that would be hard to do, being naked and all.

After a half hour of walking, Jacob came to the edge of the forest and looked out onto the main street that ran past it. Hiding behind a large tree, he looked both ways, saw no one, and casually strolled out from behind it. Stepping up on the sidewalk, he quickened his pace. He was naked in the middle of the day, walking down the street, and would be sure to attract a lot of unneeded attention if he didn't get a move on.

He heard it when he was halfway home. Not a popping sound but the distant rumble of an automobile engine closing fast behind him. At first, he wanted to take off running and try to find something to hide behind, but he knew that might draw more attention to him than continuing to walk down the street. Maybe the person in the vehicle wouldn't notice. Maybe the person would be so busy talking on their cell phone or listening to the radio they wouldn't see a tall, naked guy walking down the street in broad daylight. He hoped.

A few moments later, the car whizzed by him. It was a green, two-door hatchback and looked rather good for the age of the car. Jacob figured it was probably a chick's car but couldn't be sure, and he sure as hell wasn't going to flag the person down to find out. Then the car hit the brakes. Hard. A plume of white and gray smoke erupted from the tires. The drive shifted into reverse and backed up toward him fast.

Jacob thought about running back into the woods but instead continued walking towards the car. He would just think of some excuse of why he was naked in the middle of the day. *A woman. Yeah, that might work,* Jacob thought. *I'll just tell the person my girlfriend stole my clothes and kicked me out of the house... Yeah, that's a great idea. If it is a guy, he'll be sure to believe it...but what if it is a woman driver... Shit...I'll have to think of something else.*

The car pulled to a stop at the curb a few yards in front of Jacob. He took a deep breath and walked over to the passenger window.

It was a woman in the driver's seat.

Damn.

"Excuse me," the young blond behind the steering wheel said. "Do you need help of some kind?"

"Ahhh, actually a ride would be great … my girlfriend, ya know … she kicked me out this morning after we had a fight and wouldn't give me my clothes, so I have to walk all the way across town wearing nothing but my birthday suit," Jacob said and then chuckled.

"Sorry to hear about your luck … some women can be a pain in the aaarsh, ya know."

"Yeah, I am beginning to realize that."

The woman popped the lock to the passenger door. Jacob reached down and pulled it open. He slid onto the hot vinyl seat. It burnt like hell on his buttocks and legs, but he didn't say anything.

"Thanks. I really appreciate it."

"No worries … where to?" the blond asked.

"526 Ocean Drive."

"Ah, okay … I know right where that's at. My uncle use to live down that way when I was a kid. By the way, my name is Julie."

"Yeah, it is a nice part of town. It's nice to meet you, Julie. My name is Jacob."

Jacob gave an embarrassed smile as he closed the door with his right hand and covered himself with his left. Julie pulled away from the curb and started driving towards Jacob's condo.

"There it is," said Jacob, pointing towards his tan condo up ahead.

"Okay."

Julie pulled the car to the curb and shut off the engine.

"Thanks again for the ride, Julie."

"Hey, it's no problem, really."

"Well, thanks again. Have a good one," Jacob said, pushing open the car door and starting to get out.

"Hey, do you mind if I come in real quick and use your bathroom? I normally wouldn't ask such a thing, but I really have to go."

"Nah, that's fine. Just follow me."

Jacob led Julie to the front of his building, unlocked the door, and showed her in. He pointed down the hallway to the bathroom.

On her way, Jacob called out to her and asked if she wanted something to drink. "Yes … a vodka and tonic would be great."

"Coming right up," Jacob replied, watching her skirt flutter against her buttocks as she walked down the hall.

Jacob hurried into his laundry room, threw on a pair of khaki shorts and a Bermuda shirt, and then went into the kitchen to fix the drinks. Julie came out of the bathroom and was walking into the kitchen as Jacob was pouring the liquid concoction from a silver shaker into two chilled tumblers. He handed one to Julie, took the other himself, and they walked out on the balcony.

"Wow, this is a great view."

"Why, thank you. I do enjoy it very much here."

"Have you been living here very long?" Julie asked.

"Only about six months is all. I was actually transferred from the states with the company I work for."

"Ah, I see ... had any time to enjoy the night life yet?" Julie asked.

"Not too much yet. I'm pretty busy during the week and usually have paperwork to bring home on the weekends."

"You should really spend some time getting to know the area. I've been here for about seven years, and I love the place. Plus, the night life here is to die for."

"I bet. Especially if someone has a person like you to show them around," Jacob replied, taking a sip from his glass.

* * *

Jacob squinted against the morning light filtering into the shaded windows of his bedroom. Turning his head to one side, he noticed that the side of the bed where Julie had slept was empty. He was glad he met her, and even if he didn't know her very well—except for the time they spent together the previous day—he could tell he liked her. She was someone he could actually see himself with. He hoped she felt the same.

Rolling out of bed, Jacob stretched his arms and legs and walked to the bathroom door. It was closed. He fumbled with the knob, but the door was locked. Feeling a little embarrassed he might have just disturbed Julie using his toilet, he said, "Sorry about that … take your time," and headed down the hall and into the kitchen.

A hot pot of coffee was waiting for him. The coffee maker was always set on a timer to brew his favorite roast first thing in the morning. Smiling, he took two mugs out of the cabinet, filled them both, and sat down at the breakfast bar.

He sipped the hot, black fluid, looking out the window at the ocean and how the morning light reflected off the waves. It was going to be a good day. He could feel it. If nothing else, Jacob knew it was going to be a good day because he had met a beautiful woman who seemed to like him, and he hadn't done anything crazy the previous night. At least he hoped he didn't. He didn't think he did anyway.

How could I have done anything? I woke up at home with my boxers on … no body or blood around me. Nah, nothing happened last night that I should be worried about.

That was when he heard the popping sound again.

He twisted around and looked down the hallway towards the bathroom but didn't see anyone. No Julie. Nothing. He turned back around, took another sip of his coffee and waited for the popping sound again. It didn't come back.

After about ten minutes of sitting on the stool, looking out the window, and sipping coffee, Jacob started to get concerned with what was taking Julie so long in the bathroom. Sure, he knew that sometimes women had female issues that they needed to take care of, but he had never heard of them taking this long.

He swiveled around in his chair and started walking toward the bathroom.

As he approached the door, he leaned his ear against it to find out if he would hear any movement, running water, something. He didn't hear anything.

He lightly knocked on the door.

There was no response.

"Julie? You okay? Can I get you anything?"

Nothing.

He knocked again.

At first, he thought Julie trying to talk to him, but after another few moments, he realized it wasn't her. For one, the voice sounded too masculine, and for another, it was too close to be coming from anyone on the other side of the bathroom door.

Rearing back, he flung his shoulder into the door. The wooden doorjamb exploded into a hundred splinters, and the door shot open.

* * *

A few weeks had passed since cleaning up and throwing what was left of Julie's body in the dumpster behind his condo.

During that time, Jacob spent endless hours researching his condition. It bothered him he could only remember some things that happened after meeting a beautiful woman. Six months ago, he would have assumed it was the alcohol messing with his memory, but now, he sensed it was more than that.

A lot more.

Looking through the local library, Jacob found a wide variety of magazine articles, movies, and documents on the myth of what he had become. He guessed he always knew what he was, what Dr. Stevenson had turned him into, but he didn't want to admit it until now. Hell, even after reading and watching all the movies, he still couldn't and didn't want to believe it. But he knew that what he found out had to be the reason for his late-night adventures.

Ever since Jacob had first been experimented on, he had just found it normal to be searching for hot women in the middle of the night and then forgetting what happened after that. He could always remember meeting the random woman, drinking together, and then waking up. He could never remember the stuff in the middle. Hell, at the time, he saw nothing wrong with it. He was just enjoying the company of women and living his life. He didn't know what he was really doing. All he really knew was he did things at night; woke up in relatively the same place, walked back home, put on makeup to cover the scars across his forehead and neck, and went about his daily life.

Now, something was different; something was wrong. He was beginning to remember small details of the night with Julie, and it wasn't just the good parts either. Jacob knew he had to find out where Dr. Stevenson had taken him on Jacob's first night in Tarfaya. He had to find out what happened to him that night. Dr. Stevenson told him to have a drink with him and follow him back to his laboratory.

The only person Jacob could find whose name resembled the doctor's was James Stevens, M.D. He figured it was close enough to Jim Stevenson, so he gave it a shot.

* * *

He arrived at the doctor's office a little after five o'clock on a Monday afternoon. There was a chance that the doctor had already left the office before Jacob got there, but he had to give it a shot anyway. He figured if the doctor's office was already closed, he would just break in and take a look around, though Jacob doubted that a mad scientist would keep records of strange experiments at a secret laboratory in the same office that he helped the local town folk. But he had to try something. Hell, he didn't have anything to lose—not anymore.

After pulling his small car into the parking lot, Jacob shut off the engine and walked to the front office door. It was unlocked, and he was able to enter without having to break a window. He then walked up to the receptionist desk and asked if Dr. Stevens was available.

The woman behind the desk asked if something was wrong. Jacob said he was having some stomach problems that he needed to speak with someone about. A few minutes after disappearing down a hallway, the receptionist returned and asked Jacob to follow her to the consultation room.

"Thank you."

Jacob followed her down the whitewashed hallway, entered the room, and had a seat on a bench covered with thin, white paper.

The woman closed the door on her way out.

"Good afternoon, Mr. —" the doctor said as he entered the room.

"YOU!" Jacob shouted. He couldn't seem to remember much of anything lately, but he sure as hell recognized the tall, thin, gray-haired man standing in front of him in a white lab coat.

"Ah, yes ... Mr. Satchel ... so good to see you again. Tell me, are your headaches getting any better these days?"

"Shit, no," Jacob shouted again. "They aren't better at all. Hell, I still get them all the time, and now, I am having trouble remembering things."

"Well, that could be because of the tumor, you know."

"Huh ... wha ... what tumor? What the hell are you talking about?"

"Oh, my dear ... you don't remember, do you? The tumor I had to remove from your brain. Why do you think you had those stitches across your forehead, Mr. Satchel?"

"What ... I don't understand. I don't remember any tumor or even being in the hospital for that matter."

"Of course you don't remember. That is one of the side effects of brain cancer. Patients often forget about certain events in their lives, whether it is in the past or present. There are even instances where a patient will make up a certain memory with events that never took place to begin with."

"But ... what about ..."

"What about what?" Dr. Stevens asked.

"What about ... all the weird stuff that has been happening to me?"

"What would that be, Mr. Satchel?"

"You know ..."

Jacob didn't want to say too much at this point. He couldn't be sure any of his memories were correct anymore. He didn't want to admit to killing people if the doctor didn't have anything to do with it. He sure as hell wasn't going to give himself up to the authorities when he didn't have to.

Maybe the doctor is right. Maybe I did have a tumor and my mind just made up all the stuff about meeting him in a bar, him asking me to have a drink with him, following him back to his laboratory for a side job ... all that stuff ... It might be all made up. Oh shit, I might not only have cancer, but I might have had brain surgery, killed people, and now I am going crazy to boot. What the hell am I gonna do?

The doctor was smiling at him but looking annoyed and waiting for an answer.
Jacob didn't have one to give him, so he just shrugged and said, "Dr. Stevens ... maybe you are right. I think I'm just

having some trouble right now. You wouldn't happen to know of any medication I can take to help with my memory, do you?"

"Oh, Mr. Satchel … I am sure I can give you something to help you out." The doctor smiled, pulling a white prescription pad out of his shirt pocket.

* * *

Jacob woke up alone the next morning in his own bed. There were no dead bodies around him, no blood, no torn clothes. Just him lying on his side. Rolling out of bed, Jacob walked to the bathroom, used the toilet, flushed, and then brushed his teeth. He cupped some cold running water in both his hands, took it into his mouth, and swished it around a few moments. He then spit the water into the sink and reached behind him for a hand towel.

Drying his face and mouth, he looked up in the mirror above the sink and noticed that the wide scars that had lined his forehead were gone, as were the round holes that had scarred each side of his neck. His skin was smooth, just as it was when he first moved to Tarfaya. He glided his hands over his dry skin and felt no indication that he had had an operation to remove any brain tumor.

Smiling that the good doctor had helped him in some way, he walked out of the bathroom and into the kitchen. As always, a steaming pot of coffee was waiting for him. The bitter smell of roasted beans filled Jacob's nostrils as he walked over, took a mug from the cabinet, and poured. He took a sip of the hot coffee and let it slide down his throat. It burned but tasted wonderful. He wanted to enjoy his coffee on his balcony as he did every morning, so he walked from the kitchen, through the living room, and pulled aside the blinds that were covering the sliding door.

Sitting in his chair, he saw the back of a woman's head.

Confused, he pulled the door to one side. It slid open and stopped with a thud.

"Excuse me ..."

Sitting in his white wicker chair was Julie.

Naked.

Her arms, legs, and head had obviously been sewn back on with great care. There were also extra marks on her body.

One was a jagged stitching across her forehead, and the other was two metal knobs, one sticking out each side of her neck.

He also noticed she was wearing a rock the size of a small house on her left ring finger.

Instinctively, he looked down at his left hand and saw he was wearing a gold band as well.

"What the …"

"Why, good morning, hubby," Julie said. "You were right when you thought about me liking you …"

"How … what … when …" Jacob slurred.

"Oh, honey, it's okay. Now, we'll get to be together forever. Remember, after all … I'm your bride."

END

MORE FROM STITCHED SMILE PUBLICATIONS

In the best of times, loneliness is difficult. At the end of time it can be deadly.

Hank Walker is alone and struggling not just with the undead but with depression that threatens to swallow him. Searching for the family he sent away at the beginning of the rise of the dead, Hank is left to deal with loneliness, desperation, and his own memories that haunt him.

The dead are everywhere. The few people still alive are scattered, and the ones Hank comes across may be more dangerous than the biters.

With an unlikely traveling companion, Hank's search takes him across the state of South Carolina and to the depths of darkness like nothing he has ever experienced before. Can Hank find his family and survive the biters? Or does he completely unravel in the world of the dead?

Not all monsters are made. Some are born. And sometimes, history gets it wrong.

A freelance writer is invited to an elderly man's home to witness his telling of the family history to his sons. The patriarch's reason for requesting a stranger into his home as he shares his tale is a simple one. He wants the young man to write the true history of Family Dracul, to trace the lineage back to the very first member of a family cursed. But, the old man has another agenda. He wants to warn humanity; what happened in the past was nothing compared to what is to come.

www.ingramcontent.com/pod-product-compliance
Lightning Source LLC
Chambersburg PA
CBHW060534180626
46817CB00002B/563